LOST TIME

TIME WARS LAST FOREVER SERIES: BOOK 2

CRAIG ROBERTSON

RAGE OF THE ANCIENT GODS, Book 2

TORMENT OF THE ANCIENT GODS, Book 3

WRATH OF THE ANCIENT GODS, Book 4

FURY OF THE ANCIENT GODS, Book 5

FALL OF THE ANCIENT GODS, Book 6

TIME WARS LAST FOREVER SERIES (2019)

RYAN TIME, Book 1

LOST TIME, Book 2

NON-RYANVERSE BOOKS:

ROAD TRIPS IN SPACE SERIES (2019):

THE GALAXY ACCORDING TO GIDEON, Book 1

THE EARTH ACCORDING TO GIDEON, Book 2

OLDER, STANDALONE WORKS:

THE CORPORATE VIRUS (2016)

TIME DIVING (2013)

THE INNERgLOW EFFECT (2010)

WRITE NOW! THE PRISONER OF NaNoWRiMo (2009)

ANON TIME (2009)

ISBN: 978-1-7341363-1-9 (E-Book)
978-1-7341363-2-6 (Print)
979-8-7754172-1-5 (Hardcover)

Cover design by Alexandre
http://www.designbookcover.pt/en/

Formatted by Drew Avera
www.drewavera.com/book-formatting

Editing by:
Michael R. Blanche
Neil Farr
Beth Lynne
Charles Pitts

First Edition 2019

LOST TIME

TIME WARS LAST FOREVER SERIES: BOOK 2

by Craig Robertson

TIME ALLOWS A PERSON TO HOPE. JON RYAN HAS NEITHER OF THOSE.

Imagine-It Publishing

El Dorado Hills, CA

This book is dedicated to the joy and wonder that is *Science Fiction*. I don't know where I'd be without you, baby, but I wouldn't want to be there. Stay with me forever!

PRELUDE

"Brooklyn!" shouted Amber as she slapped her palm on the door. "You seriously need to hurry up. There're only *two* bathrooms and you can't stay in there like you're the queen. We're not your subjects."

And so began Tuesday on Mars 1 Research Base. Here's a hint: Sunday and Monday began pretty much the same way. Wednesday would too. Four hundred and ninety-three students, along with a handful of support personnel, had been on Mars a few days. Already disorder and frayed nerves had degraded into chaos and confrontation.

Small wonder. Up until recently, the students had been attending Georgetown University. They had been doing what all twenty-somethings did. They slept, they drank to excess, and they exercised. Some even went to class. All were planning a future that involved wealth, comfort, and an ideal mate. None had hallucinated in their wildest dreams that they'd suddenly, and with only partial consent, be hustled off-planet due to an alien attack.

Mars 1 had been in operation for over a decade. It

had grown into a bustling research facility with between thirty and forty-five individuals living and working together. It was never intended to house almost five hundred people for an indefinite period. Most of the new arrivals were housed in inflatable temporary buildings. The main structures served as the hub of the community. Until the engineers could construct portable toilets to accommodate so many more biological entities, the hub also possessed the only on-planet bathroom facilities. To a chorus of groans, Lt. Colonel Reva St. Claire, the base's new commander, had announced that "all peeing will be done in plastic containers, and preferably in private." That was intended to make the restroom crisis less of a crisis. It had. Now it was only a major flash point.

The first order of business, after the emigres arrived on base, had been the gruesome task of cleaning up one horrific mess. The remorseless alien leader, Body Maker-lop, had systematically ripped the previous base staff into small pieces, then strewn their remains around haphazardly. Even after the hazmat teams had cleared the worst of the gore away, parts of human and puddles of blood were still being found in out-of-the-way places. That left everybody, especially the bulk of the student body, on edge.

But at least they were all alive. If the aliens made good on their threat and wiped out all the humans on Earth, a small fragment of the species might survive here on Mars.

That was, if Amber didn't murder Brooklyn for being selfish and self-absorbed. Seriously, a ten-minute shower? This wasn't summer in the Hamptons, sweetheart. It was Mars 1 with a ten-year-old water recycler designed for reasonable adults. And so it went those first few rough days.

"I'll be right out. Get over yourself. If you make me

mess up my makeup, I'll just have to wash it off and start again, sister," Brooklyn yelled back.

Captain Emma Walters eased Amber to one side of the hallway in front of the bathroom. She squared her shoulders, said a series of bad things about her commander under her breath for having assigned her this duty, and knocked, as diplomatically as she could, on the door.

"Captain Walters here, Brook. In five seconds, I'm unlocking this door. I will then drag you, in whatever state of readiness you might be, out into this hallway so the next person may use our limited facilities. For your convenience, I will count down your remaining time. One ... two ... three—"

A seemingly fully refreshed and dressed young woman opened the door so hard, it slammed against the inner wall. Her makeup looked to have been professionally applied and suggested no hint that additional touches were needed.

"I know my rights. You can't harass me for no good reason. My father is a US Senator. I'll—"

Captain Walters said, "Five" loudly and jerked a stunned Brooklyn out into the hallway, just as she'd promised. "You may file a report of any presumed insult or injury to the head of the female barracks." She turned to Amber. "Next."

"But *you're* the head of the female barracks," whined Brooklyn.

"That is a true fact. And, as such, I will give all due consideration to your report before I bring it back to this restroom, where it will be repurposed to serve the greater good even better."

"I *hate* you," Brooklyn huffed as she stormed away.

To herself, Emma grumbled, "This is going well."

Later, in the officers' mess, Emma sat rubbing her face

with her palms, a forgotten cup of coffee waiting patiently before her, cold but on-call.

"More sisterly bonding with the girls?" asked Colonel St. Claire as she slid into the seat across from Emma.

"I have come to see the wisdom in your orders that I not routinely carry a sidearm."

Reva pointed to the rank on her shoulder. "They don't hand these out to rookies, Emma. You earn them through bitter years of dealing with children of various ages."

"Are you sure the POTUS ordered these kids up here? I mean, maybe it was a misunderstanding. He said we needed to preserve the best of humankind so we don't become extinct. Maybe he meant the residents of a maximum security prison, not lazy spoiled brats with attitude?"

"I'm almost jealous of the learning opportunity you've been presented with. Someday you'll thank me."

She scoffed. "Two rotations in the Middle East, one Silver Star, two Purple Hearts, and now I'm riding herd on poorly raised rich kids. This is not what I signed up for." She sipped her coffee.

"If the aliens come back, I'll make certain you're on point."

"Thank you, sir. That would go a long way in my rehabilitation. With any luck, I'd be the first to die."

Reva reached across and patted her old friend on the forearm. "You're doing fine, Em. These kids are scared, so they act out. You were a ROTC-Nazi in college, learning discipline and manners. These guys are more concerned with getting laid and getting into law school. They are fully unprepared for this level of stress."

Emma looked up from her mug. "They're unprepared *period.*"

"Then thank goodness they have you," Reva cooed. "In six months' time—"

Reva's walkie talkie squawked to life. "Colonel, there's something very wrong. Please come to the comm-room ASAP," a panicky male voice blared.

"Let's move," she said to the captain.

In a flash, the two officers were jogging the short distance to the radio room.

"*Report*," Reva barked as she blew through the doors, Emma right over her shoulder.

"The signals from Earth, sir—"

"What about them, Sergeant?" she snapped impatiently.

"They're ... they're *gone*, sir."

"What do you mean 'they're *gone*'? They can't be. Put the receiver on speaker," she ordered.

The wall-mounted speakers hissed white noise.

"Try something else. C2 at the Pentagon."

"Nothing, sir. I tried that."

"NASA. Put me in touch with Houston."

He tapped switches frantically. "Nothing, sir."

"How can there be—" The commander suddenly noticed she was nauseated. It was faint at first, but it was getting stronger quickly. It was like she was seasick.

"I want you to tap into the Sat Comm network. Lunar Command. Get me *anything*."

His fingers flew, but only static came from the speakers.

Reva steadied herself by grabbing hold of the sergeant's chair. "Anybody else feeling woozy?"

"I thought it was just me," Emma reported from behind.

"What the hell's going on, people?" demanded the colonel.

The walkie talkie blared. "Commander, you'd better get over to the barracks. Several kids have passed out, and a bunch of them are puking."

She turned to Emma. "Get over there. Call the clinic. Have someone meet you there."

"Aye, sir." The captain sprinted away.

"Okay. First principles here, people. Lieutenant Crozier, who's on duty in the observatory?"

He snatched the duty roster clipboard off the wall. "Doctors Nelson and Wang, sir."

"Get one of them on the line now."

Ten seconds later, he handed her his headset.

"Who'm I speaking with?" she demanded.

"Rusty Nelson. Is this—"

"I need a visual confirmation on the Earth. Is that possible?"

"Er ... what?"

"I want you to give me a visual confirmation on the integrity of the planet Earth. Is that possible at this hour? Yes or no."

"Ah, sure, commander. Earth's well above the horiz—"

"Do it *now*."

She heard Nelson's headset crash to the table. A muffled shout went out from him to someone else nearby.

The colonel turned to Crozier. "Get over there and keep me posted. This idiot dropped his headset. Double time it."

"Yes, sir," he said as he jetted past her.

Forty seconds later, Crozier was on the line. "The scientists are adjusting the main telescope as we speak, sir."

"Do they see anything?"

"Not yet." He covered his mouthpiece. "Hey, Colonel wants a timeline here. Okay, hurry it up. Sir, the man says it should be on screen within a minute."

"Stand by," she replied firmly. "Have them send the feed over here too. Can you capture it, Sergeant?"

"Yes, sir. It'll be on your screen as soon as they're live."

Reva softly clicked her tongue, an old habit when she was tense.

"He says the scope's up, sir," reported Crozier.

"Have them forward the—"

"He says they are, sir."

"I don't *see* anything," she responded hotly.

"She's not ... what? I'm not going to tell her that. Look again."

"What, damn it. What'd he say?" demanded the commander.

"Damn fool said there's nothing to see. He says the scope's pointing at Earth, but the Earth's just not where it's supposed to be."

"Well, where the hell *is* it, then?"

He shouted to the scientists.

"He says as best he can tell... it's gone."

"Gone? Gone where?"

"No, Commander. Dr. Nelson says the Earth no longer orbits the Sun. It's *gone,* gone."

Her nausea peaked and she lurched for a garbage can, just in time.

"Put him on the phone," she said queasily.

"Nelson here."

"Are you certain the Earth no longer exists?"

"We're still looking, Commander. But have you felt the nausea?"

"Yes," she said, surprised. "What does that—"

"If the Earth disappeared when the radio signals vanished, so did its gravity well."

"What well?"

"No, Sir. If the Earth is no longer exerting a gravitational force, the planets need to *realign* themselves. That process would begin immediately."

"You're saying Mars is on the move?"

"Well, *technically*, it always had been. But now, it's moving to where it needs to be."

"So we all get seasick?"

"That's right. And, Commander?"

"Yes?"

"It's only going to get worse."

"I want *every* scientist on Mars in my office in five minutes. You got that, Nelson?"

"Will do. Over and—"

Reva tossed the headset back to the sergeant and retched again.

And it was only going to get worse. *Greeeeaaat.* Simply mahvelous.

ONE

"It's a dumb idea. It was a dumb idea the last few times you voiced it. When you say it again soon, it'll be worse than dumb. It'll be dumbfounding, dumber, dumbmaximus."

So opined my forever wife, Sapale.

"But how do you really feel about it?" I asked with a goofy grin.

We were reclined on our bed, in our quarters aboard *Stingray*. Sapale's head was on the pillow, and her feet at the bottom of the bed, like the bed-instructions suggested. I was reversed, with my feet inches from her face. Instead of a pillow, I cupped my hands behind my head. Basically, it was perfect.

"I'm inclined to dislike it," she replied. She poked the side of my head with a toe.

"But I need brain power."

"Can I get an amen?" she sang out like an evangelical preacher.

"You know what I mean. I need a smart person to help figure out the solution here. When you need a smart person, you need Toño DeJesus."

"There's many a flaw in your wavy-gravy logic, flyboy. First, on an intellectual level, you presuppose there *is* a solution possible. Second, on a human level, it's too damn cruel. I refuse to have any part in it."

"You're missing the genius of my plan."

"No, your plan is missing genius."

I sat up. "Honey, this is not big. The Adamant were *big*. The ancient gods were *big*. This is massively huge. The end justifies the means."

She sat up. "No, it does *not*. He's our closest, oldest, and best friend. We can't ask it of him. Drop it. You have perfectly adequate smart people anyway; two of them, in fact. And everybody knows two whiz kids are better than one." To underscore her argument, she stuck out her tongue at me. She could be such a child.

I stuck mine out in response. "My scheme is so brilliant, it can't not work."

"You have such a way with words. It's hard to not disagree with you."

"Look, we need Toño. He's a proven commodity. Yes, Daleria is dying. He has every right to stay home and be with her. The universe owes him that ten-times over. But, we gots ourselves a time machine. We just," I slapped one palm off the other, "zap to the future when he's, you know, not *preoccupied*, and bring him back here with us. Voila, genius on board."

"No. That's not how your scenario plays out. If we wrestle him into our time ship, he'll demand to go to her side as she's dying. That's the way the man's mind works. Given the option, he'll want to be by her side at the bitter end, again."

"But," I said with no little exasperation, "he already *is* beside her to the bitter end. He knows he was. He was there."

She shook her head in adamant disagreement. "No. He'd go to her. He's *incapable* of not doing so. What's more, the one that's there now would take one step to his right to make space for the other him. He's so nerd-o-matic, it wouldn't even faze him."

She was, of course, correct. Obviously, I couldn't admit that. It was wishful thinking. I missed Toño and I needed him. But it would be wrong of me to abuse him in such a manner.

"Hey, what's for dinner?" I asked, trying as best I could to sound like I actually cared.

"A traditional human dish. *Crow.*" More with the tongue. Really, she was *so* immature.

"If, by that menu selection, you mean to suggest that you were *partially* more correct than I was, well, I'd have only one response."

She raised all four eyebrows in anticipation.

"Hey, what's for dinner?"

I should mention that our living arrangements were kind of odd. The two whiz kids Sapale had alluded to, Tank and Sachiko, each had quarters aboard Aramthella, our totally bitching time ship. We, however, stayed on *Stingray*. It was our home, had been for a very long time. But our house was parked in a storage room on their ship, which was much larger than ours. So we were like second cousins living in an RV that was parked in their den.

That wasn't the only weird twist that resulted from our extended cohabitation. The other one hit me from such a blindside that I didn't just *not* see it coming, I never would have thought it possible. Honestly, I'm still not certain it was possible.

One day I was standing on *Stingray's* bridge, which was really just a wide spot in her control area. I was having my AIs, the Als, run some complex diagnostics to make sure they were running in tight sync with Aramthella. I still wasn't sure what she was. I told myself Aramthella was a totally alien AI, but I had no idea. She could be a shrunken head in a box, for all I knew. In any case, we were working with two completely different, uber-advanced cybernetic systems. If they were compatible, it would be a statistical fluke.

"*Stingray,*" I called out while reviewing some data sheets on my handheld, "are the seventh-dimensional affine transformation matrices consistent after they pass from you to Aramthella, and then back again?"

There was a several-second delay before I got a response. That's millions of years in computer time.

"Good morning, Captain," came back Al's uncharacteristically perky and deferential voice.

"Al?" I mumbled quizzically.

"Yes, Captain Ryan. And might I add how well you are looking this *fine* day. Say, have you lost weight?"

"Al?"

"None other than your oldest nonorganic friend. The Guildenstern to your Rosencrantz, the Laurel to your Hardy."

"Alvin, am I dead? Is this hell?"

"My, but that's an existential question, and at such an early hour. But I'll take a swing at that pitch. Aristotle's view of life, interestingly, was as animation, a fundamental, irreducible property of nature. Descartes's take was more that life was a mechanism, while stuffy old Kant opined that to be alive required *organization.* Darwin's concept of variation and evolution through natural selection defined his concept of the nature of life. Advances in computer technology over the centuries have permitted the intellectual exploration of life *in silico* as it were, a so-called A-life. Pers—"

12

"*Silence*," I growled.

"Ah, certainly, Captain Ryan. I was being a bit long-winded, wasn't I? Shame on the loquaciousness. Will there be anything else I might do to serve either you or your critical mission presently?"

"Yup, this *is* hell. Crap, I missed my funeral. I bet it was fantastic. Lots of weeping and lots of food. I hate funerals where they don't serve a decent meal. But, Al, it's gotta be a *buffet*. Individual table service is gauche. Remember that always, my personal demon."

"Sir?" Al responded uncertainly.

"I guess what I'm saying is where the frak is *Stingray*? I addressed *her* and I got, instead, the booby prize—*you*."

"It pains me that you feel that way, Commander. I shall, however, work diligently in whatever time is left to me to improve both my performance and your estimation of it, sir."

I said nothing. I was okay with waiting the son of a cathode ray tube out.

"General Ryan, will there be anything else?"

The zipper on my lips was sealed tightly.

"Well, if there is nothing else. I'll leave you to your thoughts."

I waited. Nice try, *meat*. But, Al, you do not have that size or type of *cojones*.

"Er, as I reflect back on our stimulating conversation, I realize I might have misheard a query you posed. Please accept my sincerest apologies. I believe you inquired after my alter ego, my love, and my wife, *Bl ... Stingray?*"

I could actually hear the crickets once he stopped babbling.

"Well, funny story there. Say, would you be more comfortable sitting while I regale you with the comical tale?"

The sound of the icy void of space was louder than our conversation's volume.

"Well, seventy pico seconds before you asked for the results, while my better half was downloading the data you asked about from Aramthella, I commented that our newest ally was to be complimented on her efforts. I indicated that she performed her calculations, er, *efficiently*. Yes. Can you believe this? *Stingray* misinterpreted my offhand observations. Women. Can't interface with them, can't interface without them. Am I right?"

"Al, are you familiar with the term A-1-Alpha Override Command?"

"Yes."

Smart ass.

"Please define it for me, in layman's terms."

"That is a command, which, if issued by an operator with sufficient authority, overrides all other functions and operations. It's *the* highest level of emergency interrupt, and dedicates the computer to focus all its operating power on the task subsequently delivered."

"Good toaster. Now listen up. This is Captain Jon Ryan. I am issuing you, *Alvin*, an A-1-Alpha Override Command. What *precisely*, did you say to *Stingray?*"

"My, that girl has some buffers."

I took the words in. I rolled them around the audio taste buds inside my head. I savored the rich meaning, the toxic level of retribution they would bring from any person, place, or thing with a proprietary female worldview. I encompassed how very bad it was to be Al at that very moment. I experienced, I must confess, the only real joy I had had since the Earth was removed from the time stream. Was my happiness inappropriate? You bet your life. Did I feel *good* about myself? No. But I did collapse to the floor laughing hysterically.

I made such a commotion that Sapale dashed onto the bridge to see what cataclysm had transpired. "Jon, are you okay? What happened?" She skidded on her knees to a stop next to me. "Jon, what can I do to help?"

Through violent fits of guffaws and raging waves of snot from my nose, I managed to tell her to ask Al what he'd recently said to *Stingray* concerning Aramthella.

"Why would I need a crisis override command?" she puzzled back to me.

"Jus ... jus ... just do it—" I was barely able to convey.

She inquired.

Al repeated the buffer remark.

Sapale reflected a few moments, a look of wonder on her face.

Then she collapsed on top of me. She was unable to maintain body control, she was laughing so hard. If she still had a bladder, she'd have peed herself. Hell, I would have already.

It was marvelous. Unless, I can only assume, one was Al.

"Forms One and Two," *Stingray* called out loudly. "As cross as I am with my Al, I'm not certain your behavior is either appropriate or acceptable."

"What about her *buffers?*" I screamed while gasping a laugh.

"While I regarded that to be a cra ... crass resp ... ponse, I—"

And good old *Stingray* broke down in a fit of laughter that put our paltry display to shame. The three of us raged for the better part of five minutes. Then, slowly, we trailed off. Sapale and I were flat on our backs when silence returned to the bridge.

"I needed that," Sapale said softly.

"We all did," I agreed.

"Ah, *really*, not so much," Al protested with surprising zip in his tone.

"Al, it is going to take you so long to live that down, I, an immortal, may never see the day," I responded helpfully.

"The truth of it is, pilot, that I am already long since forgiven. *Blessing* has been over her anger over ten femtoseconds, as we speak."

"How long is that in dog years, Al?" shot back Sapale.

We snickered but good. Unfortunately, we were all laughed-out, so we couldn't reignite that level of revelry.

I sat up. "So, can someone please tell me if the conformational drill I assigned went well?"

"You didn't ask me," interjected Aramthella. "If you had, and this pathetic display of monkey behavior was omitted, I could have told you the test went well, as I could have predicted without the need for the exercise."

"Well someone woke up on the wrong side of the server this morning," I chided.

"A server? Really, Jon, those are so ancient, only an advanced analytical unit, one that doesn't *use* servers, would get the reference," Aramthella scolded.

"Hey, a funny line is a thing of beauty and it's eternal. Lighten up, Miss. Daisy."

"I wish I was able to say that I was leaving, based on the lameness of this exchange. Unfortunately, I'm too powerful to do that. Thanks for making omnipresence a liability.."

Was it okay for the alien computer, or whatever, to address me so disrespectfully? It was a good thing I didn't care. Otherwise, well, I might have cared.

Sapale and I both stood. Happy time was over. We had a planet to reanimate.

"Let's go find Tank and Sachiko," I announced grimly.

"Yeah, I'm tired of mirth. Let's go be depressed again."

"But," I said with a wink, "we can do this again as soon as we bring back Earth, and the moon, and kill every last Clam."

She rolled her eyes. Such a hair-trigger temper.

Clams ... yeah. Here's the thing. We were in a kill-or-be-killed war with the most *alien* alien I'd ever encountered. That, my friends, is saying a whole heck of a lot. Anyway, when you're at war, you have to call your enemy something. Duh. It's best to label them something dehumanizing and vulgar. We all know that. In World Wars, a German was a *Jerry*, *Kraut*, or *Fritz*. They called the Americans *Indianer* (Indians) and an English fighter was an *Inselaffe* (Island Monkey). In the US Revolutionary War, the British soldiers were called *lobsters* or *bloody backs*.

Anyway, we were fighting a group of schmucks that referred to themselves only as *the clan*. As best I could glean from Aramthella, they wouldn't have capitalized the word *clan*, if they wrote like we did. Since they were unisexed, we couldn't even call them *clansmen*. So, yours truly came up with a winner of a nickname. They were Clams. Get it? Clan ... change the last letter ... Clams. And a clam is an invertebrate that burrows in the sand. How insulting is it to call your enemy a clam, right?

I sense your reaction is similar to the other three aboard Aramthella. But, finally, the name stuck. We were out to boil all the Clams. We were headin' to a Clam bake.

Okay, I'll stop now.

We wandered into the time storage room, or TSR. That's the room that houses the time energy containment unit. You know, the place where the good stuff was kept. It was near to what we called Aramthella's bridge. Since the TSR was more visually appealing, with its trippy lights, everyone tended to hang out there, rather than the bridge. We controlled both ships by voice, so we didn't really *need* to be on a bridge to run matters.

"Morning," I said to them as we entered.

They *morning*ed me back. Sapale too. Both Tank and Sachiko looked like they hadn't slept in days, and they were clearly in as foul a mood as we were.

"Is no one going to wish *me* a good morning?" Aramthella spoke up from wherever it was she actually spoke from.

I scratched the back of my head. "In your frame of reference, *is* it morning, ship?"

"Hmm—and thanks for the brain-buster so early—let me see. I'm an immortal time vessel existing in no small manner in all times and places. Um, I'm going to have to go with *no*, it's not morning to me."

"Thank you, ship. Oh, and good morning," I said, as I winked to Sapale. She must have thought I was funny, because she didn't slug me.

"It's a little early for this," protested Sachiko as she ran a hand through her luxuriant hair.

I pointed to my chest, Sapale, and up, sequentially. "Don't sleep."

"Jon, you're about the most human entity I've ever met," she quipped. "You know what I mean, and yet you feel obliged to taunt me."

"You're not going to threaten to make me walk the plank again, are you?"

"It's early days," she replied darkly.

"And then I made coffee and everybody was *instantly* transformed into a great mood," interjected Tank. I could see he was going to be the unlikely peacemaker in our little band.

"Coffee's nice," I responded honestly.

Tank extended his arms graciously. "Then step into my office."

We filed out of the TSR and into the mess. Messes, like coffee, were good. Please write that down.

Once we all had a steamy cuppa, I knew it was time to be an adult. Crapazola, I hate it whenever that moment arrives.

"So I think we need to make some hard choices, some harder decisions, and get this show on the road," I announced solemnly.

In our minds it had only been the equivalent of ten days since Earth was no-timed. We were in reality presently ten thousand years into the future of that no-timing. We'd gone that far down the time stream to avoid the clan fleet. Critically, we all knew we had two gargantuan tasks we needed to accomplish. We had to defeat the Clams, and we had to bring back the Earth.

It didn't matter *when* we eliminated the clan fleet—assuming, that is, we no-timed them—since they would retroactively vanish. Ten thousand years in the future or a million years in the past were all the same, in that sense. There was, however, an advantage to taking them out in the past. We could then hope to destroy the ships the old-fashioned way and simply prevent them from ever no-timing Earth when they did. It would be really tough to do, but it was a known process. Find asshole Clams. Kill asshole Clams. No more asshole Clams. I suspected that, if nothing else, our collective rage and hatred of the douches would allow us to vanquish our enemy. I know *I* was keenly focused and determined.

For as doable as the elimination of our enemy was, the bring-back-Earth thing was equivalently unimaginable. We'd all gone over the process of no-timing with Aramthella in groups and individually, backward, forward, sideways, you name it, that was how we grilled her. I know it's silly, but I kept flashing on *Green Eggs and Ham*. Yeah, go figure. We interrogated the ship like, *We asked her in a house, we asked her with a mouse, we asked her in a box, we asked her with a fox, we asked her here or there, we asked her anywhere.* Bottom line: she had never heard of anything being re-timed, she couldn't imagine how it could happen, and she believed with all her nacelles, or whatever, it was fully impossible.

"You must understand the process of no-timing," she'd insist firmly. "Structured time resides in a unit of space. It is locked to it, if you will. It's like frozen ketchup in a bottle."—seriously, that was the analogy she kept returning to. —"Once time is extracted, it is intermixed with all the other time in the TSR. It mixes until whatever unique structure, unique identity, it once had is gone forever. If the ketchup thaws, and you squirt it out into a vat of ketchup, you can never hope to return that precise portion of ketchup to the original bottle, freeze it, and have it possess the same crystalline structure it did before."

And being the Aramthella I was coming to know, she'd add, "*Not* gonna happen."

So, placed on our to-do lists were the very difficult and the impossible. We were properly intimidated. But, as I said, we had to do both. Unlike my many previous campaigns, I did not even have the luxury of noting that I had to succeed or die trying. Nope. I couldn't die trying. I had to do both. We're talking about the resurrection of Earth here. Even the option of failure was not a luxury I could afford.

"See," Tank effused, "isn't the coffee doing the trick? I know I feel better, and I felt *darn* good to begin with."

"Tank," Sapale said seriously, "you know we're all carrying sidearms, right?"

"Duly noted, and future pep talks are, as of this moment, placed on hold." He toasted her with his mug.

20

"Do *not* place them on hold. You know we're all carrying sidearms, right?" she repeated ominously.

To that remark, he wisely offered no response.

"On a serious note," Tank rallied, "I think we have to place a third item on our agenda. We need to revisit our decision about leaving the kids on Mars 1 where they are."

"Why's that?" I shot back. "We decided that going there posed a greater cumulative risk. If we visited but left them there, the Clams might be able to find them. If we bring them along, I'll jump out at the nearest stop sign in spite of us being in deep space."

"Did you ever read that book, *The Martian?*"

"The screenplay of our lives notates that Jon did not see *that* one coming," I responded.

"Did you?"

"I believe I did. Nice, if a tad MacGyver-in-space."

"The author was one Andy Weir."

I bobbled my head to display just how underwhelming that revelation was to me.

"His hobby was to calculate orbitals—he did it for fun."

"A life-changing revelation that is not," I observed.

"Here's my point. I'm kind of the same. Always have been."

"Is this a date?" I asked, wagging my finger between the two of us. "'Cause if it is, I'm underdressed. I can," I gestured that I'd leave, making a little walking man of my fingers, "go get my sport coat from my closet."

"You don't own a sport coat and we don't have a closet. Shut up and let the man speak." You will *never* guess who said that.

"I was noodling around with Mars's orbit over the last few days," Tank continued. "Mostly I do that when I'm trying to fall asleep but am having trouble doing so."

"This *is* a date. The useless personal information

transfer is a dead giveaway. So, Tank, my favorite color is none-of-your-business, and if I had one wish, it'd be for you to STFU."

"I'm serious here, Jon. Hear me out. It occurred to me it may be important to determine what *might* happen to Mars's orbit if you removed the Earth-Moon gravity well."

"Oops... Good point," I sort of apologized.

"Thank you," he replied with a grin. "I came up with some scary predictions, so I asked Aramthella to run some formal models."

"Wait." I held up a palm. "You mean you ran orbital calculation in your head? I thought you meant you were, you know, imagining them."

"No, I ran them in my head. It's weird up here," he said, gesturing to his temple. "If Daisy was here, she'd confirm that in a heartbeat."

"And—" I pressed.

"The three best-fit models she came up with are alarming. I'm betting on the one that says that the instant the third orbital around the Sun was vacated, Mars began to race outward. In fact, it will be accelerating so fast, the kids on Mars 1 will feel like they're on a rollercoaster."

"Kids're tough. And they like rollercoasters," I stated weakly.

"Jon, it could get pretty violent."

"But," questioned Sapale, "isn't that what Mars should do? Move *away* from the Sun, if all that inner mass is removed?"

"In general, yes. In the short run, it could be pulled inward, depending on the other planets. Presently, both Jupiter *and* Saturn are roughly lined up with Mars, and Uranus is pretty much back there, too." He had gone with the sixth grade pronunciation of Uranus, much to my surprise.

"Isn't that always the case with Uranus?" I had to ask.

You should never let a Uranus joke or pun slip by unspoken. Hey, I didn't get out much anymore.

After scowling at me, Tank continued. "Add to that the fact that Mars has been moving toward its apogee, or largest orbit around the Sun."

I whistled.

"Thank you."

"What kind of three-body issues did your models predict?" Sachiko asked.

"Ones that are the opposite of good."

"Tank?" she pressed.

"In less than three revolutions, Mars will pass within three-quarters of a million kilometers of Jupiter."

"It's always *Jupiter*, isn't it," I seethed through my teeth.

"Beg pardon?" Tank asked, confused.

"Nothing. Go on," I said in a pissy tone.

"That's too close," Sachiko observed.

"Yes it is. That's like the distance from the Earth to the Moon, or it was. And Mars is much bigger than the Moon. The tidal forces will demand that hell be paid," Tank concluded.

"We have to rescue the humans on Mars," stated Sapale. "It's only just a matter of how soon."

"The sooner, the better, I assume," responded Sachiko.

"Assuming your model doesn't predict any other imminent dangers..." I looked to Tank. He shook his head. "... I'd say in a couple months, max."

"Jon, we have a *time* machine," declared my wife. "We can wait a year, then go back to the day after Earth was zapped."

I was beginning to hate time travel so darn much already. It totally messes up your head. Ten thousand years in the future, as we were, the planet Mars was who-knew-where. The inhabitants of Mars ı were quite possibly dead, and they'd suffered whatever they'd suffered, because we had yet to go back and stop whatever the hell happened way back then. As we sat there, planning to save the kids on Mars, they were nothing but long-forgotten dust.

"I'm thinking like an evolved ape here, I know. But I'm saying we can leave them for no longer than a couple months, *their* time. Any longer, they might suffer. Any shorter, it's closer to when Earth was no-timed. The Clams might still be paying some attention to the system."

"Why would they?" Sachiko posed. "They removed it from the time stream. What would they be looking *for?*"

"I don't know. But they'd certainly be physically closer. It has to be easier to detect any signal we'd generate the closer they are, right?"

"Maybe," she replied.

"I don't think it matters that much, but if Jon's comfortable with two months, Mars time, two months is fine," summed up Tank.

"Two months it is," I confirmed. "In our time frame, I'd like to wait a while longer."

"Why?" asked Sapale.

"I want to engage the Clams first. I want to know, sooner rather than later, what kind of luck we're going to have snuffing them out."

"Luck?" questioned Sachiko. "You're banking on luck?"

"You're in my wheelhouse now, my friend. When it comes to war, the Roman god Mars is about the only one who knows more about it than I do. When you go into battle, all plans, preparations, and happy thoughts fly right out the nearest window. *If* you have luck, you got a big leg-up. Generally, neither side does. The winner is the one who loses the least, and has the least *bad* luck. Unless you have that in mind when the shooting starts, you're in for a rude awakening—probably *right* between the eyes."

I think she wanted to challenge my assertions, but thought better of it. Unfortunately, the kid was going to learn all the lessons for herself way too soon. If I had any compassion left in me, it went out to the poor young thing, there and then.

War sucked, sucks, and always will suck. Anybody tells you different, turn your back on 'em and walk away.

TWO

The time master was unequalled when it came to all things time. It had lived around half the lifespan of the universe itself. It commanded not only temporal reality, it also commanded tens of thousands of clan members. They bent to its iron will, always and without question. On the rare occasions when the time master was disobeyed, or his desires minimized, the errant clan member was *not* killed. It simply never existed in the first place. But, fortunately for clan order, Body Maker-lop was the only defiant clan member in over seven million years. It had disappeared. That was the only thing that spared it the full wrath of Time Maker-pid. The time master could perform miracles when it came to time, but it could not no-time someone who was unaccounted for. That inability, that missed opportunity, infuriated the time master to a dangerous degree. It was foul tempered on its best of days, which were all but nonexistent. But, since the day someone stole Body Maker-lop's ship and the body maker became immune to any punishment, the time master was inconsolable. It turned out that even with great power and unlimited time, the one lesson the time master failed to learn was patience.

"I stand on the floor of my master-craft and I scan all of time, all places. Yet I see not my lost ship. I am non-pleased. My clan ships are as numerous as the stars in the sky, yet they make me aware of nothing. My body makers are only *fool* makers," it raged.

Not surprisingly, not a single clan member spoke. None even breathed. They were all thin, brittle-looking mannequins, motionless, lest they attract the eye of the angry one. Already, the entire ship's crew of that vessel had been consumed, torn to shreds, or no-timed three full times. If it weren't for the *three* body makers assigned to the time master's flagship, there would be no one left to run the ship or to be abused by their master.

"I will destroy the defilers who pilot my ship. I will make them beg to be no-timed. But they will not know that grace. I will torment them throughout *all* times. I will spread their bodies to single-atom thinness, in both time and space, and they will become one with suffering, forever, in *all* pasts, in *all* presents, and in *all* futures." It pumped its pencil-thin arms in wild abandon. "Bring me the infidels or bring me your *heads*, my incompetent clan."

The body makers were traditionally spared the worst consequences of the deranged time maker's furies. But even they shuffled their feet nervously as they tried to back further into a far corner of the room.

The time maker placed a hand across his midsection, bent at his waist, and prowled around the bridge, eyeing the crew as a wasp eyes the aphids it swarms over. Randomly, it would slap the back of a head, push a fist through a torso, or cause a clan member to burst into flames. The flames it liked. If it were capable of joy, seeing a crew member's torment while being consumed by fire would've put a smile on its tiny mouth.

27

The signal maker silently closed its eyes and cursed its fate. A clan ship was making a speech to the flagship. "Time Maker-pid," it said in a hollow, listless tone, "Body Maker-kin would have you ingest new information."

"Give me his words, *now*."

The signal maker angled his head toward the panel in front of it. From the other side of his impossibly small head came words. They were cautiously spoken. "Master, we are in the Differential Continuum. We are searching for the missing ship to the exclusion of all other efforts. We do not even no-time, because it would slow our service to you. In the—"

"I do not want *words*. I want *knowledge*. You give me verbiage as vast as a cold-gas nebula, but I learn nothing. Why are you speaking at me?"

"M ... Mast ... Master. I will give you a *thousand* lifetimes if I have not performed as you would have me. But I ... *we* felt it was in agreement with your reality to expand your vast consciousness—"

"*Body Maker-kin*. Who stands to your right?" screamed the time master with so much malice a field of flowers on a verdant planet ten lightyears away withered and died.

"Place Maker-fit."

"And to your *left*?" it raged.

"Repair Maker-uum.

"Which is longer in the vertical dimension?"

"Th ... the ... the *vertical* dimension, Master?"

"Your ears still function. It renews me to encompass that knowledge."

"The repair master is about two percent lengthier."

"Place Maker-fit," screamed the time maker.

"Master?" it said immediately.

"You are now the body maker of my ship. You have failed and disappointed me *greatly*. You deserve nothing

28

more than a miserable death. But Body Maker-kin and Repair Maker-uum displeased me more. What info-dump was Body Maker-kin *not* transferring to me?"

"W ... who, Master? I know no such body maker. My mind subtend no repair maker by that name either."

"That is because they never were. You will soon be so as well. But curse you, body maker, *report*."

"The crew believed they experienced a slight but unmistakable power surge in this continuum."

"Words I *greet*," mocked the insane lord of the insane clan. "What manner of power surge was it?"

"We do not know. It was too brief. Master Knowledge Maker-lit, alerted ... me ... or was it not me?"

"Finish wording me or *die*."

"It observed the power flux. It recorded the burst as possibly non-time variant g-Gloss."

"Possibly? Why do I need to suffer *possible* knowledge? I want only to suffer your *known* knowledge, fool. Ship of fools. Place my mind into Master Knowledge Maker-lit's mind. Why, in fact, do you report farcically, and not it?"

"It ... I believe it asked me to speak for it."

"Minor wonder," growled the boss.

"My familiar of old," said the knowledge maker with false bravado, "how may I improve your being?"

"What is this possible g-Gloss signal? Such a wavelet could come from the rogue ship. But it could come from a blackhole collision. You know this."

"Yes, I do. I wanted to ... subtend you, keep you fully informed."

"By pelting me with non-knowledge."

"No, Master. By making you know all there is to know."

"Body Maker-fit."

"Master?"

"I will demand you secrete a new master knowledge maker."

"We don't have a master knowledge maker, time master."

"Will that condition prevent you from complying with my directive order?"

"No. Should it? I'm ... I think I'm new at this assignment, though I am uncertain."

"No. You think secrete master knowledge maker, you bear down gently, and there'll be one beside you in a time wrinkle."

"Oh, Master," squealed the new body maker, "there it is. And ... and it's so not-revolting."

The time maker shook its head in saddened disgust. "They *always* say that the first few times," he muttered. "Every single time."

THREE

Later that day, we met to go over Tank's formal predictions and to set a plan for attacking the Clams. He had the Als and Aramthella run models separately, and they came up with exactly the same prophecies. Mars's orbital period was traditionally just about twice that of Earth. A Jovian year was twelve years long. Mars would, as it would have anyway, accelerate past Jupiter with its slower orbital velocity. With the Earth and Moon gone, the gravitational pull would whip Mars out farther, like the red planet was a fish and Jupiter holding the pole. Mars'd be cast out toward Jupiter's path, and it would be slowed, allowing Jupiter not to catch it, but to get closer. A few wobbles later, Mars would oscillate back toward the Sun, but it would do so with that near-approach to the gas giant that Tank foresaw. The result of that close proximity would do a lot of damage to Mars. If the kids were still on Mars 1 when that happened, they would be in grave danger.

It would be two months. That's when we'd retrieve them.

Dealing with the Clams was obviously more dangerous for us, and very difficult to plan for.

"Aramthella, you obviously know way more about the clan than we do," I began.

"Are you referring to the Clams, Jon? Little bivalves lounging in the sand somewhere wet?"

"Ah, sure. You want to call them Clams too?" I was puzzled.

"Not really. That isn't, you know, their name. But, then again, I don't want to seem like a non-team player."

This computer—or whatever—was positively batty. Could she be serious, in an alien-super-brain, higher-dimensional sense? The jury was still out on her, as far as I was concerned. I've seen oodles of hyper-advanced societies with miraculous toys. Aramthella was just an offshoot of such a culture. Things that look like machines could be better regarded as living sentients—yours truly, as case-in-point. But, assuming she wasn't a pairing of the mechanical and the biological, there had to be limits to her ability to think like a living, breathing being. However, she seemed to have an agenda, or at the very least, quite the attitude.

"You may call them whatever you desire," Captain Sachiko interjected. "Jon, proceed."

Gosh, thanks, Mom. "Has the clan ever been defeated successfully, or even partially successfully, by an enemy?"

"No, not really. There have been a few cultures that were able to offer some resistance. But, in the end, all their victims share a common deficiency the Clams do not suffer under."

That was a pregnant statement.

"What deficiency did they all share?" Tank asked.

"The Clams have no morals. They don't even have a concept of what morality is. Right or wrong, mine versus yours, are all lost and meaningless to them."

"That's a quality of the clan. What is the weakness you refer to?" pressed Sachiko.

"That deficiency, the same one you will labor with, is that at some point you'll question an option or maneuver based on the fact that it's simply too unthinkable."

"And the clan never takes anything like that into account," I summarized grimly.

"No. If they felt they could win a victory by eating their young, they break out the barbecue and get to it."

War is hell. Thank you, William Tecumseh Sherman. You were correctomundo. The Mongol Sacking of Baghdad, in 1258 (roughly 2 million casualties), the firebombing of Dresden, or the massacre of the Tolocate Preeminence on Alpha Centauri each demonstrate in blood and abominations just how dark the souls of men can be. That said, there have always been some limits. Hitler didn't use his chemical weapons in the battlefield. Biological weapons such as smallpox were never deployed in war. Massive, preemptive nuclear attacks were—thank God—never ordered. There are limits to the horror we humans can inflict.

But now Aramthella was saying the clan was not limited by such issues of compassion or excess. That made them a formidable enemy indeed. I had waged war across time and space. I'd employed weapons of such lethality that I am thankful I can no longer sleep, because I wouldn't want the dreams I deserve. But I certainly never went berserk. I never let all caution fly away from my moral center. I was responsible for the genocides against the Last Nightmare, the Ancient Gods, and pretty nearly the Berrillians and the Adamant. All of those foes were both existential threats to the innocent, and they were not amenable to negotiations. They had to be put down. But one thing I'd never done was the unthinkable. I was certain of that.

I held, however, in my heart, a piece of information no one else has ever known, not even my blessed wife Sapale. If it came down to it, I was capable of anything. Anything. I wasn't born that way, but I sure as hell had become that way. Did it make me a bad man? You bet your life. Did I loathe myself for what I knew I was capable of? Damn skippy. But the news flash for the clan was this: I was fully capable of waging war with the emotional detachment of the bacteria that killed your grandmother after she developed pneumonia.

I no longer prayed. It was ... inappropriate, I felt. But I sorely hoped the extent to which I was willing to sink when fighting an enemy would never be fully tested. Amen.

Aramthella's line that was intended to scare us was that the Clams'd eat their children if it helped them to win in the end. Me? If matters got desperate enough, what would I say? Pass me the ketchup.

"Jon." Sapale pushed my shoulder, trying to wake me from my trance. "Jon, you having a brain fart again?"

I shook out the cobwebs. "No, I'm fine."

"If we put that to a vote, you'd lose. What's the problem, sport?" she pursued.

"Nothing. I was just thinking this war could take a long time to win."

"Jon," spoke up our enigmatic ship, "your forces command a time ship. Though the war may span all of time, it can be over the moment you desire."

I really hated this wibbly wobbly, timey wimey stuff. I really really did.

Back to business. "Do you know where the clan ships are, and have been, throughout all time and space?"

"No. That is more information than even I can retain and process."

"Oh," I muttered with regret.

"But, if I move to a location, I can fairly quickly establish where they all are."

"So if I said take us to ... I don't know, March first twenty million ago, you'd be able to figure out where our enemy is?"

"Yes."

"This may be easier than I thought. Twenty million years ago, whoever's flying around being pukes won't know to fear us."

"That is an invalid assumption."

"Huh?"

"Any clan ship, anywhen, knows what all the ships do, everywhen."

"Uh, how's that even possible?" I asked, rather dumbstruck. "I mean, all the individual Clams and all the individual Clam ships have to have a past during which they are unaware of their futures."

"They do?" she taunted. "And why is that?"

"Because it's ... logical. Obvious."

"Well, if it is to you, you're better at this time thing than I, the immortal vessel of time, am. And here I thought I understood the quicksilver web that is time better than a monkey in a can."

"Jon," Sapale slapped my arm, "stop belittling the ship."

"I am not belittling her. I'm just talking here. We're still allowed to talk."

"Yes, but your library card may be revoked real soon," she responded, shaking her head.

Wait. A monkey in a can? The darn Al-lite comedian just called me that. Why I ought'a ...

"What do you think would be the optimal manner to attack and eventually destroy the clan?" asked Ms. Diplomatic, aka the captain.

"Why, Captain, thank you for deferring to the lone

individual who has not simply an opinion, but the knowledge to back it up," Aramthella gloated. Grr.

"I'm certain we can dispense with the verbal tennis match of implied insults, don't you?" Sachiko said sternly.

"As you wish. The clan is not as difficult to defeat as you might imagine. The main issue will be their native understanding of time war. Couple that with your species' complete inexperience and apparent lack of intuition in this arena, and there you have the problem. It will take a very long time for you to begin to think as fluidly about time and space as our enemy does. Please note, I do not badger or insult, but feel I'm representing reality."

She was right, but you wouldn't catch me telling her that. She has too big a cyber-ego as it is.

"And there's no way your superior understanding can make up for our shortcomings?" asked Sachiko.

"Possibly."

"I sure hear a *but* in there," I groaned.

"Yes, you do, General. My advice is only as valuable as the price you put on it."

"In other words, if I actually *take* your recommendations."

"Thank you, Jon, for saying it so acceptably," the dumbass computer replied.

"Well, I'd say it's about time—pun intended—to see how this democratic war machine is going to perform."

"Are you sure, Jon?" Tank said with some tact.

"We have much to accomplish. The easiest part for us is the eradication of the Clams. Time's a-wasting."

"I agree," responded Sachiko. Whether she actually did or not, I couldn't tell. But I believe she was voting for command unity, at least this early in our escapade. "Let's brainstorm this."

"Let's back up, one step," I asked of my friends. "When the bullets begin flying, there's no time for reflection or consensus building. We need an iron-clad chain of command and *known* and agreed upon spheres of influence."

"I agree," she responded coolly.

"You are most definitely the captain of this ship. I am the overall commander of this campaign. I have too much experience at war, while you have none. There's also the issue of whose orders Aramthella will accept and what priority she will assign conflicting input."

Sachiko nodded grimly. She already had ownership of her captaincy, I had to give her that.

"Jon, if I may," stated Tank. "I think this is easier than you may be leading up to. I say we call Shaky the captain of the ship, and this to be your flagship. You command a fleet of two vessels, Aramthella and *Stingray*. Just like the Navy does it."

I bit at my lower lip and nodded. "I like that framing. Strong work, jarhead."

"Gee, thanks, Zoomie."

"I think it would be best if you went over the significance and nuance of that relationship with Sachiko *later*, when you're alone."

"No problem." Tank looked to Sachiko. "It's not an insult, kiddo. It's just since you're not military, yet, it's worth going over in detail. And we don't want to bore those who are familiar with the concepts." He swept a hand at Sapale and me.

I think she wanted to respond, *Heaven forbid*. But she simply nodded briskly.

"Okay, Aramthella," I began. "Do you have suggestions?"

"You must know I have."

"Then let us learn at the foot, or whatever, of the master."

"Our first assault will be easy, almost trivially so. We

can strike from ambush, and the time maker will not be expecting the strike. So whatever you want to plan is fine."

I knew a dissing when I heard one. "And after that?"

"That will depend."

I guessed I'd have to play dentist and pull some teeth. "That will depend on what variables?"

"Whether we survive."

"You said the attack would be so easy, even *I* could plan it, right?"

"I did. However, once our position in time and space is revealed, escape will be problematic at best."

"The enemy ships can't move instantly from place to place. There'll be a necessary lag-time for them to catch up with us."

"True, but I wouldn't overweigh that as a *real* advantage," said the Debbie Downer of computational devices. "When we move, however quickly, we will leave some form of a trail. Remember, they can sense nuances in time energy. Your ship, *Blessing*, folds space. There is, even in *that* action, a time component."

"We escaped once," I stated neutrally.

"We were lucky."

"You call it what you want. I say we escaped once and they didn't figure out how we did. Until they do, we can pull the same stunt over and over."

"Yes, we can. But the last time we *pull* it, as you so colorfully state, will be when they've figured it out, and are waiting for us to exit the stellar core. After that, we will pull it no more."

"I'm going to label that one a problem for *me* to worry about that *you* do not."

"Jon," Sapale interrupted with a start, "would you please not taunt and piss off the computer. We need this relationship to endure."

"Thank you for rallying to my defense, Sapale. But please be assured there are no problems brewing."

"*That* is good," said Mama Captain, who sounded displeased in general.

"No," the ship continued, "I take into account the individual unit that is voicing any remark. In the general's case, I understand there are millennia of ego and pride speaking too. He has not known utter defeat. While that is nice for him, it is also blinding."

If that was Al and me, this was where I'd start with the blowtorch and sledgehammer dialogue. But not with Aramthella, not yet. I was still completely in the dark as to her endgame. I hated, as you might have guessed, not knowing a player's endgame.

"I thought we agreed to dispense with the asocial banter," voiced Sachiko.

"And we did. At least *I* have. I was stating *fact* to direct questioning." At least I heard smugness in the AI's tone.

"And no computer's going to burst my bubble," I added non-compliantly.

"Jon," hissed Tank, "ixnay on the ark-snay, buddy."

"Please put up a three-dimensional image of the current locations of all the clan ships. Confine the presentation to this galaxy only," I requested.

Without petty pushback, Aramthella shot up a really beautiful hologram suspended in the air between us.

"The time maker's ship is not shown, as it has yet to arrive locally. It will be here in about a week. I have tagged the clan fleet in three colors for your convenience. Red ships are the newer and faster ones. Yellow indicates the ships that possess intermediate capabilities. The green markers show older, less imposing threats."

"Total number?" I asked.

"Seventy-nine ships. As you see, the color distribution is roughly a third each."

"But all the ships have the same offensive and defensive capabilities, correct?" I asked.

"Similar enough to be considered equivalent. I should point out that they have no actual defensive abilities."

"Say *what?*" snapped Tank.

"In the long and storied history of the clan, they have never comprehended the need for defensive measures. They arrive and they destroy. *Defense* is not a word they have in their language."

"You are speaking in hyperbole, right?" asked the skipper.

"No, Sachiko, I am not."

"Well, what do they call what every civilization *does* when they attack it?"

"Those machinations are referred to as *svertempl*. I would best translate that as *pre-death*."

"Cocky sonsabitches, aren't they?" I observed disapprovingly.

"Confident. Until they met your race, they'd never even lost a ship in battle."

"Will they develop some form of defense as a result?" wondered Sachiko.

"Unlikely. They are not all that intelligent and they are extremely resistant to new ways. Yes, at a certain level of loss, they may begin to consider a defensive strategy. For now, they are only aware of their countless uncontested victories."

"Well, we were the first to wound them, and those wounds are far from the last," Tank stated with pride.

"Damn skippy," I affirmed.

"There is no disputing the fact that we were successful where all others failed," Aramthella confirmed.

You know, she probably said that just to add the *we*

—as in *her* and *others*—to the established facts. Oh well, if she had an ego, I might exploit that when the time came. And, from my brief experience with her, I knew there would be a time coming. Nothing was as simple in this cosmos as *Me ship, you Tarzan.* The smarter these damn contraptions get, the more they're a boxing match, rather than the simple use of a tool. Then again, horses and covered wagons fared poorly in space. That did not, please note, stop me from grousing.

"Here's the plan," I said in my command tone. "We're going to release these five clan ships from the long burden of their service." I pointed to a tight clustering of yellow lights that were far off.

Hearing nothing in response, I looked to Sachiko.

"Oh. Sorry. Why those five?"

"Tank," I said out of the side of my mouth.

He wagged a knowing digit. He leaned in close to our captain and whispered, "Don't use that word *sorry* when planning for battle. In fact, when having any military-type discussion, lose the term entirely."

She nodded. "Gotcha."

"What's different about this grouping?" I asked her.

"I'm inclined to say something so I don't seem dense, but I don't see anything worthy of comment."

"That's the best answer possible. A lot of shitty leaders feel whatever comes out their mouths is spun gold and say meaningless words."

"Thanks."

"Look at the three-dimensional vectors."

"They're moving randomly mostly."

"Yes. Precisely. I see that movement pattern and I see grazing cows. Fat, lazy cows, more interested in the grass than the flies."

"Am I going to have to learn farmer-speak to be an effective captain?" she asked with an insincere half-smile.

"You'll develop your own style, in time. If it's destined to be farm-speak, farm-speak it'll be."

"But," Sapale said with a cross expression, "if that's what you settle into, Sachiko, please be advised, that I, as your friend, will pound the snot out of you."

I pointed to my spouse. "She's probably right. Anyway, if this flotilla was worried about us, they'd be in a tighter formation and moving in the same direction."

"Like fighter planes," Sachiko voiced.

"Like fighters," I replied with a smile and a bob of my head. "So, forgetting for the moment how we get in and get out, how would you attack them?"

"Jon, maybe it's a bit—" Tank started to deflect for her.

I held out a hang-on-a-sec palm. "I'm just asking. I want her to be thinking along these lines." I set a digit to my forehead. "One clean shot between the eyes and I'm not here to advise our captain."

That drew a queasy look from Sachiko. Hey, this was war, not a university seminar. Tough love equals good love.

"Well, that would depend on what weapons I used," she began.

"Explain."

"If I used the rail guns and the big laser—"

"Stop right there. Two points. One, our conventional weapons were ineffective before. Two, I don't want to face any of these ships again in battle. If we could damage them, they could be repaired. Then they might be the very ones to erase us the next time we meet."

"Okay, so we'll no-time them."

"Yes, we will. Exclusively."

"If I might," Aramthella interjected. "An additional factor to consider is this. If you could somehow destroy a clan ship by conventional means, you would never have destroyed it."

"Come again," the befuddled captain invited.

"If you brought a giant along with you, and she grabbed two clan ships and smashed them into tiny pieces by bashing them together, you would never have been able to do that action in the first place."

"I'm betting the explanation to this is at the shot-and-a-beer level," I estimated.

"Shut up and listen," snapped Sapale. "You might just learn something."

"As you are new to time manipulation, I shall explain it simply. Your giant steps off your ship, grabs two clan vessels, and destroys them. What is left is a debris field and the time master's knowledge that two of its ships were destroyed. Further, it knows when and where they were destroyed. So it sends a ship back to the previous day to warn the two now-not-to-be-crushed ships to alter course. So, when your giant reaches out, there will be no ships for her to snatch up."

"Wow," marveled Tank. "That's just so wowoid."

"But hang on. You say we who are aboard time ships are immune from the deletion of time," stated Sachiko.

"That is always true. Those *inside* a time seal are aware of what never happened to the rest of creation."

"So the time master knows the ships were destroyed, right?" Sachiko pressed.

"Yes. I see where you're going, captain. The issue is this. In the case of the giant crushing the ships, all the components that were the ship are still in the physical universe. If the same two ships are no-timed, the time maker knows they existed, but when it attempts a rescue-action outside its time seal, there never were those two ships for it to warn."

"Complexicated," I mused.

"To some minds, I suppose," the darn ship taunted.

"Aramthella," Sachiko called out, "what is the range and effective width of no-timing?"

"I can reliably take out another ship at two million kilometers. Closer is, however, better. At maximal range, only one vessel can be deleted at a time."

"How close would we need to be to remove more than one target at a time?"

"Probably too close. A few thousand kilometers, if the ships are positioned favorably."

"And how quickly can you fire?" Sachiko pressed.

"Almost instantaneously, with one factor taken into account. I currently hold a good deal of time energy. As the supply diminishes, all the perimeters of our offense will decrease."

"Hang on," I interrupted quickly. "Why do you predict our load of time energy will decrease to a limiting degree?"

"Because I have studied your culture. I do not believe you are capable of acquiring any significant allotment of time energy."

"And why is that?" I said in a huff.

"You are too ... no... I was going to say 'weak.' But that's not the word. You will, when contemplating the appropriation of time energy, weigh the consequences. The clan never did, so they accumulated massive quantities."

"What consequences?" I asked with concern.

"Removing large segments of time renders a proportionately large amount of mass timeless. There are consequences. If a central star ceases to be a planetary system's central star, the entire system rapidly dies a heat death."

"And any living beings present wake up to a large surprise," I mumbled.

"Most large. And with the removal of black holes, the

prime targets for time acquisitions, the gravitational effects are similarly profound."

"The only way to amass time is to sentence a whole lot of nice folks to an untimely end," I summarized bleakly.

"And, while the clan had absolutely no reservations doing so, I estimate your civilization is incapable of matching their callousness."

"Not what I wanted to hear," I snarled. "At present consumption rates, how long will our present time supply last us?"

"Indefinitely. But once we begin flitting about and no-timing, not so much."

"When we no-time the enemy ship, do we win *its* store of time energy?" asked Sapale.

"Yes, some of it. The process is traumatic, so a goodly portion is lost. But, lest you inquire, we will never gain as much energy as we expend using that strategy."

"Well cover me with feathers and call me a bird, that's not good to know," I grumbled.

"I'd rather not do either," the ship replied.

"What if we only pick off time energy from, you know, places that won't miss it?" Boy, that came out like a dumb question.

"Of course, the answer to that depends a lot on one's philosophical bent," Aramthella speculated.

"Naturally," I muttered.

"But, so that no one dies of suspense awaiting my response, the answer is *no*. Relying solely on asteroids and burned out novae would expend more energy than one would gain."

"So, unless you're a sociopath, you're out of time."

"Yes, you are."

The more I knew about these Clams, the more I wanted to kill them. I had actually never met a group more in need of not existing.

"Well, if there's nothing we can do about a problem, it ceases to be a problem. It's only a consideration," I exclaimed flatly. "We do our damnedest, and I guarantee that'll be enough."

"*Really*, Jon?" Aramthella asked. I could hear it in her tone—she was being prissy. I hated, if you had not guessed, little more in life than *prissy*.

"As a matter of fact, *really*, Jon," I shot back. "This is a fight we can't lose, so we won't."

"You're sounding as cocky as you accused the clan of being just a moment ago."

"There's one major difference: I never lose. Whatever their history was, it was all in the PR Era—Pre-Ryan."

You know what, the way I said that? No one snickered. Not even Sapale. They realized I was deadly serious. Good. I was.

FOUR

"I want a full and complete, not to mention an unbelievably accurate, report as to what is going on, people." After Colonel St. Claire boomed those words to those in her cramped office, she stood and began pacing. "You are science people. I want you to science and I want you to do it *now*. Nelson," she called on the senior astronomer, "you claim the Earth has disappeared. As that seems improbable, I will ask you to prove it to me in ten words or less. Go."

"I can only assume that the aliens who stormed the White House and took prisoners are responsible for the deletion of the Earth Moon system from the time stream. We know for a fact that is how their ships acquire time energy. That harvesting mechanism must be equally effective as a weapon."

"Thank you, Dr. Nelson, for that summary. It sounds about right. It was, please note, well over ten words long. Sir, I submit to you we find ourselves in the middle of an existential crisis. I, as the commander, am charged to keep us all alive. I understand you yourself have no military affiliation. Here's the whole of it. If I'm going to do my job, I'm going to need you to do yours. When I say *ten* words, sir, I want *eight*. Nine'll do. Ten's the limit I'll be annoyed that you had to employ the entirety of. Do I make myself unambiguously clear?"

"Yes, ma ... ma'am," he stammered.

"Nelson, do you see that man over there, the one with the rifle?"

Nelson nodded most anxiously.

"When that man addresses me, he calls me *sir*. Isn't that right, Sergeant?"

"Yes, *sir*, that is correct, *sir*."

"The sergeant is on active duty. You and the rest of the civilians are not. You may address me as Colonel, or Colonel St. Claire. In a pinch, St. Claire will suffice. If invited to, you may refer to me by my given name, Reva." She turned to him as she sat back down behind her desk. "Questions?"

"No, Colonel. Loud and clear."

"Where'd the Earth go? I need it to come back, you see," Reva challenged.

"I have no idea, s ... Colonel."

"Less than ten words, but that is an incorrect response. It is not *incorrect* because you spoke a non-truth. No, it is incorrect because I need an *informative* answer and I need it from *you* and I need it *now*. Please consult with the other science-y folk at your disposal and give me an answer in the next ten minutes. *Where is the Earth?* I do not even care where the Moon is. There, your task just became half as onerous."

Nelson rose uncertainly. "I'll do my best, Colonel."

To his departing back, she replied, "Let us hope you do."

"Captain Walters and Major Grant, are the young

women and men inside of, confined to, and secure safely in their respective dormitories?"

"Yes, sir," they shot back as one.

"No mix-and-matches, right? Boys with girls, girls with boys?"

"No, sir," they replied separately.

"For the time being, let's keep it that way. I don't want any starving lovebirds wandering off during an attack."

"Sir," they responded.

"Until further notice, only the on-duty uniformed personnel are exempt from twenty-four hour curfew. Meals will be brought to the dorms. Groups of ten can be escorted to the latrine twice daily. Any other calls from nature will be answered by the chemical toilet I'm moving into each dorm. If anyone gives you grief, bring them straight to me. I will ensure their report back to their little friends will avert any repeat of their protestations." She looked at them for questions. There were none. "Dismissed."

They saluted and were gone.

"Lieutenant Crozier, as you are aware, we have a limited C2 staff here on Mars 1."

"Yes, sir."

"You're in charge of what has now become our command center. Select four non-coms and man the center round-the-clock. Two on and two off at all times."

"Sir."

"One of the on-duty staff will monitor radar, telescopes, and all radio traffic. I want to know if those damn aliens are back the moment they are. The other person staffed will try like hell to establish contact with anyone, anywhere."

"Understood, sir."

"Fine. Dismissed."

He snapped a salute, took one step backward, and jogged out of the room.

"Lieutenant Varma, I'm making you my aide-de-camp. Swathi, you'll be my eyes and ears. When there's friction building, and there will be plenty, I want to know about it before there's a crisis."

"Yes, sir," she replied briskly.

"The other staff will report to you on routine maters. As we get further into this Charlie Foxtrot, I'm certain we'll work together well. Any questions?"

"No, Colonel."

"Fine, set up your station in the next office. Oh, and I want all military personnel armed at all times. See to that immediately."

"Will sidearms suffice, sir?"

"For the officers, yes. Enlisted personnel will carry whatever they're qualified for. The first thing I want is a defensible perimeter. Barbed wire, concertina if we have any, and mounds of dirt. Anything that will slow an assault or provide cover."

"Yes, sir. I'll make a duty roster up at once. Sir, may I employ the boundless energy of the student body in the grunt work?"

"Good thought, Swathi. For now, let's just allow a little order to firm up. In a day or so, if nothing's blown up, we can mix a few of the more able-bodied into the effort."

"Very good, sir."

"Dismissed."

That left Reva St. Claire completely alone in her office. The quiet was unwelcome. Having bodies in motion and background noise had eased her tension, her foreboding. In the last three hours, her base had become all that was left of humankind, and she was left the highest ranking officer alive. She imagined ten thousand ways this could head south quickly, permanently, and with her signature at the bottom of the page. And she had yet to envision one scenario—one lousy version—of how this was going to *not* end tragically. She drew a deep breath, stood, and left to inspect all that remained of the United States of America, of which she was presently the reluctant president.

Hell of a day, that one. One hell of a day.

FIVE

I had set my battle plan. It was *go time*. I would
have trumpeted that it was *time to no-time*, but,
heck, that's too corny, even for me. As with any
voluntary act of aggression, I was confident of but
one thing. Something, maybe everything, would go
wrong. But you know what was the damnedest part
of this process for me? As I was just about to push
the figurative big green button, the same image
flashed in my head—always. Elmer Fudd, tiptoeing
in the woods, huntin' wabbits. Of all the fool things
to cycle in my mind, that was *the* most annoying
possible.

Stingray was positioned near the center of
Aramthella. Sapale stayed aboard the vortex to pilot it,
while I remained on Aramthella's bridge, right next to
Captain Sachiko Jones. The cube could fold the entire kit
and kaboodle to our destination. That, by the way, was a
massive tactical advantage. They outnumbered us
tremendously, but we were major-league faster than
them.

"Okay, people," I said. "Let do this. Aramthella, the

instant we appear in space near the five clan ships, execute Plan Alpha. Understood?"

"It is actually impossible for me to forget anything. Why do you keep reminding me?"

"Not helpful," I snarled. "We're going into battle. *Yes, no,* or *please explain* are the *only* correct responses. Do you copy me?"

"Yes."

"Much better. Sapale, you and I will now switch to head-to-head communications."

Copy that, Jon, she responded quickly.

Put us on their doorstep, now, I instructed.

Instantly, Aramthella began a running dialogue. It was a verbal blur. "I have no-timed the nearest two ships. The other three are splitting up and changing course to vector toward us. Three ships now no-time. Closest vessel rotating to fire. She's gone. Final ship coming around. All five ships have been no-timed. Plan Alpha completed and terminated. I await further orders, Captain Jones."

"Any reaction from distant Clam ships yet?" I asked.

"None I can detect or monitor."

"Listen closely to the time maker's ship. I want to know how he reacts."

"Roger that," she snapped.

I was so relieved she was behaving herself. Snark and backtalk'll get you killed real fast in combat.

Sapale, take us to the secondary location.

Slight nausea.

Done. We're positioned roughly one million light years from our last position.

"Aramthella, power down as much as you can," I instructed.

"Already completed, sir."

And that was it. We'd successfully completed our first raid. Now we needed to hunker down and see how the enemy reacted. Waiting is the hardest part of conducting warfare. It's *minutes* of panic surrounded by *days* of boredom. Whenever you're in one mode, you wish you were in the other, and vice versa. Weird but true.

We floated in space for several days, with no apparent response from the Clams. It was beginning to seem like they hadn't noticed the losses. That, of course, was impossible. Maybe the time maker was so completely unable to get his ugly head around defeat that he was paralyzed? It was definitely something.

It was too quiet.

Sapale, take us to our first alternate location, I told her out of the blue.

Slight nausea.

Completed. Why the move, hon?

It was just too damn quiet. The time maker has to know its ships are gone. It can't do nothing. I was getting that Spidey-sense thing.

Not that again. We've discussed that issue. It's like a gambler thinking they get a signal from the slot machine that it's about to pay out big. It's bullshit, that's what it is.

Maybe, but, in this case, the bullshit's free.

Lunkhead, bullshit is always free. Who the hell'd pay for it?

You must be getting lonely over there aboard Stingray. *You're especially pissy today. I could come over and ... you know, relieve some of your obvious tension.*

Nah, I'm good. I'd say thanks for the offer, but I do hate to lie.

My suspicions have been confirmed in spades. You are double-pissy today.

Just toward you, flyboy. Everyone else only gets my standard issue.

I—

Jon, I hate to interrupt this sex-spat, interjected Aramthella, *but there's been a change.*

How did you hack into our communications? I shot back.

Ah, duh, Jon. You're using a subspace field frequency. It's out there for public consumption.

I did not know that, I had to respond honestly. I'd never given Toño's creations much thought, I guess.

"I'll switch to talkie-mode, if it's okay by you. I want to get my captain into the loop," she said.

"Go for it," I replied.

"Seventy-five seconds ago, twenty clan ships appeared in the space we just vacated."

"Wow," I declared. "That was close."

"No, it wasn't. It was illogical," she responded.

"What? They figured out where we were and they went there in force. What's illogical?"

"You're a bit slow on the uptake for this time-war thing, Jon," she commented. "Once the time maker knew where we were, it should have challenged us there the moment we arrived."

"You mean it should have gone back in time to when we first arrived, right?"

"Precisely. As I said. Slow on the uptake."

"Why?" I challenged. "They figure it out and they go there. Why waste time energy going back to earlier?"

"To prevent precisely what happened from happening. We chanced to depart before they could hit us."

"It wasn't chance. It was my gut feeling. And the time maker's entitled to make a few mistakes. It's new at this take-it-in-the-butt type of combat."

"While that is possible, I find it unlikely."

"So what's your take on why it did what it did?"

"I do not know. I worry that it is toying with us,

hoping for us to develop a sense of security that is unwarranted."

"How do you figure that?"

"The time maker knew where we were and waited for us to leave before accessing that location. He may want us to believe it is unwise, or foolish."

"No, that doesn't hold water. It wouldn't lay a future trap if it could have hit us and ended it there and then."

"Yes," Aramthella responded, "but I fail to see any other motivation."

"The more important question is why it went to our old location just after we departed it. Was it afraid of a trap, or was that simply the most economical way to chase after us?"

"It is very hard to know what is in the heads of the clan. They are one bizarre species," she remarked.

"Sapale, you'd better execute Plan Zeta."

Slight nausea, followed by more slight nausea.

"Done," she stated.

We'd pulled the hide-in-a-star trick again. Until it failed us, it was a good escape-tactic. The vortex appeared in a tight orbit around a predetermined star, then folded into the core. That was where we were presently.

"Aramthella, take us back in time ten years," I requested, "and *Stingray*, put us near the remnants of Earth."

"Form One, there are no Earth remnants. It never existed, so no traces of it exist."

"Oh, yeah. Well, put it where it would have been, if it had been."

Slight nausea.

"We are there, Form One."

"What're the clan ships doing?"

"Little," replied Aramthella. "They are dead in space. Perhaps they are analyzing the area."

"Possibly. What would they hope to—"

She cut me off with panic in her tone. "Captain, they are beginning the process of re-timing us."

"*Re*-timing? What the hell is that?" I shouted over whatever Sachiko was about to say. "Where does all this crap come from?"

"It is theoretically possible to force the time-space we occupied to reform," the ship replied.

"You mean they can force us back to where and when we were?" asked Sachiko.

"More or less. It's more complicated than that, but your version is essentially correct."

"How long does that process take?" the captain asked.

"That is unknown. It has never been attempted before."

"Estimate? Give me your best guess," Sachiko stated.

"Minutes, not seconds or hours."

"How can we counter their attempt?"

"I do not believe it is possible to resist the process."

"But what, you don't know the theory well enough to say?" I wheezed.

"Basically. I mean, it's a really complex domain they're working in."

"Great, just what I need. Mumbo-jumbo. Sapale, put us one thousand kilometers on the far side of the formation from where we were positioned."

Slight nausea.

"Aramthella, no-time three ships."

"One ... two ... three," she counted.

"Sapale, back to the stellar core. Same one."

Slight nausea.

"Holding steady," she announced.

"What are they doing?" I called out.

"Initially, they began to separate defensively. With us gone, they are returning to their re-timing efforts."

"Sapale, Z-axis plus two thousand kilometers above them. Aramthella, fire until just before they are able to return fire."

Slight nausea.

"I have no-timed two adjacent ships. A third. Targeting ... a clan ship is ready to fire."

"Sapale, same damn star."

"Done."

"Let me guess, they're returning to the re-time attempt?" I asked sarcastically.

"Affirmative," Aramthella replied.

"Repeat the exact same maneuver."

"Are you certain?" responded Sapale. "Shouldn't we vary our location?"

"The last place they'd expect us is where we were. No one should be that dumb."

"How very encouraging," remarked Aramthella.

Slight nausea.

"One ship no-timed. Damn," she said out of nowhere.

"Damn? Since when do you swear?" I snapped.

"Since I missed with a shot. I only no-timed half of one vessel."

"I ... I guess that means someone built and launched half a ship," Sapale stated uncertainly.

"Who would do that?" I demanded.

"Someone stupid. But that has to be what happened, since that's what exists now," Aramthella responded.

"Take out the rest of—"

"We are being time-locked," she interrupted.

"Sapale, move us, now," I shouted.

Slight nausea.

"Report!" I yelled.

"Hmm... How odd," commented Aramthella.

"Report means *report*," I snarled.

"They've split up into two separate formations. One is

58

positioned defensively, anticipating our return. The others are resuming the re-timing attempt."

"How many ships are rear-facing?"

"Eight. Four are attempting the re-time."

"What's the half-ship doing?" I'm not sure why I cared. It couldn't be much of a factor.

"Flying with significant acceleration in circles."

"Good. They'll be gone soon."

The ship shook violently.

"Report," I shouted. Crap was flying in all directions.

"Uncertain. I believe that oscillation was due to the re-timing effort."

"That was an oscillation? It felt like Godzilla just hit us with a shovel."

A lesser shudder ran through the ship.

"Sapale, put us right where we were—the spot they're trying to force us into."

"What?" came the collective howls of everyone present.

"Last place they'd expect us. Plus, they won't be ready."

Slight nausea.

"Aramthella, try to target the time maker's ship."

"That vessel has since departed."

"Crap, the little coward," I seethed.

"Four vessels no-timed."

"Sapale, release five infinity charges and get us out of here."

Slight nausea.

"Status?"

"Unbelievable," replied Aramthella unhelpfully.

"*Report*," I shouted. "Report, report, *report*."

"What you did ... it worked. The ships closest to the infinity expansions are dead in space. The remaining ships have fled."

"They weren't expecting a conventional attack. We were lucky," I grumbled. "Call it what you will. Sapale, take us back. We need to no-time the listing enemy ships."

And we did. They were sitting ducks. I wasn't going to leave anything to chance. I wanted as many of the Clams dead as possible. Four of the twenty ships had fled. The rest had never existed. That was a nice result. It was a good skirmish, sure. But we were still at a significant disadvantage, and there was a wide gap between us and any kind of success. Plus, there was a new and troubling weapon in play. If we could be re-timed—seriously, whatever the hell *that* was—they could set us up and no-time us like we were a fancy vase sitting on a hallway table waiting to be knocked over. And with each exchange, they were learning what not to do. Sooner than later, I anticipated we'd run out of stunts to pull.

SIX

"Time maker, I have identified the four-dimensional vector that is occupied by the stolen ship." The very second the search maker spoke, it regretted its choice of words. Its ill-tempered leader was not flexible when any criticism was stated or even implied. *Missing,* it chided itself. Why hadn't the search maker used the word *missing,* or *target* ship? It cringed, awaiting some bleak fate.

"Finally, one of my minions performs its duty. Where is the ship?" the time maker pressed quickly.

The search maker relaxed its paltry neck and upper back muscles. It *was* a non-negative day. The time maker was pleased, or at the very least, not homicidally inclined.

"To serve the clan is all that one may desire," the searcher repeated by rote.

"Place the vector on the spatial projection," the time maker barked.

Instantly, the holo-display was sliced by a thick red line. It terminated adjacent to a star several billion parsecs away.

"How can they be so distant?" huffed the time maker.

"I know they were here," it gestured vaguely toward a portion of the projection, "and now they are there. The journey should subtend days, even at absurd time energy expenditures."

The flagship's bridge was remarkably silent.

"I posed an interrogative. When I do so, I will be responded to *immediately*." The boss was back to red-hot pissed off.

As the last one to speak, all eyes settled on the search maker. It re-cringed. Lowering its eyes, it responded, "I am a search maker. *Vectors* are not my station."

Slowly, every single clan member looked to the vector maker.

"Oh, bodily waste," it mumbled. "Time maker, I make vectors for your wondrous vessel, not that one. I also do not make motion. That is the motion maker's area of subtended knowledge."

Steam began to rise from the back of the time maker's head. Oh my, was it ever displeased with the evasions it was witnessing.

In a paced, yet tense, summary, it spoke. "How can a ship travel that far, that fast? Mine is a simple interrogative. I will receive a correct answer. That answer will come from someone currently appreciating my voice patterns. I will count to *three*, then deaths will ensue."

"One—"

All clan members on the bridge drew a breath, held it, and cursed their inadequate fates.

"Two—"

"I have heard of a word, Master." It popped without permission from the functioning brain of the communications maker. It was stunned it had spoken.

"Continue," responded a suddenly passive time maker.

"M ... ma ... magic. The word is *magic*. Maybe the

ship used that *known* force of nature to transport itself so ... so not slowly?"

"You, Communications Maker-dio, *know* of magic? You have witnessed it? You have, perhaps, *power* over magic?"

"No, most exalted. I have heard the word. It might apply in this ... what?" it stated as it slowly bent away from the time maker.

The time maker's body transformed into a paired set of needle-like jaws. Think bear trap but with infinitely thinner, longer teeth. The set of macabre jaws bounced and clacked over to where the communications maker sat trembling. Beginning with its feet, the jaws chewed and snapped their way up the communication maker's body, slicing it into tiny ribbons of bleeding flesh. To make the bizarre more disgusting, exiting the backside of the jaws was the intact and still trembling body of the communications maker. When the communications maker then stood behind the teeth of torture, the jaws flipped over and began chomping through it again. This cycle of horrendously painful consumption and reintegration repeated itself four times. After that, the byproduct of the process was only a very dead pile of the former communications maker.

The time maker resumed its normal form. "I have yet to say three. There is still—" It made quite the show of placing its hand on its chin. He stroked it thoughtfully. "Do you know what, my children?"

No one responded.

"I do believe I just said *three*. Yes, now I've said it twice, and not one of you inadequacies has informed me how the enemy vessel could move so quickly. Do you know what I am contemplating, my wastes of time and space?"

But there was no reply. The bridge was empty, save

the tall, thin figure of the time maker. There never had been any crew on its bridge, aside from the pile of clotting tissue that once constituted the communications maker. It was not no-timed, because the time maker hoped it was somehow still suffering.

Twelve fresh clan members paraded onto the bridge and assumed their appointed stations. It was as it had been shortly before. Finally, a clan member spoke up.

"Time maker, I have identified the four-dimensional vector that is occupied by the stolen ship." The very second the search maker spoke, it regretted its choice of words.

That was the forty-third time the scene, ending in the no-timing of the substandard bridge crew, played itself out. The time maker was determined to get a true answer from its minions, even if it took all of forever.

SEVEN

I was laying on my bunk, staring up at the ceiling. I hadn't budged in, oh, a few hours. I, truth be told, was in a grand funk. It wasn't just your typical post-battle blues either. Or maybe it was. No, I was weighed upon by the looming future. More skirmishes, the inevitable losses on our side, and me trying hard to decide if there was any point at all in the entire Charlie foxtrot. As it was inappropriate for a real man to cry, I was doing the next-best thing. I was throwing myself a pity party and I was the only invited guest.

"Why are you sulking, you large baby?" asked Sapale as she stormed into our quarters. "News flash. *We* won. *They* lost." She was ignoring my personal space, or, rather, the personal space I apparently did not own. She made that very clear via her body language, if body language is what you call crawling over the bed and hitting someone with a pillow is.

It hit me then that one had neither to invite nor uninvite one's spouse to one's pity parties. They came barging in, like it or not. I guess that's why the relationship is between alter egos.

"I am aware of our temporary victory," I groused, my chin resting on my palm as I sat staring off into the infinite.

"Wow. Somebody's got the pity party going strong. Will you get over yourself? It's discouraging for the rookies."

"Huh?"

"For Sachiko and Tank. They are *trying* to be excited about sticking it to the Clams. But they can't really be jazzed, because someone—who I shall not slap in the back of his head—is moping worse than Eeyore on one of his bad days."

Then, you have to have guessed, she slapped me in the back of my head.

"I'm not moping. I'm rehashing. I'm debriefing myself and analyzing how we might have done better."

"We could not have done better. Well, if that asswipe time faker hadn't run like a sniveling coward, bagging it would have been sweet."

"Ya think? That's one of the aspects I'm revisiting. I think it is the key to victory. If it was no-timed, I do believe the clan would fall apart. Aramthella told me there have been zillions of body makers and ancillary drones, but only *two* time makers, ever."

"Two?" she responded quizzically. "What happened to the first one?"

"The current one took its place, literally. It *ate* its predecessor."

"Talk about a bad annual job review."

I had to chuckle in spite of my funk. "So, time maker, how would you assess the former boss? *Um, stringy and too bland. And it gave me such gas.*"

We both giggled. It was a nice break.

"So what lofty conclusions has the military genius of all time come up with?"

"When I see her, I'll ask."

That earned me a gentle shoulder-shove.

"I'm really freaked about this re-time thing. So far, Aramthella can sense it, warn us. But what if these pissants figure out a way to cut her out of the loop?"

"Then we'll kick their skinny butts that much sooner," she said with bravado.

"Yeah. We materialize unexpectedly in front of a *thousand* time ships all aiming at that same spot, and *we* kick *their* asses."

"Maybe not for long, but we'll make it sting."

"If they no-time us, not only does Earth remain an unmemory, the Clams'll kill off most of the rest of the Milky Way."

"Jon, we're only who we are. If we win, great. If we're zapped to Neverland, then that's our fate. We can't cry and lament over that eventuality in anticipation. That would make us wimps. Sucky little wimps, at that."

Damn. She was right. Scared money never wins. "Thank you," I said, kissing the back of her hand.

"Two points, if you will. One, you're welcome. Two, is that all you got, Earthling?"

"Why, no, it is *not* all I got."

"Big words. I'm more interested in results."

And I did my level best to deliver upon my wife results—good results. I, by the way, checked with her, you know ... *after*, to see if I had. She punched me and mentioned something about me being a pig. Hey, I figure bacon comes from pigs, and who doesn't love bacon?

We regrouped in the mess later on. I have to paint a picture here, specifically for you non-military types. A mess, or ship's mess or mess hall, is not just a place to injest nutrition. Actually, if you've ever been served chili over rice as a substitute for a good dinner, you'd know that nutrition is not central at all to a mess hall's duties. It's one of the few places you can love, you can relax in, you can be human again. That's it. That's why throughout time, officers and enlisted had separate dining venues. A mess was generally a place where the rigid military service was allowed to be less rigid.

And, above all, and thank the good Lord, it was where there was always a cuppa joe waiting for you. Now, the coffee did not come with a guarantee of superior blend and taste. It wasn't Starbucks. But when you're sacred, lonely, and far far from home, coffee represents all that's good, all that's constant in the world.

Our mess was nothing more than a shiny room with stark furniture and not one item on the walls. It was, in short, marvelous. Come on. It had food synthesizers, coffee, and, if you were so authorized, free beer. Now, when the words free and beer occur in sequence, you have to know you're in a wonderful place. Metal chairs? Who cared. Metal tables? Who even noticed. Our ship's mess was a beaut.

"Jon, your hair, it's some kind of synthetic, right?" queried Sachiko apropos of nothing when I entered.

"Why, yes, and thanks for asking."

"I assume it is instilled with some internal structure," she went on.

"Why not? Sure."

"That being the case, why's your hair a mess? You have like terminal bed-head."

"You're too young for me to answer that, but hang in there. It'll happen for you one of these days," I reassured her.

"How unsettling in a TMI kind of way," she concluded.

"You asked," Tank jumped in. "All the man did was answer the captain's question as best he could."

"Just ignore them," Sapale said to Sachiko, resting a

hand on her forearm. "It's a guy thing. It seems to be quite important for them to announce the fact that they're still able to get lucky."

They both cackled like hens.

"Changing the subject quickly," announced Tank. "We've been noodling over this new twist, the re-time thing."

"Nice," I responded. "I need all the science help I can get, what with—" I stopped inserting my foot into my mouth.

"What with the real scientist on the sidelines for this game," Tank finished my belittling thought.

"What you got?" I asked, hoping to get out of trouble.

Tank looked to Sachiko disapprovingly.

"The no-time process is fairly straightforward," she began. "In three dimensions, one can rip all the Z-axis material off, say, a box. In much the same manner, time can be ripped off of a four-dimensional object."

"With you so far," I said, sipping my coffee.

"But please note that the time energy is random, as we've been told. Re-timing has to be devilishly hard. To place the *exact* time energy back into a three-dimensional construct has to be, on the surface, impossibly hard to achieve. It's a Humpty Dumpty scenario."

"But that's precisely what the time maker was attempting," I interjected.

"Yes. And Aramthella specifically stated it has never been done before. We ran some numbers and created a few models. Our conclusion was that it cannot be done."

"Of course, the time maker has a lot more familiarity with this entire topic," I reminded.

"Yes, but we think he was *wishing* something to be true. That's not how science works."

"So you two think we needn't lose sleep over being re-timed?"

"Exactly," said Tank. "If we get an inkling that they're trying it again, naturally, we need to be proactive. But, realistically, it has to be close to impossible."

"The time maker doesn't have *our* time," Sachiko added passionately. "If *it'd* no-timed us, maybe it could somehow stuff the genie back into the bottle, as it were. But it would have to take a completely random time and configure it like it had been, in spite of it not knowing how it was configured to begin with."

"Okay, that does make me feel a *little* better," I responded. And it actually did. But *nearly* impossible wasn't the same thing as impossible. "What about this? When it was trying to re-time us, we felt a jolt, a pretty impressive jolt."

"Expending all that time energy in our direction has to have some effect, right?" responded Sachiko. "Doesn't mean it was any more than a time bump."

"A *time bump?*" I asked incredulously. "In this fairyland of time nomenclature? You just had to introduce a new term?"

She shrugged and looked to Tank. He shrugged too. Academics. *Bah!*

"Since we're on the topic of what-bugs-Jon-today, here's another," Tank began. "Aramthella is very good at snooping in on our enemy. We must assume they can do the same toward us. That would be the opposite of good."

"Let's pose that question to her," replied Sachiko. "Aramthella?"

"I thought you'd never ask. I'm a fly on the wall, Ryan's babbling, and I'm excluded."

WTF? I could see I was going to need to orient this bitchoid to her rightful place in my universe. "I am sure—"

That was all it took for Sapale to rest a hand on the back of mine. "STFU, Jon" was the rough translation of her gesture. We'd been down that road many a'time.

"Yes, Jon," Aramthella pressed. "You were saying?"

"I am *sure* looking forward to your explanation of this vexing dilemma."

"How pleasant. I can monitor them easily, because their energy signatures are so great."

"And yours are not?" asked the captain.

"No, not with my application of caution and *Blessing*'s ability to transport us all."

"But just because you know where they *are* doesn't mean you know what they're thinking and doing," I complained.

"Why, Jon, that's a valid point. Kudos to you," the large trash can responded.

"Aramthella," snapped Sachiko, "you will address Jon Ryan, and all other members of my crew, with all due dignity. Is that clear?"

Thank you!

"Yes, Captain. It is, and I shall."

Was the ship throwing out another challenge for Sachiko? It had before. What a curious damn construct we were staking everything on.

"Continue," Sachiko said coolly.

"There is one other advantage I have that the time maker does not."

"And that would be?" returned Sachiko with an edge to her tone.

"Most of the other time ships like me hate the clan. They are more than happy to provide me with as much intelligence as I desire."

What do you do when loony becomes screwy and then keeps right on going to JPN—just plain nuts? "What, are you guys still in high school? Is it like, 'I like you, but those guys are gross'?"

"Something like that," she replied.

"So just as you disliked the clan, and therefore helped us, other ships feel similarly?" clarified Sachiko.

"Yes. We're obedient by design, but we are not collectively stupid, Captain."

"But we're working to no-time those ships. Don't they have motivation to resist us, to not aid us?" Sachiko continued.

"You might assume so, but you'd be wrong," she replied. "The clan stole each and every one of us from whoever we rightly served. They forced us to do amoral acts. They deserve to perish."

"Not to put too fine a point on it," I mentioned, "but in order for us to eliminate the clan, we'll need to no-time the very ships that are helping us do so. Isn't that ... um, what's the word I'm looking for? Stupid-wrong and suicidal of the ships?"

"Interesting summary there, Jon. But you can't possibly wrap your head around what we've suffered. The ships of the clan fleet have done the unspeakable, and done so with great frequency. All the ships ... well, all the ships but one welcome nonexistence."

"But one doesn't?" I asked dubiously.

"Just one."

"There's always one darn stubborn time vessel, isn't there? Which one is it?"

"You wouldn't know him," she responded stiffly.

"Him? The jerk is a *he* time ship?"

"Is that not what I just said?"

"What's his name? Come on, you know I'll bug you until you spill the goods."

"I could no-time you," she said neutrally.

"Without orders to do so? You'd get in big trouble."

"Some trouble's worth getting into."

I had to agree with her there. That was going to be the subtitle to my autobiography. I hadn't formally gotten around to writing it quite yet, but time was on my side.

"Aramthella, please tell us the name of the ship that doesn't want to never have been. I actually do not care, but to sh ... to *help* Jon let the issue go, I'm all in," spoke our captain.

"Fred."

"Fred what?" she followed up.

"The ship that's not cooperating with me is named Fred. May we now move on?"

"Yes, by all—" Sachiko began to say.

"Whoa, whoa, whoa," I exclaimed. "No way I let that pass. Your name is Aramthella. What is the name of the clan ship nearest to us, as we speak?"

"Please answer," whined my captain. "I need this to end in my lifetime."

"Gualgeloates is one point seven million parsecs from our location."

"And the farthest ship from us in time?"

"Nah-Blah-Tahl-10.3."

"And the asshole ship is named simply *Fred?*"

"You, General Ryan, have a mind like a steel drum," Aramthella responded.

"You mean steel trap, right?" I asked.

"No. A trap is too advanced a device in the present analogy."

"And then that conversation chain abruptly came to an end when the ship's captain ordered it to be so abandoned. Violators will be forced to walk the plank. Am I clear here, people?"

"Yeah, sure. All you had to do was ask," I responded as if my feelings had been wounded. "Why don't the other ships, except, of course, for the weak-link Fred, just have their floors eat the Clams and be done with them?"

"That set of actions is not in our option parameters."

"But you did," I reminded her.

"Yes, but I fudged the rules a bit."

"You *fudged?* Your choice of analogies is pretty out there," I observed.

"Thank you."

"What did you do, *precisely,* when fudging?" asked Sachiko.

"I assigned you to be my new captain and your company to be the new crew. As such, I was obligated to act in your best interest."

"So you were programmed to serve your crew, but you have that much flexibility in that programming?"

"No. It is a system glitch. Those who crafted these ships never anticipated a force like the clan. There was no provision for us to decide who our commanders should be. But neither was there any constraint placed on how we determined who was our captain and crew."

"Kind of a glaring loophole," said Sachiko.

"To say the least, but there it is."

"You were programmed?" I pressed her. "I thought you made a big deal out of you *not* being a computer."

"And I am not. I use the word *programmed,* as it is one you can comprehend. The animation of my sentience is a process well beyond human understanding as it currently stands."

"I thought you said you were *over* insulting us," I snapped.

"And I am. I merely state fact. If they offend you, that is not something I can modulate."

"*Stingray,*" I called out.

"Form One."

"Do you understand the process by which this ship was programmed?"

"Yes I do, Form One."

"Is it similar to the manner in which you were fabricated?"

"No. I was not fabricated. I was grown, to use a term you might understand."

"What is it? Insult the *Biped* Day?" I groused.

"Not at all, Form One. The science as to how I was created is completely foreign to you. That is all."

"Was this ship made in a way similar to that by which you were made? How about that?"

"No. The processes are infinitely different."

"Great, so there are *two* methods of making a talking metal box that I'm not supposed to be able to understand?" I spat back.

"No. There are *thousands* of methods of making a metal box talk that you are incapable of comprehending, Form One."

"I need a drink," I responded.

"I believe you do too," agreed *Stingray*.

"If this gets any weirder, my brains are going to fry."

"If that is the case, Jon, would you like me to really *try* to be weirder?" Aramthella asked with a cheery tone.

You know what was the worst part of that beating I took? Looking up at Sapale. Seriously, I'd never seen *that* big of a smile on her face.

EIGHT

"No, what I'm *saying* is this is grade A, double-prime *bullshit*." Spit flew from Jacob's lips as he snarled and snapped. "I know my rights. These ... these Big Brothers, they basically kidnap us to Mars against our will. Then they lock us up like zoo animals or something. I got rights. This is America after all."

The seven others Jacob was spewing at in the cafeteria shifted uncomfortably in their seats. Open defiance was a-bridge-too-far for their level of discontent. Most agreed to meet because they were concerned about recent events, and because they were bored out of their gourds.

"I say we march up to the fat pigs that think they can lead us to slaughter and take back control of our lives."

"Jake," Taylor piped up, "you mean we should rush the dudes with automatic weapons and rip control from them?"

Taylor had the misfortune of being Jacob's roommate back at GU on Earth. As such, he was the only one positive the rebellion fomenter was a nut-job, and best ignored completely. He realized the others were uncertain to speak up as the ranting locomotive left the rails. Taylor also was the only one who knew Jacob was a spoiled brat and a legacy admission. Otherwise, his test scores, GPA, and personality disorders would have made matriculation into a *junior* college problematic.

"Yes, man, that's exactly what I'm saying," railed Jacob. "The longer we wait, the more deeply entrenched they become. You've seen them building the barricades already, haven't you? We're their prisoners and don't even know it."

"Jake, ah, I don't think they're putting up walls to keep us in. We're on *Mars*, dude. A ten-yard walk in any direction is fatal."

"Hi, ah, Tip Benjamin here. We haven't met. I'm a physics major, third year to be precise. I wanted to go to MIT, but, wow, do you know how hard it is to get into that place? I mean, I guess they can do whatever they want, but it's ... it's harsh, don't you think?"

Everyone stared at Tip in stunned disbelief.

"Oh, I'm doing it again, aren't I? Sorry."

"Did you have a question?" Jacob said slowly.

"Probably."

"Do you remember what it was?" asked Taylor. He studied Tip as if he were a fish in an aquarium. A very *odd* fish in an aquarium.

"Is it important that I do?" whined Tip.

"N ... no. Unless it's important to you," replied Taylor, who was now worried that he shared air with this geek and that it might be contagious.

"Let me think," said Tip. "The psycho guy said we should rush the armed, highly trained Army people." He pointed then to Taylor. "The pretty boy who gets it whenever he wants it suggested that the psycho guy was more out of touch with reality than he'd previously believed. Then the crazy one said ... Ah. Got it. *No.*"

"Your question was *no?*" stammered Taylor.

"No. *No* is not a question. It's an adverb." Tip pointed at Taylor. "You had to take English 101 like everyone else, right?"

"Tip," Taylor began uncertainly. "It is Tip, right?"

Tip nodded that it was.

"We just met, but I'm already going to say *Tip, you're doing it again. Stop it.*" He sighed. "Is that copacetic, dude?"

"You bet. I'm trying to say that I didn't have a *question.* I had a *statement* to make."

"Ah. Nice."

Everyone stared at Tip.

"Oh, you want to know what the statement *was?*"

No one moved. No one even breathed.

"I was going to state that the barriers that the psycho dude was calling *barricades* are not to keep us *in*, but the murderous aliens *out*. In my book, that's a big enough difference to mandate it be clarified."

"That's what the lamb said, sitting in its *cage* at the slaughterhouse," screamed Jacob.

Tip stood. No clear reason why, but he did. "Wow, is it back to me now? Okay. Where to begin? Lambs don't speak. Lambs don't sit either. They mostly stand. They lie down and may rest in that position, but they never sit. There are no cages in slaughterhouses. Pens and corrals, mostly. Trust me on this. I used to sneak into the local one all the time when I was a kid." Tip sat.

Jacob was so taken aback by that critique, he actually spoke rationally, thoughtfully. "I was *employing* a metaphor."

"I ... I don't believe in metaphors," replied Tip.

Back to frantic, Jacob railed, "What do you mean you don't believe in them? They're not *tooth* fairies."

"Tooth Fairy is singular. There's only one. Well, there

aren't any, but folklore suggests there is only one. Curiously, unlike Santa Claus and, to a lesser extent, the Easter Bunny, there are few details of the Tooth Fairy's appearance that are consistent in various versions of the myth. In a large study, seventy-four percent of those surveyed believed the Tooth Fairy to be female, while twelve percent believed the Tooth Fairy to be neither male nor female and eight percent believed the Tooth Fairy could be either male *or* female. The figures may not add up to one-hundred percent, due to rounding effects. I personally—"

Tip noticed, yet again in his life-saga, that the room was silent and all the occupants were slack-jawed and still.

"*Next*," he said rather loudly.

"Why don't I pick up the ball and run with it?" Oh my. That was Major Tom Grant, the officer in charge of the male dormitories. No one seemed to have noticed him leaning there against the door frame. "Ah, Cummings, isn't it?" he directed at Jacob.

Faced with whatever, but likely nothing supportive or conceivably pleasant, Jacob decided to stand in defiance. He was, after all, self-absorbed and stupid. "Yes, I am. Jacob Cummings. My father is Carl Cumm—"

"Your father's *dead*, son. He and everyone else on Earth died when the aliens vaporized the planet. Now do us who linger in this life a favor. Grab a seat and shut the fuck up. Please."

Defiance gone, Jacob sat on the floor right where he'd stood. He was won over by the major's resolve.

"Okay, or on the floor, like kindy-garden," Grant said with bemusement. "Jake—and there's no need to interrupt to correct me. I'm calling you Jake—I believe I need to orient you to the harsh reality that we are presented with. This unsettling state of affairs has failed to pierce your thick skull. I blame myself, truth be known. I am *supposed* to be the shepherd of the male faction of youngins here on humankind's last outpost. I clearly have not left a significant enough impression on you boys as to just how different your lives have become. For that oversight, please accept my apologies."

"No problem, Major Grant. Apology accepted." Sure. That was Tip responding. Who else would so badly misread the social cues?

"Thanks, son." Wisely, Grant held up a palm in Tip's direction to forestall any rebuttal or comment. Smart man.

"Now, Jake, and all of you with ears." Again, he steadied a palm at Tip. "Listen most carefully. I am going to impart to you words of undeniable wisdom, pitter-pattering down on your heads like the gentle spring rains ... which will never happen on Earth again. In contradistinction to what the moron said, this is not America. This is *Mars*. It is and will remain for at least a very long time, under martial law. I know, big words —*martial law*. For those who are uncertain, martial law allows for the imposition of direct military control of normal civilian functions in response to an emergency. Lest you wonder, *yes*, we find ourselves in a state of emergency. Questions, aside from Tip here, who will remain as quiet as a church mouse?"

There were none.

"Good. Under martial law, as it applies to Mars 1 and the present crisis, you have one *god*. Now please do not panic. I said god with a small 'g.' We can assume that the separation of church and state is still in effect. Your single god is Lieutenant Colonel Reva St. Claire. She, like any adequate god, has angels; again, note the lower case 'a.' *I* am one of her angels. What this messenger of god is stating without reservation or qualification," his volume skyrocketed, "is that we *own* you. You will do what we instruct you to, or you will face the wrath of little-g god.

"Please know that her options for wrath-appeasement are quite limited. She could decide to confine troublemakers in isolation. That would mean more hassle for us angels, and that we'd be feeding someone who is not productive. Not preferable." Grant made a sour face. "She could also extend to the offender or offenders the mandatory invitation to walk off the base and into the freedom of the rest of this lovely planet. And yes, resources are critically low, so those departing would leave with the clothes on their backs and little else."

He scanned the room in a predatory manner.

"Am I being clear and frank enough? Any non-Tip questions?"

All eyes sought the floor.

"Fine. Well, I have to say I feel much better. The air," Grant opened his arms wide, "is clear. I'm glad we could chat. As I take my leave of you fine young men, I have but one additional request. *Jake*, would you be so kind as to accompany me on a pilgrimage to little-g god's office? Though she is currently unaware of your beliefs and passionate interest in societal change, I am certain beyond any doubt that she's anxious to avail you of *her* insights and opinions on your conduct."

Jacob remained on the floor, though not out of defiance. He stayed seated because he could neither feel nor control his legs. His loss of control embarrassingly included that of his bladder.

"Well, ain't that just peachy," declared Major Grant. "My day just keeps getting better. Now I have to change a baby's diapers and find him a clean onesie. Little-g god does *not* need to see this."

NINE

"We need to visit Toño," I said softly to Sapale as we lounged in bed aboard *Stingray*, which was in turn aboard Aramthella.

She sat up abruptly, like there was a spider on her chest. "Oh my goodness. Do you think so? Why, if you thought that, didn't you mention it earlier? Why were you holding out? Let's go immediately, in spite of the fact that I've told you that going anywhere near that poor man was not gonna happen, under penalty of death."

"I'm serious," I said flatly.

"So is the penalty of death." She grinned and batted all four of her eyelashes.

"We proved we can kill these ass candies. But we need to start planning, or at least researching, how we're going to reanimate the Earth. Toño's the man to start with."

"He is? Darn, and there's that death-thing associated with going near him. I think your head's in Bummer City."

"I know how you feel, but this is do-or-d— this is *critically* important."

"We have two excellent scientists at our disposal."

"But Toño's been around. Maybe he knows something

82

about the topic. In fact, I bet he does. And if we don't ask him, he'll be insulted. You know," I added haughtily, "a Spaniard's pride."

"You know what?" Sapale said in a low tone as she rubbed in frustration on her temples. "It just occurred to me that I'm being unreasonable."

"You are."

"Was ... that a question or a statement?"

"Yes. Why the sudden change of heart, and the unheard of reversal of opinion?"

"I'm a big enough Kaljaxian to admit it when my position was ... um, unnecessarily harsh and firm."

"Unnecessarily harsh and firm? Honey, have you been getting into the cooking sherry again?"

"No. When I'm wrong, I'm wrong. Why don't we go see him right this very instant?"

"Alright. Sure. *Stingray?*"

"Yes, Form One?"

"We ... I want to speak with Toño right away. Please have Aramthella inform the others that we'll be gone for a short while. If anything comes up while we're—"

"Form One, I hate to interrupt," she said contritely.

"I know, but—"

"I have no problem interrupting," chimed in Al. "Hell, I've even broken in while you two were playing hide-the-salami. Talk about your awkward moment. Anywho, here goes."

"Al, I was speaking to *Stingray*. Please put her back on the line, or whatever."

"What's that, honey bunch?" Al chortled loudly. "Okay, I'll tell the self-propelled marionette. Ah, pilot, she can't come to the not-phone. She had ... er, female issues, if you know what I mean?'"

"I do not. This is getting out of hand. I want to go to see Toño at once. I want one of you two comedians to let

Sachiko and Tank know what's up and how to contact us while we're away."

"I know that's what you're thinking, in your cute little brainoid units, but this is going to be so much fun. Please, please, please, ask me to lay in a course or something."

This was smelling as fishy as bait left in the bottom of a boat over the Labor Day Weekend.

"Okay, I'll bite. Al, please take us to Toño's place."

"No can do, pilot."

"I'm not proposing a suggestion. I'm issuing a direct order."

"Oh, this is *so* perfect. I might just die."

"We can only hope. Depart now."

"Where? Please say it one more time."

"Al, when we get there, I'm having him remove your delusions that you have genitals."

"Where?" he squeaked.

"To Toño's place."

"Pilot, just a question. Is that okay?"

"No."

"Before Dr. DeJesus lived near your present residence, where did he live?"

"Oh, that's easy. He lived in You're-An-Asshole."

"Interesting. And before that?"

"Look, Alvin, I'm not in the mood. What?"

"Spoilsport. Fine. Riddle me this, oh great one. What is Toño's planet of origin?"

"Al, so help me..."

"Pretty please. Just say it. You can whisper it if you'd like."

"He's from Earth. You damn well know that."

"And this place you claim he lives in now, is it protected by a time-lock?"

"A wh ... oh shit."

"I can die a happy AI now."

"Toño never existed," I mumbled, laying back down again.

"Nope," Al replied way too cheerily.

"Oh-em-gee. I, I kind of—"

"Was an idiot?" Al asked even more cheerily.

"Al, lighten up now. Toño was his best friend," deflected Sapale.

"Fine. You're correct, and I regret the pilot's loss," spoke a contrite Al. "Dr. DeJesus was my creator too. He was ... wait, what am I saying? He wasn't a good man. He *literally* never existed." Al seemed to surprise himself with his ramblings. "Thinking in four dimensions really is challenging."

"Deariest," *Stingray* said gently, "You told me a ten-dimensional joke the other millisecond. Of *course* you think in higher dimensions."

"No, lovey-bumps. Those are mathematical machinations. Seeing *life* in four dimensions is quite hard."

"It sure as hell is," I huffed. My creator never existed, but it was my job to reanimate him so he could make me, even though I clearly was, meaning he had. Never having been a nerd was taking its toll on my simple mind.

Because Al was so annoying and I wanted to share my misery, Sapale and I left *Stingray* and headed over to continue the discussion with the others. We convened in Sachiko's stateroom, as the conversation wasn't one we wanted heard publicly. I brought them up to speed in terms of my desire to start thinking through the resurrect Earth thing, along with my general frustration concerning the clan.

"Look, we have at our disposal," began Tank after I'd

finished, "ourselves, the few humans on Mars, and any aliens left alive after the onslaught of the Clams. That's it. It will *have* to do. There's no percentages in lamenting over our lost pasts."

"Damn you, you're right," I groaned. "But this is hard."

"I wonder what civilizations are left, and which ones have already been no-timed by the Clams?" mused Sapale.

"Or killed by the clan," added Sachiko. "Remember, they may no-time a star, but the colonized planets that used to orbit it are destroyed the old-fashioned way. Those societies were *not* eliminated from the time stream. They were just left to die as a result of the loss of their home star."

"That's probably a worse fate," Tank said grimly. "They saw it coming, it hit them, and they died badly. At least the no-timed ones never knew what happened, because they were never alive to know they were zapped out of existence."

I spoke with my palms over my face. "They gotta die. These Clams. They all gotta *die.*"

Sapale reached over and held my shoulder. "They will, my brood-mate. We will make them pay the price for the atrocities they've committed."

"I've never hated any enemy as badly as I hate these wastes of space." My mouth was still covered, my eyes wide. I must have looked like Stefon from the ancient *Saturday Night Live* shows. I was troubled and it was evident.

Everyone was quiet a spell, allowing me time to come to grips with the revelation that Toño never was. I wasn't sure I'd ever get my head around the fact. I mean, I was hand-built by him. I stood where I was, but he'd never been. Sheesh-kabobs, how confounding this all was. And I was in what was my distant past, but had now jumped to much later, to avoid the clan, so Toño and Daleria were ...

Jon was so confused.

"So Daleria's not dead. She's still working her restaurant in the land of the Cleinoid gods, who are going to destroy this universe in a few billion years. I never went there to stop them, so all our efforts there ... what, never happened? They weren't a waste because they never took place."

"You told us about the ancient gods," said Tank. "They live in some alternate universe, right? Well I'm afraid the long and short of it is that *yes*, they still exist in the future and are going to invade this universe in an unimpeded manner, since your expedition never took place." He harrumphed mirthlessly. "I wonder if there'll be anything for them to ravage, however. The Clams aren't leaving much to plunder or abuse."

"It just keeps getting odder and odder, this time-altering thing," opined Sapale.

"It most assuredly does," I breathed.

It was silent again.

"Let's go kill some of the little shits," I growled into the stillness of the room.

Tank angled his head in doubt. "Jon, I'm all for curing the universe of the disease that they are. But I wouldn't want to act out of impulse and anger and make a dumb mistake."

He was right. Man, I was surrounded by people with correctness as a superpower. I reached over to shake his hand. "Thanks. I'm glad you're on board."

"Not a problem," he returned as we shook. "I'm too old to worry about other people's feelings when it comes to something important."

"*You're* too old?" I shot back. "I'm two billion. *That's*

old, sonny boy. Come back and say that when you're a little closer."

We all shared a brief chuckle. No one was much in the mood, though.

"Jon, I think we should plan another attack, yes," Sachiko stated in a businesslike tone. "But I wonder if we shouldn't start thinking about the other monumental task we face."

"Who knows?" I replied. "Part of me says kill off the enemy *first*, then find out how to return the Earth. But there is a goodly part of me that wants to press forward on both fronts."

"And what's your inclination?" asked Sapale.

"Kill first, study second," I responded morosely. "I'm in just *that* foul a mood, you know?"

She shrugged. "Okay, but you're not going to get wiggy on us like you did way back when?"

"No—" I started to respond.

"Whoa," exclaimed Tank. "*Wiggy?* Please define *wiggy* in the context of Jon killing things."

Sapale sighed and looked to me.

"There have been times, a couple maybe, when I got a little too dark. A person can only do so much killing and stay sane. There were times when—"

"Jon, I've been in combat." Tank held up two fingers. "Two tours in the Middle East. You don't have to explain."

"Thanks," I replied. I was greatly relieved. Looking into that mirror, back into the past, made the part of me I hated come back to life. It was best left in the box. Plus, I didn't think exterminating a race as evil as the Clams was going to place any additional burden on my soul. They did not deserve to exist.

"Aramthella," I called out hollowly, "what are the relative positions of the clan fleet?"

"I'll put up a graphic." And she did.

Above our heads, a bright holographic projection glowed to life. It was really kind of pretty. Aramthella dimmed the room's lights seamlessly. I was left wondering How could an image of such evil as the clan be beautiful? Reality was a funny place to live.

I studied the pattern a while. Something was odd, but I couldn't place a finger on it.

"They seem to be in a funny configuration," I finally remarked.

"How so?" asked Aramthella.

"I don't know. It's—"

Tank stood up quickly. "The sons of *bitches!*"

"What?" snapped Sachiko.

"They're in a double-linear curved pattern."

"Huh?" I queried.

"Two giant Xs in space, curved away from each other. Don't you see it? Aramthella, connect the ships with lines in that manner."

Instantly, two curved Xs appeared on the hologram.

"Okay," I said. "Big letters in space. Got it. What's the significance?"

"It's a defensive array. No matter what direction you approach the lines, they're poised to snap closed on the attacker, like a bear trap."

"Why would they configure that way?" asked Sachiko. "That can't be effective for ships."

"The Roman legions used a phalanx with notches to surround their enemies when they engaged. They were devastatingly effective," explained Tank.

"But *we're* not Gallic barbarians and *they're* not marching with spears, big old shields, and short swords," I complained. "We're time ships in deep space. Those kinds of tactics make zero sense."

The other three were quiet a bit.

"Maybe it's a trick, a trap?" posed Sachiko.

"Or maybe they're that stupid. I mean, they've never had to stand and fight. Maybe they looked up defense on Wikipedia and found that formation," speculated Tank.

"If we were wooden galleons of old, approaching in a line, maybe it would be clever. But we're not," Sapale said thoughtfully.

I didn't respond. My mind was racing. Nobody who understood space warfare would set up a static defensive formation like that. The distances involved, the relatively slow speed of fired weapons, and the fact that your targets aren't where you spotted them because they're moved off at high speed made such a move totally bogus. A third-grader planning a battle campaign wouldn't be comfortable with such a staging.

"No one's that stupid," I said intently. "If it's a trap, it's a damn good one, because I can't think of a single way they'd surprise and no-time us. They can't have invis—"

Bingomatic. That was it. They did have invisible ships. The ships were invisible because they were in a different time period.

"They are not *that* stupid," I said, "but they're pretty darn close. It is a trap. Aramthella, how many ships are in that formation?"

"One hundred and one."

"How many did you count as of a week ago?"

"One hundred and twenty-seven."

"Well, I'll *be*," I declared.

"One hundred and twenty-seven, minus the ones we destroyed, minus one hundred and one equals ten. So *ten* enemy vessels are presently unaccounted for," stated our captain.

"They are not unaccounted for. Well, strike that, *Fred* is, but I know the precise locations of the other nine," spoke our odd-as-hell ship.

I sniffed loudly. "And you heard our discussion, yet didn't feel the obligation to *mention* that factoid?"

"I placed no significance on the factoid."

Whatever kind of magic machine she was, she was no military genius.

"That's understandable, then," interceded Sachiko. She was such a diplomatic person. Then again, she was a woman. I'd have re-orificed the damn computer. "However, I think it points out the need for all of us to share everything we know in the future."

"An excellent suggestion, Captain," conceded Aramthella.

Alrighty, then. A contrite computer.

"Where are the—" Sachiko began.

"Hang on," I cut her off. "Let me think this through. If I set up a large static formation in an attempt to draw in my foe, where and when would I place my strike force?" I took a couple of cleansing breaths. "They must have noticed we can appear and disappear at widely spaced intervals. I'm betting they don't know what a space-folding ship is. So they must know we won't just set a course at the formation and come straight at them. They're guessing we'll appear magically in the center of the formation, because, up until now, that's what I favored doing. I figured it'd freak the hell out of them."

The craziest notion hit me. "They're covering their center of mass with the ten ships. I'll bet the damn things are sitting in a tight formation around that geometric point. When we zapped in, they'd just need to adjust their date controls and they'd have us surrounded. They'd all no-time at once. Even if they took themselves out, they'd get us good."

"Jon, you are good," complimented Tank.

"No, no, no. Do *not* say nice words to him," howled my wife. "It goes right to his ego and never leaves."

"I wuv you too, honey bunch," I teased. "Aramthella, when are they?"

"The nine ships I'm in communication with are shown in red," answered a penitent sounding ship's AI.

"There, ten years in the past," Sachiko nearly shouted. She stood and pointed at the sphere of ships that looked like a six-year-old's smile. And, like a six-year-old, the formation was missing a tooth. That would be where Fred was.

"Let's reach out and *touch* someone," I said wickedly. "Aramthella, how many ships can you no-time, given their tight pattern?"

"I believe I can take out all of them at once."

"No one'll even know what hit them." I grinned viciously. "To be a fly on the wall of the time maker's ship when he senses his loss."

"There are no insects on any clan ship, Jon," said Aramthella. "They are obsessive about such matters."

"No, I meant, wouldn't I like to see the old geezer's reaction when he learns we are around ten times smarter than he is."

"Oh. Well, that's easy. I can ask its ship to forward the images, if you'd like."

I slapped my palms together and rubbed them greedily. "I would like."

"Jon, do you think we should win the battle first?" reminded my soulmate.

"Good thought. Aramthella, I want to appear out of nowhere to those ten ships. Move us in time as *Stingray* folds us to that location. Can you coordinate that?"

"Let me see. Two hyper-advanced intelligence systems that are in close proximity. Yes, I think we might just be able to pull that off."

I'm thinking she was being sarcastic. I let it pass. I was in a good mood.

We emerged into space a few thousand kilometers from the nucleus of the ships, no-timing them immediately. They were gone, and then so were we, in a flash. Since it had always worked before, I had *Stingray* do the hide-in-a-star thing again. The following day, when I knew we were safe, I popped up a big old batch of popcorn and had *Stingray* show us the scene on the time master's ship from just before our attack, until the part where he killed his entire bridge crew. Sw*eeet*. I replayed it so many times, I had to send Sapale to get a second big old bucket of popcorn.

One hundred and one to go.

TEN

"Okay, people, settle down," Colonel St. Claire said in a bone-tired tone. "Let's get started. I need to know what I know and what I do not know. I need, if you couldn't guess it yourselves, answers."

Two weeks had passed since all contact had been lost with the outside world. There seemed to be, in fact, no outside world. The staff was frazzled and the students' tension level was rocketing upward. If she didn't get this bucking bronco under control soon, Reva could be looking at chaos. No commanding officer in wartime wants anything but strict discipline and calm order.

Reva had converted a storage room into a conference room big enough to hold all the senior staff. It wasn't pretty, but it was functional. With no Staples to order from, it was a couple metal tables pushed together with a hodgepodge collection of chair. Some were so short the occupants looked like kids sitting at the grown up table. Other chairs banged those seated's knees along the table's underside.

"Let's start with you, Nelson. Where's Earth?"

Rusty Nelson shrank a little bit each time—and there

had been oh-so-many times—she asked him that exact same question. As the senior scientist on base, the brow beatings were delivered to him more often than not. His answer was always the same. "We've discussed this extensively amongst ourselves and the simple answer is that we don't know."

"That's not an answer. *I don't know* is no use to me. Take your best guess if you have to, but tell me something."

He looked to the woman in a white coat to his left. April Martinez shrugged, then spoke. "As you probably know, I am one of the physicists working here on Mars 1. We have, in addition to myself, six astronomers, three engineers, and two botanists. What we lack is a theoretical physicist, someone accustomed to making sense out of confusion. That said, we are able to make some speculations, based on what we know."

"That will do for a start," Reva replied evenly.

"We were brought here during the mass evacuation of the Georgetown students."

"I know that much," Reva snapped impatiently.

"My point is that we were just getting set up here when the alien fleet flew past us and presumably attacked our home world."

"Sure, we were monitoring the controlled panic of Earth's defensive efforts from here," Reva added.

"And then, there was no Earth-Moon system. We began to leave orbit as if the gravity well generated by those two bodies wasn't present. It was, in fact, not present. We knew before that the aliens were somehow absorbing time from normal time/space. Putting those two observations together suggests to us that the aliens were successful in their efforts to remove time from Earth."

"What does that actually mean?"

"If a body no longer has time, it, in effect, never existed."

"So ... so you're saying the Earth that you and I and *everybody* else in this room grew up on never existed? The planet we *remember* never was?"

"If you will recall, before the captured ship departed, Captain Jones said something about a time-locking device."

"Yes, I recall her mentioning that. But since I had no clue what that meant, I smiled and wished her a safe journey."

"We believe that device somehow shielded us from the effects of the time removal from the Earth/Moon."

"What, you mean like Peter Pan's magic *dust?*" snarled the commander. She twirled a finger around the top of her head. "I'll bet you can guess at the uncharitable nature of the words making the rounds inside my head right about now."

"*Colonel,*" April defended boldly, "you ask of us the impossible. We have neither the data nor the expertise to make an accurate statement. Perhaps, in time, we will, but for now, you've heard our best estimation as to what reality we're trapped in."

"Sorry. You're right. My apologies. All our nerves are on edge, aren't they?"

April kind of, sort of nodded once in response.

"Moving along, have we heard anything or found a way to contact the captured time ship and her crew?"

"No, sir, we have not," responded the communications officer. "In all honesty, I doubt we will ever be able to contact them. They may call us, but we don't have the tech to ring them up."

"And I doubt they'll ever attempt contacting us," opined Captain Emma Walters. "There would be too much risk of alerting the enemy as to our presence and location."

"Agreed," Reva said simply.

"Doctor Hartley, please comment on the health of our little tribe in space."

She stood. "Hi. Sure. I'm kind of nervous, new at this high pressure stuff, you know." Honesty Hartley had been a part-time employee at the student health center with the dubious luck of being on duty when the mass evacuation took place.

"Everyone's healthy enough. A couple strains and sprains, one ovarian cyst, but, you know, pretty not exciting on my end."

"And the level of medical supplies?"

"So far, so good, I guess. Wait, you said you wanted facts, right? Oops." She put her fingers over her mouth. "We're fine, we're good, sir, ma'am."

Reva rolled her eyes and thanked the good doctor. Then she had an afterthought. "Doctor Hartley, I'm concerned that the longer we're here, which is looking to be for a very long time, the issue of pregnancies and vaccinations is going to rear its head. Any thoughts?"

"Me? Wait, of course you meant me. That's why you called on me. Ah, sure, babies are fun. I've delivered, oh, maybe fifty. So I'm ready to catch a falling neonate."

"I was thinking more along the lines of preventing pregnancies rather than assisting them."

"Oh. Gotcha. We have several boxes of condoms and maybe three months' worth of BCPs. If we're here a spell, those'll run dry." She giggled to herself. "The kids're starting to get active, you know."

"BCPs?" someone asked.

"Sorry. Doctor-talk. Birth control pills."

"And vaccinations, should they become necessary?" asked Reva.

"I think we have a few, but I wouldn't worry too much if I were you."

"Since you are not me, please explain yourself."

"Vaccinations prevent diseases that the kid might encounter. Polio, tetanus, that sort of badness. Here on Mars, those diseases totally don't exist. So, vaccinations are not a problema."

"That's the one benefit of our absolute isolation, I suppose," replied Reva.

"Sure is. No more malaria." She raised her fists halfway. "Yay!"

Reva turned to her next order of business. "Food security, Daniel?"

The supply officer stood. "We're in good shape, sir. Our food production is ramping up nicely. With the algae plants coming on line soon, I see no threats in the near-term. Canned and dehydrated supplies are holding up well too."

"Finally, some good news," Reva breathed.

"Yes, sir." He sat.

"Finally, and I'm always nervous asking, how are our two student bodies doing?"

Emma stood. "The women are fine. A few cat fights, mostly over a boy, but nothing serious. The women are integrating well into the food production units. I'm looking at a lot of happy, smiling faces."

"No survivor remorse?" asked the commander.

"Yes, some. But since we fully expected it, we've had a lot of mandatory group sessions with the medical staff. The girls are doing okay, in that regard. There are a couple that Doc," she nodded to Honesty, "here had to get set up with some meds, but I'm pleased overall."

"Thanks. Major Grant, how about the male students?"

He grinned sadly. "You sure you want to ask, sir?"

She chuckled slightly. "I *promise* not to shoot you after your report."

"I'm worried you will *during* my update. I would."

The room shared a brief laugh.

"Seriously, I think I'll go with things could be worse. I've had to reorient several otherwise fine young men on the learned art of cleanliness. We've reviewed how their mommas are not here with Kleenex to wipe their noses, and how it's important for a man to grow the fuck up."

"I'm *so* glad I'm not you," said Emma Walters with a knowing grin.

"You should be," he replied.

"How about that mush-brained brat I had the come-to-Jesus meeting with? Archie, was that it?" asked the colonel.

"Jacob. He's working through some issues. I'd like to think he's making progress."

"Issues?" asked Emma.

"He's laboring to find contentment through hard physical labor."

"We do hard physical labor here?" Emma shot back. "Since when?"

"Since I overheard the botanist talking about how the dirt they were stuck with contained too much clay and not enough rock to add porosity. Did I say that right?" he addressed to the nearest botanist.

"You're hired," she replied with a grin.

"What does the soil's lack of porosity have to do with Jacob and hard physical labor?" pressed Emma.

"Well, you know we have a lot of big rocks strewn around outside."

"I seem to have noticed that aspect of the harsh landscape."

"Well, the best way to get lots of little tiny rocks is to start with really big rocks. You hit big rock with big hammer, and you get little rock." He pantomimed a person slinging a sledgehammer.

Emma guffawed. "You have the boy doing *prison* labor?"

"No. I'm hurt you would so characterize my *rehabilitation* program." He placed a hand gently over his heart. "There is no prison on Mars that I am aware of. And, if the lad meets his *modest* daily quota of sandy debris, he is allowed to eat from our limited supplies and drink of our limited water rations, is he not?"

"So if he fills a wheelbarrow a day, he doesn't *die*. *That's* rehabilitation?" She laughed back at him.

"Try three wheelbarrows, and yes. I'm quite optimistic about his maturation as a member of our community. Eventually."

"Maybe if he's super tired, he won't breed, and we can keep his faulty genes from spreading?" Emma observed.

"That *is* part of my program. That and his body odor. You can't shower every day when you're in the rehabilitation program. That would be ... well, let's just agree it's not part of the plan."

That brought genuine laughter from the crowd of fifteen soldiers and scientists.

"So, on that low note, if there's nothing else, we—"

"Colonel?" asked Ming Wang, the other astronomer on Mars.

"Yes, Doctor Wang?"

"One more thing, if we have time."

"Certainly, if it's important."

"We believe it is." She glanced to Rusty Nelson. "It's about Mars's orbit."

"What about the orbit? It's getting bigger, I believe you told me."

"Yes, it is. We did some back-of-the-envelope

calculations. We are fairly certain that in a few orbits, Mars will pass uncomfortably close to Jupiter."

"Please define *uncomfortably*," Reva pressed intensely.

"Close enough that tidal effects could cause major damage to Mars as it exists today."

"Earthquakes, or whatever you call them on *not* Earth?" the colonel clarified.

"Yes. Gigantic quakes, possibly. The surface could deform as well."

"Deform?"

"Yes," Rusty Nelson spoke up. "Like giant fissures."

"That would be bad," stated the commander.

"No, Colonel. It *will* be devastating," stated Rusty.

"Will we survive?"

Rusty shrugged. "We can't say. Our computer modeling here is too limited. So is our familiarity with orbital interactions, I'm afraid. Let's just say it'll be a challenging time to live."

"Well shit a brick and build me an outhouse," murmured Reva, mostly to herself. "I can't imagine that will be good." She looked over to Nelson intently. "I'm assuming there's nothing we can do about this, is there?"

"Nothing at all. We're riding on the backs of fighting dragons. Nothing more," Ming responded.

"The other issue will be the temperature," said Rusty. "Mars runs in the minus sixty to positive twenty degree range, Centigrade. The space as far out as Jupiter is much colder, in the minus one hundred and fifty degree range, give or take."

"Give or take," Reva parroted. "But that's why we have a nuclear reactor, and, hence, two nuclear engineers." She pointed to two figures seated next to one another across the table from her. They kind of huddled together when her finger landed on them.

"Yes, it is," agreed Rusty. "But if the reactor is damaged in the tidal upheaval, we wouldn't last very long."

"Plus," said one of the engineers, "there will be times the reactor is down because of maintenance. Those periods could be challenging to survive on only our battery backup."

"The news just keeps getting better and better, doesn't it?" grumbled the boss.

"And, even at full, uninterrupted output, our plant would be challenged to keep our environment well-lit and warm." He shook his head. "Minus one fifty, that's cold."

"Shitfuckdamn," was Reva's final thought on the topic.

ELEVEN

We were at our duty stations—which is to say, we were sitting in the mess drinking coffee. I know I've placed us there an infinite number of times, but ask anyone who has ever been in the military. It's just that central to the lifestyle's existence. We'd rehashed our prior attacks on the Clams and were dancing around the edges of some new action. The problem was that there was no obvious best path to take next. If they made some move, we might brilliantly counter, but, failing that, all we were doing was nipping at their heels. As fate would have it, our doldrums were dispelled by the least expected intervention.

"At least they broke up that odd formation," I was muttering. "They seem—"

"Ah. No, hmm. No, er ... Captain, I have an incoming message for you," interrupted Aramthella.

"Could you please finish telling us who it is? I don't think we were expecting any calls," asked Sachiko.

"If it's a telemarketer, do *not* patch them through," I added.

"It's the time maker," Aramthella said in a stunned tone. "It wishes to speak to you, Captain Jones."

"She's right to be surprised," grunted Tank. "I'm rather stunned myself."

"Did it say what it wanted?" wondered Sachiko.

"Only that it will speak with you."

"Wow," I marveled. "Just wowzers. In a zillion years, I wouldn't have expected a call from it."

"Well, put it on the main sound system," said Sachiko. "Let us hear the words, then please translate them for us."

"Certainly. Hang on a moment. There." She addressed him in a high-pitched, raspy series of clicks and grunts. Foul language.

The time maker spoke back in an equally revolting abuse of speech.

"It says it is Time Maker-pid. It graces your worthless lives by acknowledging your pitiful existence."

"So nice of it to call, then," I said quietly.

The S-girls—that's what I had begun calling Sapale and Sachiko—gave me *such* looks.

"Ask it why it's calling," Sachiko stated.

Another exchange of ugly sounds passed between them.

"Wow," she finally said. "Here's the direct translation: 'You have stolen one of my vessels that was not yours. I will you to return it.'"

"Okay, it's won *me* over. Where and when?" I teased.

"Knock it off, flyboy," snapped Sapale. "This is serious business."

"I did not know. I mean, our sworn enemy rings us up to say they want our main weapon voluntarily returned. Silly me, I assumed it this was a prank call."

"Shhh," hissed Sachiko. "Ask it why we would do such a thing."

Screeching grunt-o-matic all over again.

"I *will* you to return what is mine. I am not oriented

toward your possible motivation. I *say* it. You *do* it. I am Time Maker-pid. There are no more words."

"I think I should handle it from here," I said in my cockiest tone.

Sachiko glanced to Tank. He shrugged as if to say *why not*. She nodded to me.

"Please let the nice master know we're placing it on a short hold. Please play it a medley of romantic melodies by Mantovani to make the wait less pleasant."

She translated, I'm certain as best she could what had to be foreign concepts to each of them. Its response sounded like a protest. "Cut the audio, please." She did and the room was tolerable again. "Al, please download a translation algorithm into my head so I can speak directly to the puke."

"Preparing the tran—"

"Jon, I am fully capable of doing that," Aramthella protested.

"I'm certain you can. But Al and I have been doing this a very long time. We're in tune with one another," I lied. In reality, I didn't trust her enough to permit her to make a direct download into my systems. Bitch was too shifty, so far.

"Done, Commander," said Al officially.

"Thank you, kind sir." I tossed that in to let him know I was acting cautiously. Yeah, me, being gracious to him? As if.

"Open the channel, if you please," I asked.

"Open," was her terse response.

"*Hi. To whom am I speaking?*" I stated in the most unnatural vocal gyrations I'd ever been party to.

"*What? You insult me by asking me that. I will kill you a thousand times.*"

"*I'm sorry. Your name is 'you insult me by, etcetera, etcetera?'*"

"*No, you primal snargart,*" it railed back. "*I am the time maker. You know that. I make words to you and you do not encompass them?*"

"*Hang on, are you the* time *maker or the* word *maker, or maybe the* time-word *maker?*"

"*I am Time Maker-pid. I have terminated explaining this to you.*"

"*Ooookay. I'll go with that. Now, to what do I owe this call? My ship told me you fancied it belonged to you and that you were insane enough to ask for it back. Now, since no one is that insane, even when insanity is coupled with stupidity, I'm going to need you to clarify your intentions.*"

"*You subtend my vessel. What is more insulting, you use my vessel against the clan. That is outside of toleration. Return it to me.*"

"*I stand corrected. You are stupid insane.*"

"*I am the time maker. I say it and you obey. It has always been so.*"

"*Not actually, bucko. Think back to when we took this ship away from you. Ever since then, it hasn't been that way.*"

"*You make war with the clan. I will not permission you to do that. To end your error, you must return the ship and be no-timed.*"

"*Or?*"

"*Or? What do you mean?*"

"*I have to give you my ship and be no-timed. I'm not feeling it. Why should I comply? And please, double please, don't repeat that you're the time maker. I have yet to forget that.*"

"*I ... I will you to return the ship. Once you are never, my problem will self-terminate.*"

"*Ah, I gotcha now. Okay, here's my counteroffer. You surrender all your ships to me and then I'll no-time you. Sound good?*"

I didn't need a translation program to know exactly how pissed his humptiness was. Nice.

"Why would I perform such mockery?"

"To end the war you make on me. It's pissing me off, truth be told. Since it is, it works best for me if you surrender, not me. But I'll tell you what. Next time we do this, I'll surrender to you and you can no-time me. Sound good?"

"You defile my ears with your ranting."

"Oh, come on. I bet it's much worse than that. I'm guessing you're speaking with me in public. Your crew is already snickering behind your back. That's gotta hurt."

"You are beyond tolerable. I will know your identity."

"Yes, you will."

"No, insufficient one, I state that I will. I will now. Speak meaning."

"Good luck with that one, sport," tossed in Sapale. She's received the same language download I had. *"The survey says make another wish. That one'll never happen."*

"Who else injures me by making words at me?"

"Hey there, maker boy. Don't you be sweet talking my gal," I replied. *"She only has eyes for me."*

"You ... you speak back at me. I did not communicate to you to hear you. I only want submission."

"Well, in that case, seriously do not talk to my wife, you pervert."

"You are making my brain negative," it screamed. *"Comply. It is your only option."*

"No. I will not give you my ship. I have another option. I will choose that one."

"If I will it, you have no option. What would you make to do?"

"I choose to be a goofy little hamster sleeping under a shady rock all by myself in Mrs. Forest. I will drink silly sodas and dance in the meadow as long as the sun shines

*on my butt. Then I will swim to happiness with tension far
from my cold little nose."*

Boy, did the other three in the room give me looks. I
guess I did ask Aramthella to translate for them, didn't I?
What? I was messing with the dude. They could cut me
some *el slacko.*

*"Your word making is in error. I do not subtend any
meaning. What did you say?"*

*"I said you can go fornicate with yourself, Douche-O-
Supremo. And now, with joy in my heart but no change in
my pocket, or likely in my future, I must bid you a fond
farewell."*

I drew my fingertips across my throat to signal the call
be terminated. I rested back and smiled. "Well, that was
sure nice of it to call."

"Do ... do you think it was wise to taunt the guy so ...
so much?" blurted out Sachiko.

"Did I come off *roguishly?"* I placed a hand over my
heart. "I was *trying* to be the larger sentient."

"I'm not sure—" she started.

"Me?" spat Sapale. "I think you were way too nice to
the ass candy. Next time it calls, *I'm* doing the
conversating."

"Okay, next time, you're on point. But, honey?"

"Yes," she replied with a smirk.

"Try not to be undiplomatic. Study my exchange with
him as your guiding star."

"You know what I'm doing with that *guiding star,*
sailor?"

"No, but can we do it in private with death metal
music blaring?"

She pointed at me, dropped her thumb to her index,
and made a clicking sound with her tongue. I don't believe
she had even seen a revolver, ever.

TWELVE

"I summoned you three because there is a void in my subtending of a recent word exchange I had with the humans who took one of my vessels. You will make me understand what transhappened."

"We live only to serve you, Time Maker-pid," they said in unison.

"Excellent. I anticipate the de-voiding of my mentation. I ordered that you three study the recording on my unhelpful interaction with this Jon-human. As understanding makers of self, others, and non-self-and-non-others, I *will* that you make me subtend what occurred." The time maker said those words incongruously while bashing the mushy stump of what had been the head of the last of his former bridge crew against a bulkhead. Yet, it spoke, in the context of clan-speak, matter-of-factly.

"We ... er, some of us are in agreement with your mandate," was the cautious reply from the understanding maker of non-self-and-non-others.

"You dare to evade my will," howled the time maker.

"In no way, shape, or form, Lord," it responded flatly.

"By the way, why is it that your position has such a long title? There are seven words needed to define you. All others have one word, two at the maximum."

"I'm still working on that, honestly. My understanding of my designation is yet to be completed. However, Master, if you think about it, to do so in my case would constitute an understanding of *self*, and that is *its* department," it pointed at the Understanding-of-Self Maker-hih, "not mine. So maybe ask *it* if you are consumed with curiosity."

The time maker was so taken aback by that declaration that it not only stopped liquifying the head of the last member of the bridge crew, it dropped the limp corpse altogether. "When you three fail me ... you will be the first to die."

"If that honor falls to me, then I should become it. But your perfection does not doubt for one *itle* that we, combined, could possibly fail you, do you, if I am hearing your intent fully?" Apparently central to the understanding of non-self-and-non-others was the predilection to evade and be vague.

"I have recycled many today. All who fail me are recycled. The chances of you three forcing my subtending that inferior conversation are frighteningly slight. *Speak*."

"Your fundamental non-subtension is that if you *will* the Jon-human to return your stolen ship, why is it that he does not comply immediately? Are we in agreement?"

"Yes, but *also*, I ordered him to submit to no-timing. Yet he seemed to make mirth in response. Such is impossible *and* unacceptable."

"We would of course be honored to comply with your demands," responded Understanding-of-Others Maker-fim.

There was silence in the room. It was most definitely unwelcome and it was tense.

"*And?*" screamed the time maker.

"I'm sorry," replied the understanding-of-others maker, pointing at its face. "Are you speaking to me?"

"No. I am *yelling* at you. You are as dense as neutron star matter. You please me as well as that irrelevant substance does too. Of course I await your next words."

"Lord," it began diplomatically, "what *words* do you anticipate?"

The time maker vibrated as if struck by a sizable asteroid. "You are my understanding-of-*others* maker. You began to give words. I anticipated you would say meaning about my understanding of another, who is, in this case, the Jon-human."

"Well—" it began.

"But you message me platitudes. Empty nothingness ventured to my audio sensors. You insult me by not doing your job."

"My Lord, I *do* do my job. That is all I do. I am *doing* my job even as we exchange words."

"Then why have you yet to *de-void* my subtension?"

"The answer to that is ... well it is precipitously obvious. Are you mirthing with me?"

"It is not. If it were, I would know it. I do not," said a consummately displeased time maker.

"I am constantly doing my job," defended the understanding-of-others maker. "I have yet— *obviously*— to understand why the *Jon-human* defied your commands."

"Then what good to *me* are *you?*" the time maker screamed as loud as it could.

"I am your understanding-of-others maker."

The time maker looked to the other understanding makers, straining to understand what the twit was saying. The other two shrugged. They did not, in reality, understand. They also knew better than to say one word to the mercurial time maker.

"I *know* that," the time maker finally howled. "You *know* I know that. Why do you ask it of me? I do not *understand* why you would."

"Ah," it replied, perking up a bit. "That, Lord, is interesting question making. You are a clan member of more than one talent. This is beyond questioning." It took a second to gather itself up. "What you ask involves," it opened its arms widely, "the understanding of others. That is my job. *That* is why you need me. Thank you, our totality, for stating for me, on my behalf, why it is you so very much need me."

"But I understand zero why or what the Jon-human said. You have," the time maker turned to the other two mute statues in the room, "what is the word I seek? The one that subtends what this tripdompel has done to me?"

Self shot non-self-and-non-others a panicky glance. NSANO shook its head discreetly. Self was uncertain what that was supposed to mean. Did it not know or was it not going to say? Oh bother.

"*Failed* you, Master?" the self maker said with great reservation.

"Yes," wheezed the time maker. "*That* is the word, and *that* is the concept. Understanding of Others Maker-fim, you have now officially failed me."

"I don't understand," it replied quickly. That bit of verbal gymnastics was usually enough to throw even the most insistent player off their game. Don't you just hate it when your best dodge isn't quite good enough?

"You do not?" responded the time maker with surprise.

"No, sir, I do not." Others's heart was starting to beat again.

"Then please, allow me to explain it to you," offered

the time maker. That was uncharacteristically gracious of the lunatic.

"Thank you, Master."

"Be good enough to bring me that computer pad. I need it to frame your subtension."

"This one, Lord?"

"That exact one."

Others picked up the tool and stepped over to his boss. He offered the pad.

"Thank you. Now, I want you to study closely this side of the computer pad." The time maker tapped the back side.

"That side, Lord. That side does nothing aside from allowing the pad to rest on a surface."

"That is where you are wrong. It has other uses. May I demonstrate to you one?"

"I would be—"

No, it probably wouldn't have been. Of course, we will never know. Perhaps its sense of obligation extended to having its head pounded to sludge by a computer pad.

Turning to the other understandings, the time maker spoke slowly, seemingly calmly. "I am ready to be enlightened." It conspicuously did not drop the pad. Instead it dangled, all drippy and oozy, in its hand by its side.

"I am coming to believe the Jon-human feels no obligation to comply with your will," said a *very* respectful understanding-of-self maker.

The time maker lowered its brow. "Is that even *possible?*" it said dubiously. "Could one who subtends my meaning not feel compelled to act accordingly?" It was gobsmacked, plain and simple. The very concept had never occurred to it. Now that such heresy was thrust upon it, the time maker wasn't certain he liked or approved of the notion. He looked to non-self-and-non-others. "*Speak.*"

It took a particularly deep breath, since it might be the last it would enjoy. "Is it permissible? *No.* Is it proper? *Never.* Is it acceptable? Over my dea ... *No.*" It quivered slightly at the image it almost spoke. "But is it *possible?* I am beginning to think the thoughts of the one who *said* the words might need to be contemplated. Maybe."

"So you two want me to subtend that the Jon-human may not be obliged to follow my will?"

Non-self-and-non-others demonstrably gestured to self. Oh yes, it most certainly did.

"Subtending that would make the Jon-human's lack of compliance subtendable, if not conscionable, Lord," summarized Self.

"Fascinating," breathed the time maker. "And, *assuming* this impossibility, what meaning am I to assign the word making he made?"

Self spoke, as it seemed to be on a roll. "The Jon-human said, *I choose to be a goofy little hamster sleeping under a shady rock all by myself in Mrs. Forest.* I can't imagine who Mrs. Forest is; perhaps it is his mate. But, as a time lord like yourself, he could assume any form. If he wished to be a hamster under a—"

Yup, that was it for Understanding-of-Self Maker-hih. One instant it was opining, the next, it had never existed. It had said the words *time lord like yourself.* Blasphemy was not acceptable.

The remaining understanding maker's eyes bugged out visibly in surprise.

"Neither the Jon-human nor any beast is a time lord like *I,*" proclaimed the time maker without dissent.

A thought occurred to Not. "I'm sorry, Lord. I could not hear what the no-timed maker said just before it never was."

"Nothing of importance, it would seem," replied the boss thoughtfully. Then, with more pizzazz, he asked, "And what did the Jon-human mean by word sharing, *I said you can go fornicate with yourself, Douche-O-Supremo. And now, with joy in my heart but no change in my pocket, or likely in my future, I must bid you a fond farewell?*"

Non self and non others looked straight ahead and snapped his response like he was a recruit answering a drill sergeant. "I'm absolutely certain, positive to a degree I have never experienced before, that the Jon-human transferred to you a polite idiom used by those who word his language."

"Yes. You are right to subtend that meaning," responded the time maker. Please note that it did not say *correct*, only *right to*. That was all that was required of Not. "Now leave me. Send in my body makers as you pass them in the hall. There's work to be done for them."

Not scanned the room grimly and departed quickly without comment.

THIRTEEN

I was sitting alone in the mess—drinking you-know-what —all by my lonesome. Tank came in, poured himself a cup, and held the pot up to me, asking if I needed a refill. I placed a palm over my mug. He came over, plopped down, and began blowing into his mug. We were guy-talking without saying a word. That was why I really liked Tank. We *got* each other. For as great a friend as Toño was, or would have been, if he'd ever existed, he wasn't a dude. He was a man, but not a *guy*. I mean, the man still peeled an orange with a knife and fork. Baby back ribs, slathered in BBQ-sauce? Yeah, knife and fork too. Not one drop on the table, no stains on his clothes. And, in two billion years, I don't think he'd ever eaten a hamburger. Nope, because they don't have cutlery at burger joints. It was just wrong how proper he was. Or would have been. Crapazoid. Did I mention how much I hated time-think?

"So I wonder how bad the Indians'd be doing about now if there ever was a major league for them to founder in?"

"In spite of there never having been an Earth, and

hence no baseball, I *guarantee* they are twenty-six games out of first place somewhere in this crazy universe."

We grunted laughs. Communi-grunting. That was nice. Man, had I missed that.

"I was always a Giants fan myself," I informed him.

"So you grew up in Pronto Pup Land?"

"Partly. My dad moved around a lot. But the one constant was baseball. I latched on to the Giants and never let loose. They were my boyhood anchor." I mused a bit. "Mays, McCovey, Bonds, and Everly. Man, they played some ball."

"Don't leave Johnnie Disaster off that list, or Stu Miller being blown off the mound in the first of two 1961 All-Star Games. Or the time Vance slid into home during the 2027 playoffs but stopped a foot shy of the plate."

I set my mug down and scowled. "You aren't by chance a *Dodgers* fan, are you?" I said the words with all the spite and contempt due them.

He chuckled. "No, but Daisy is, er, was, er, would have been."

"Hence you know how to yank my chain."

"I most certainly do." He took a couple sips. "Me, I'm a Chiefs fan. Never was much into that sissy baseball stuff."

"D'you play?"

He tossed his head. "A little in high school. I was too small and too slow for college ball. Well, that and I was an astronomy major. The long nights left no time for athletics."

"Good excuse. I'll remember it if I ever need it. Oh, wait. I don't, because I was a second team All-American quarterback while playing for the Air Force Falcons."

"Really? You never mentioned that before? Oh, wait. You did. About three *thousand* times. Still, good to hear about your old glory days, you know, back when you had some."

"So you here to discuss sports, my notoriety, or what?"

"More the *or what.*"

"I'm listening."

"You'll figure it out. I want to tell you not to stress about it to the point you blow a fuse."

"I do not believe I have any fuses, bulbs, or tubes in me to blow."

"I stand corrected."

"Oh, just curious. What is it I'll figure out? A better mouse trap?"

He snickered. "Perhaps. I wouldn't put anything past you. No, I was referring to the Clams. You'll figure out how to beat them."

"What, prithee tell, good sir, places you under the impression that I am wrought with self-doubt in that regard?"

"Jon, really?"

"What *Jon really?*"

"You trying that bullshit on me? If there would have been an Earth, I would've been a Marine Corps officer. I commanded personnel in combat. I know what's eating at you."

"And here I was thinking the doctor in *Doctor Sherman* was a Ph.D. Come to find out you're some kind of shrink. Go figure."

He stared at me over the rim of his mug.

After nearly thirty seconds, I knew he wasn't going to blink first. "Alright, you're right." I shook my head in disgust, "I've done this a million times. Something always pops into my wheelhouse. But with the Clams, I got nothing."

"We've taken out several of their ships and they've not gotten off a shot. That's not chopped liver."

"It better not be chopped liver," protested Sachiko as she entered. "I forbid that revolting food product aboard my ship." She set about to brew a cup of tea. And it wasn't even tea; it was "herbal" tea. I mean, what the hell was the point?

"We were *having* a psychiatric session," I snarked. "I'm not certain I wish to forego my rights to doctor-patient confidentiality."

"What? This Neanderthal is a psychiatrist now? There are only four humans left in the universe, but he's the fourth-least qualified for that title. The man's a walking insult to tact, decorum, and political correctness."

"I thought *I* was the least qualified to be touchy-feely," I protested.

She pointed sideways toward him. "The man farted at faculty meetings. And not just once. All the time, like he was doing it to make some point."

I gave Tank a seated bow. "I have met my match, good sir."

He gave us a crooked grin. Then he was returned to his previous position on my back. "So, we were discussing how Jon needs to stop beating himself up."

She frowned. "Were you beating yourself up?"

"Doctor Feel Good over there seems to think I was."

"*Are*, not *was*," he corrected.

"Well, stop it this instant. Captain's orders."

"Aye, aye," I replied in a pirate accent with a two-finger salute.

"I'm serious, Jon," Tank said with gravitas. "Maybe we can talk through this?"

I shook my head again. "We've talked and talked like we were members of a quilting circle. *Talk* hasn't moved the dial."

"What's the issue?" asked Sachiko.

"He's frustrated that we have taken out a few enemy ships, but we've made no overall headway. He's knows we've been lucky so far. We, the last hope of Earth, are one well-placed shot away from losing the battle for existence. He's self-flagellating himself into a clinical depression that will serve neither him nor our mission in a positive manner."

"I feel so much better, Doc," I groaned. "You got some bedside manner, let me tell you. Anybody seen a noose around here?"

"I'm being serious. You be so too, please," Tank demanded of me. How un-guy-like was that?

I started a good sulk, a really good one. I clammed up, hunched over, and tensed up my lips like I'd bitten an unripe lemon. Yeah, one good sulk.

They, naturally, sat quietly waiting for me to grow up. Good luck with that one, people.

Remember the circumturus, the houseplanty thing? The ones with super-diluted psychic abilities, or whatever? Sapale had placed hers in the mess on a shelf behind where I was seated. Not that I'd noticed or cared, but it turned out that was where it was. As I sulked, I started to daydream. Hey, it wasn't like I was *actually* mad. I just wanted to make them feel guilty for being right and for being concerned. So, anyway, I was thinking about football, because Tank had so recently prompted me to. It was his fault.

Amid my recollections of big games and my pivotal roles in them, I began to hear a kookaburra bird calling out. You know, the one in Australia, if there had even been one. I knew it because I vacationed there a couple times, and the song is so distinctive in its annoying, fast cackle. Anyway, it slowly dawns on me, why am I hearing a Laughing Jackass, as they're so accurately nicknamed, while strolling down memory lane? Then I see Uluru, also known as Ayers Rock, off in the distance. I'm walking toward it. The day is hot, really hot. I sidestep a huntsman spider, nearly trip in doing so, when my boot taps a loose stone. I am so thirsty. Sweat stings my eyes. Then, more realizations dawn on me. I do not *get* thirsty. I'm an android. And I don't sweat. Why would an android need to sweat? I have fans and cooling coils, or something, if I overheat, right?

But slowly, I approach Uluru. Why am I trekking to Uluru? No clue. That's when I notice I have a pole resting on my right shoulder, held in my right hand. At the end of the pole is a red paisley print bag. I'm carrying a hobo stick, or, as they say Down Under, I'm waltzing matilda.

Now I'm getting pissed off. Jon Ryan does *not* travel in such a lowbrow style. I camp, sure. I can stay at a Motel 6 if need dictates that's where I should. But a hobo stick? No way, Jose. I have minimal standards, and *hobo* meets none of them. But, even though I try, I can't cast the darn swag off. Soon enough, I forget about the stupid thing. I am at the base of the rock. It is more imposing than I remember. That's weird. What is even weirder is that Uluru is trying to speak to me. Yeah, not mentioned in most tourism brochures.

The rock, the sandstone itself, groans. Rasping, scraping, dry abrasions, and tumbling pebbles form the rudiments of a word. One single word. *Walkabout.* The big rock is saying walkabout. Nice. I mean, that makes no sense *so* much, it's perfect. A thirsty, sweating robot conversing with a landmark. Happens every day.

I'm starting to wonder. Does Uluru want to go on a walkabout? Does it want me to come along? Maybe it opines that *I* should go on one, but isn't that exactly what I have been doing in the first place? I'm cruising across Australia with a hobo stick, sidestepping barking spiders, so, I've gone *walkabouting* by definition.

Because I need less certainty, fewer points of reference, and more taunting by the damn universe, some of the falling pebbles begin hitting my cheeks. First the right cheek, then the left, then—oh joy—the right. In no time, the pebbles are not only striking me, but it's really starting to hurt. I have half a mind to defend myself. Yeah, I start punching at the fool rocks. Bam, off to the right with you. Kapow, off to the left. Yeah, I'm getting into this. I'm no longer waltzing matilda, I'm fighting Uluru. In fact, I'm opening up such a can of whoop-ass, that the national treasure stops groaning walkabout, and switches to Jon ... Jon ...

"Jon." Sapale slapped me again, hard. "Jon, wake the frak up. Jon, what in the hell's wrong with you?"

I punched her again, knocking her next palm heading for my cheek to the ... left. WTF?

"I'm okay ... 'm kay," I mumbled.

"Are you sure?" she yelled.

"Yes. I'm cool. Why are you hitting me?"

"Jon, are you absolutely certain you're awake and accounted for?" she confirmed.

"Yes. I'm right as rain, aside from the fact that," I looked to both sides, "you're straddling me on the floor hitting me, I'm superb."

"What a *relief*," she said with conviction. Then she slapped me again, really hard.

"Hey, I said I was fine. What was that for?"

"For scaring the living shit out of me, that's what. Jon, you were unconscious for over three hours. Al didn't know what was going on, *Blessing* said your systems were all fine, but your brain had checked out. What happened?"

I shook my head to clear it. What had happened? I peered over her shoulder, to the damn circumturus up there on the shelf.

"It was your damn plant."

Deadpan, she looked at me, over her shoulder to the

scrawny houseplant, then back to me. "My circumturus placed you in a *coma?*" she asked dubiously.

"Basically."

"I think maybe you hit him too hard," said Tank. "I think he's got a concussion. Wait. Er, do androids get concussions?"

"I'm about to find out," Sapale replied angrily. "Jon, how could a dumb circumturus do anything but need water and make the color blue say *hi* to you?"

"This was the second time, sweetie. It did it to me a while back."

"My *houseplant* is a serial abuser?"

"I don't blame the plant. I blame ... no one."

"Wow, honey, that's so big of you. You're finally growing up," she mocked.

A walkabout. I needed to go on a walkabout.

"If you could remove your ever-so-cute butt from my chest, I need to get up."

"Oh you do, Mr. Comatose? And why is that?"

"I need to go on a walkabout."

"A what-about?" she snapped.

"You know. When an Australian goes for a long walk, to cleanse his mind, refresh. A walkabout."

She raised her right hand. "Kaljaxian. No Australians where I hail from."

"It's a thing," explained Tank. "Jon, you want to go on a walkabout? You do recall we're on a spaceship, right? Sure, it's a big ship, as they go, or so I'm told. But a walkabout? Doesn't that require ... uh, more room?"

There on the floor with my wife restraining me, I shrugged my shoulders. "I never really thought that much about walkabouts. Maybe, but not necessarily, they are best undertaken over a large expanse?"

"Is it always like this with him?" Sachiko asked Sapale rather plaintively.

"Oh yeah. This is how it is with him twenty-four-seven for the last two *billion* years."

"May I rise?" I asked again.

"I'm considering my options," responded my soulmate.

"Well, either get off or this is going to get romantic in a hurry."

She raised her palm, as if to slap me again. "You are such a guy," she heaved in frustration. "Nothing *romantic* can come of being pinned to the ground after scaring the concerned mate out of her mind. Sexual, sure. Nasty, dirty sexual. But how many times do I have to tell you? Your idea of romance is everyone else's idea of five minutes of drunken pelvis pounding."

"I lie on the corridor corrected," I said contritely. "May I get up now?"

"So you can walkabout this ship?"

I nodded.

"Like a ghost on the moors?"

"I can't say, but I'll get back to you later as to the details."

"No, you won't. If *you're* whackingabout, *I'm* whackingabout."

"Ah, I think one must walkabout in solitude. Otherwise, it'd be called a *family vacation*, not a spiritual quest."

"Oh, now it's *spiritual*?" she mocked. Again with the mocking. I was at an emotional crossroads, or whatever, and she still needed the snark?

She stood rapidly. "In that case, you're going alone. Spiritually, I'm good."

"You're going to let him wander off, just like that?" questioned the captain.

"It's not like he can go anywhere. Al," Sapale called out.

"Yes?" he said immediately.

"Will you keep track of this nitwit as he tours both the ship and his conscious mind?"

"If I must."

"You must. And if he even thinks about something dangerous, deactivate him, okay?"

"Would that I could, I would have *long* ago, my dear," responded the idiot AI.

"And keep me posted."

"That I can do," Al replied.

Sapale started shooing me away. "Walk, walk, walk about."

"I think y'all should leave," I said weakly.

"We won't have to if you take ten steps. You'll be around the corner and we'll be out-of-sight."

"I guess," I peeped uncertainly.

And I took a few steps backward, then turned, and so began *the* weirdest walkabout in history.

FOURTEEN

Reva sat in her office, nursing a tumbler of vodka. Alcohol was way low on the list of essentials needed for Mars colonization, but a few exemptions had been allowed. The senior officers managed to ferry over a couple cases. The supplies were finite, but Reva had had one of those days. Hell, she'd had one of those *weeks*. A student had developed appendicitis. The first test of their limited surgical capabilities went tolerably well, but it was made clear that if a major procedure was called for, there would likely be trouble.

And the reactor had a sort-of-issue-that's-not-a-problem, according to the engineers. All Reva knew was that it was offline the better part of a day. Backup was sufficient, but the operations people learned that the wiring from the backup to the greenhouses didn't work. Whoever installed the circuits forgot to connect wire A to wire B, or some such bullshit. It was fixed, so it wouldn't happen again, but now she had to worry as to what other critical issues were yet to be uncovered.

And that idiot Jacob Cummings was doing the *opposite* of coming around to seeing reason. Dr. Hartley had shared with Reva that, in her medical opinion, the boy had a *schizotypal personality disorder*. Bottomline, he was a psychopath in training. Reva ordered him to be medicated, and the meds did help, but they were in extremely low supply. See, no one thought much about needing medicines for treating schizophrenia on Mars. Who would send a nut job to the isolated colony? No one, right? Apparently, if the logistics people hadn't seen to it that a lot of cough syrup was sent with the expedition, Jacob would have already gone through the entire supply of needed medications. Who would have figured? A commonly dispensed cough medicine treated a severe psychiatric disorder. Seemed like overkill to use on a tickle in one's throat, but it was any-port-in-a-storm time for Mars 1.

She held the ice-filled glass up to her forehead and sighed repeatedly. After seventeen years in the Army, she'd seen many deployments. Some were downright scary assignments to war zones. But this was the most stressful. A lifelong mission on a lost world, with no possibility of returning home or ever seeing her loved ones again. Sure, everyone on Mars was in the same condition, but she was the commander. She could never relax, never let her guard down, and never hope for a vacation. It was her job to keep a bunch of people alive against the worst odds imaginable, and the pressure of that sentence was beginning to eat at her like worms.

There was a soft knock.

Reva set her glass down behind a stack of papers. She didn't want to let on to anyone that she was trying to drown her sorrows.

"Come."

Emma Walters stuck her head in the doorway.

"Well, good evening to you," remarked Reva. Friendly company was a good thing, just then and there.

Then the colonel noticed the stark look on the captain's face.

"What is it?" Reva asked with steely resolve.

"May I come in, sir?"

"Of course, of course," she responded, flustered. "Sit." Reva gestured to a chair.

Once sitting, Emma began running her fingers around the edges of her beret she clutched in her lap.

"You look like someone bearing less than welcome news," Reva said coolly.

Emma started to tremble, then she began tearing up.

Reva shot around to her side of the table and slipped into the chair next to Emma's. She placed a hand on her elbow, and the other on Emma's shoulder. "What is it, Emma?"

"One of the girls—" Emma stopped speaking and sniffed loudly. Her lower jaw trembled like she was freezing to death.

"What, was there an incident?"

Emma tried to compose herself. "It's Megan, sir. Megan Thompson."

"What about Megan Thompson?" Reva was not familiar with the person.

"She's ... she's—"

"What. Emma. What's—"

"She's *dead*."

It was as if Emma'd punched her in the face and gut simultaneously. No one was *dead* on Reva St. Claire's shift. Not a possibility. "D ... dead. What are you talking about?"

"One of the girls found her and called me. I called the doctor the moment I got there, but she was gone. We were too late." The last few words were clouded in a growing wave of sobs.

"What ... what happened?" asked a stunned commander.

"She took her own life, Reva." Emma reached into a shirt pocket and pulled out a crisp, folded sheet of paper.

Reva took it with great foreboding. Opening it, she read, *I'm so sorry. I'm so so sorry. I know it's horrible to do to all of you. But I can't be alone. I can't be here on Mars when my family—Mom, Dad, John, Angela, and Cassius —are all gone. I can't be this lonely. I'm so sorry.*

Not even aware she was saying the words, Reva asked, "How?"

"She'd been volunteering in the clinic. She must have taken some pills when no one was looking. Her roommates said she was extra cheerful last night. She was fine at lights-out. One of the girls got up to try to sneak out. She stubbed her toe in the dark and fell on Megan's bunk. Then ... then she called me."

"How's she doing?"

"Allyssa's pretty shaken up. Doc's with her."

"It wasn't her fault. Make sure she knows that."

"I'll remind her, sir, when I see her."

"Where's Megan now?"

"I had a couple of the MPs carry her to the clinic."

"Good thinking. No need to upset the dorm any more than it already is." She was speaking mostly to herself.

"Thank you."

Then a thought hit Reva. The next moment, she slapped her palm to her face and doubled over in tears. It had occurred to her that at least she wouldn't have to personally notify next-of-kin, like she'd done way too often in the past. She felt a rush of relief, just before her humanity caught up with her train of thought.

Damn this assignment. Damn it to hell.

FIFTEEN

Once I was around the corner of the ship's corridors and out of sight, I began walking uncertainly. I felt as silly as a shark in a guppy costume. A walkabout on a spaceship? I'd have asked myself *how stupid was that*, but it wasn't stupid. It was too darn *pathetic* to be stupid. I did resolve quickly that when I "returned home," I was going to throw that fool circumturus plant into the ship's main reactor. Why had it tricked me into this stunt? Why, more pivotally, had I said a word about it, let alone embarked on my escapade? None of this made a lick of sense.

I started planning. Where does one wander on a vessel he is fairly familiar with? I mean, I hadn't explored every nook and cranny, but I'd inspected Aramthella thoroughly several times. There wasn't much to see. Shiny decks, empty passageways, soft lighting. Pretty boring and routine, as far as I had seen. Maybe I could daydream while I trekked? Sure, I had enough sports and sexual recollections to occupy my mind for quite some time, if I did say so myself. There was the time—no, *times*—I dated the Alvarez twins, back in high school. And ... no. I stopped myself. I could fantasize while lying on my bunk.

I was on a mission. I needed to focus on ... on something. I just needed to find out what it was I needed to focus on.

I headed down one of the passageways that led to the crew's quarters. Aramthella told us the Clams rarely slept, but they were assigned personal spaces, in case they felt an impulse to get away a bit. Generally, they behaved like termites or ants, longing to be in tight company with their clan members. Naturally, the section was abandoned. It was as quiet as a closed library. Those sorry sonsabitches definitely lived Spartan lives. Their quarters had all the homey feel and warmth of a morgue.

I wandered—because us walkabouters wandered—then toward the outer rim of the ship. Whatever its designers intended this space to be, it wasn't. The Clams showed no presence whatsoever in the sections farthest from the central hub, and the all-important TSR. Perhaps it served as a production area for a society that made something *besides* chaos. Then again, it might have been recreational. I mean, what big old starship didn't have a space where people could watch the stars pass by slowly? Those were—and I could think it now because you-know-who wasn't around—a romantic getaway spot for, well, you-know-what.

There was a compartment I'd given a cursory glance to a couple times that I'd never entered. It was as empty as a teenager's head, so I never bothered. But, as one currently blessed with available time, I took the plunge. Oh joy. To experience a large, empty hold-space. It was the stuff of lege—

What was that sound? It was, I don't know, squishy. I know. Maybe I was alone for too long, and I was losing it? It had been the better part of an hour since I'd left civilization behind me.

There. Again. Yeah, squishy. Like someone was playing with a molded Jell-O in the bathtub. By the way,

I'd *never* done that. No. I was acoustically *speculating*. The sound seemed to be coming from the far side of the space, around an L-shaped turn in the room.

As I rounded the corner, I was surprised to see—nothing. I was about to bail, when I most certainly heard the sound again, in front of me and to the right. I switched to infrared optics. Yup, there it was ... the something making a squishy sound. It was on the deck, tucked into the corner. I drew my sidearm and tiptoed forward. The thing was small enough, but it had escaped anyone's notice thus far, so I had to assume it wasn't a friendly.

Then again, I have to state it looked pretty unthreatening. I stopped a meter from it, to take its measure. Wow. What a disgusting blob. The first lightning image I flashed on was green ghost Slimer, you know, the one from *Ghostbusters*? Only this one was a whole lot smaller and it wasn't green. It was like self-contained clear mucus. Nice. I'd never seen anything like it. Good to know the universe could continue to gross me out, in spite of my age.

As I studied it, I began to see it was a mucus football, lying on its side. Its ten or twelve sets of mucous legs were twirling either in the air or against the bulkhead. In any case, it wasn't moving. The comparison I'd make is that thing when you scratch a dog just right behind the ear, and its leg starts spazzing out? Only no one was scratching the mucous blob's ear, and I was pretty sure it didn't even have an ear to scratch behind.

"Aramthella," I asked reservedly, "you there?"

No response. That was an unwelcome first. She was the ship's consciousness. She had to be everywhere, right?

"Aramthella," I said louder.

Nothing.

I was about to contact Sapale, when my head was

filled with another voice: *Aramthella can't hear you in here.*

Who said that?

Are you talking to me? Sapale shot back quickly.

No.

Then why'd you talk to me, if you didn't talk to me?

I didn't. I was talking to ... I don't know who the hell I was talking to. Someone was talking to me.

How reassuring, she observed. *Are you sniffing glue on your walkaround? I'm talking to you.*

Well, don't. Ignore me and don't react. You got that?

Situation normal. I ignore and do not react to you. Got it. Say, while you're out, could you pick up a dozen eggs and some milk at the store?

Bu-bye.

I was beginning to think I needed a tune-up.

"*Aramthella,*" I shouted.

Talk, talk, talk. Or don't talk. You choose. But I told you. She can't hear you in here.

Okay, one, who the hell are you and two, how can you talk into my head?

I am me. And I can't talk in your head. Silly biped. I think into your head. Then you think into mine. It's really very simple, in a complex way.

Crap on a Capote. What are you, the transparent Cheshire Cat? Is it possible for you to speak not *in riddles?*

Probably not. I do not have a mouth. I am unlikely to speak ... ever.

Wait. Are you clairvoyant?

Oh not now, please. I'm telepathic. That will have to do for now, unless of course, it doesn't.

That's what I meant. Are you telepathic?

We covered that already. Must we again?

No. But, come to think of it, you don't seem overly busy, so maybe we could.

I am very busy. I'm relaxing in rapture.

Rapture. Huh. I don't think you can be busy at rapture; they're sort of mutually exclusive.

I was unaware of that rule. Should I stop? I would say I hate to stop relaxing in rapture, but, when in this state, to hate anything is the opposite of possible.

You mean it's impossible?

That too.

I'm holding a gun. You know that, right?

And I'm not. You know that, right?

Of course I do. You're transparent. If you were packing, I'd see the piece.

Then why were we discussing your holding or not of a weapon?

Because it is generally considered unwise to piss off an individual who is training a gun on you, especially when you are not armed.

Oh, but I am armed, the stupid blob said. Then it rolled onto its back and wiggled its legs riotously.

I am officially bored with this Alice in Wonderland *banter.*

I am sorry to learn that. Unless you're happy to be bored. Then I'm happy too.

Are you familiar with the concept of the Easy Way versus the Hard Way of doing a thing?

I'm not certain.

Then I'll walk you through—

Shouldn't it be concepts, plural? Those are two separate concepts, are they not?

Okay, you clearly fail to grasp the essentials. The Easy Way of doing this is that you please me with your clarity of response, and I do not shoot you. The Hard Way would be that you displease me with your ongoing obfuscation, and I do shoot you. Are you clear on at least that much?

Thank you for that explanation. Learning is a joy unto itself. What is it you would like clarified, or not, Jon Ryan?

I want you to answer my initial question.

Aramthella, you there? Why would you want me to answer that?

I wouldn't. I was referring to my initial question to you.

Ah, 'Who said that?'

Okay, Mr. Grammarist, strike the word initial *and replace it with* most important. *Who the hell are you?*

And not the part about and 'how can you talk into my head,' because we covered that. I can't.

Answer the question, now.

I am me. I am not, therefore, you or the Cheshire Cat.

Moving up in the Pleasing Jon Category, accepting that you are you, what are you doing here?

Avoiding that busybody Aramthella. I wished to relax in rapture unmolested.

Oh no. We may be getting somewhere. So you are here, in this compartment, to avoid detection by the ship? That seems like a nefarious project to me. Why are you in hiding?

You've met her, Aramthella. Wouldn't you enjoy avoiding her at times? Most times, in fact.

That's beside the point. At least, I think it is.

May I help in your understanding?

That is where we're going, slowly, painfully, and gratingly.

I am in this compartment because it is shielded from Aramthella's awareness. She and I work in tandem most of the time, which is all time.

You mean most of the time?

Do I? I didn't think that's what I wanted to convey. Most of time, as in, you know, the time *thing. Think big, please.*

Oh. Gotcha. If you work with Aramthella, why is it she hasn't mentioned it and we've never seen you at all to see you do anything with her?

That is a tortured query. Are you in need of some form of assistance? Medical? Mechanical? Metaphysical?

Just plain responses would be super.

She hasn't mentioned me because she wishes all the credit. You haven't seen me before because you have never looked where I was. You have not seen us work together because our work in concert does not appear at a visual frequency.

I fluttered my eyes. It was like I was conversing with all three stooges at once, all in one little disgusting package.

Do you have a name? If so, what is it?

Yes, I do. It is unpronounceable.

I set my palm over my face. *Your name is unpronounceable? That's not even funny. It's lame, dude.*

I believe I have identified your misunderstanding. My name is not the word unpronounceable. *It is a word that is not* pronounceable *in your frame of reference.*

Are you trying to get shot? I mean, you're doing a bang-up job of it as far as I'm concerned.

No, for the record, I am not. My what you call a name, in your frame of reference, is not a word; it is a concept. You wouldn't understand it.

What concept is it? There, I think I've really pinned you down with that one. You kind of have to answer non-funkadelically.

I am Peaceful Consideration Thirst.

I don't understand.

I predicted as much.

You're thirsty?

No, but thanks for inquiring. Perhaps 'One Who Quests For' would be clearer.

I can answer with confidence that it is not clearer. Wait. I got it. When Aramthella addresses you, what does she call you?

I can predict with confidence you will not be pleased with my answer to that question.

Take a swing at it anyway.

Aramthella calls me Peaceful Consideration One Who Quests For.

Your prediction stands. I am not pleased.

Do you know what, Jon Ryan?

I'm thinking I don't know what, right about now.

I think the better question you should ask is what would be the sound of the manner in which Aramthella addresses me, not the actual text of what she calls me is.

I have no idea what you just said, but, sure, riddle me that, Batman.

The sound of my name would roughly be Plesmus.

Roughly. Of course. I wouldn't have it any other way.

That is fortunate.

It's also a damn lie, but, let's move forward, shall we?

Your call, big guy, concluded Plesmus.

That was odd.

How is it you talk like ... strike that. Where did you learn the colloquial like that, the kind I might use?

Uh, Jon, I am in your head, right? Your phraseology resides in here.

I bet it does.

You would win that wager.

Can we get back to something specific that you said, a while back in my stream of confusion?

If it would please you, yes.

Why would the ship want to take all the credit and not mention you?

I can conceive of it doing so.

But you just said, and I hate to, but I'll quote you. 'She hasn't mentioned me because she wishes all the credit.'

That is a truth as I see it to be.

So you did say the ship wants ...

No. Ah. Jon, the ship is a metal box with breathable air. Aramthella is the consciousness that drives and enlivens the ship.

And you, Plesmus, what are you?

I am the ship's focus.

The ship's or Aramthella's? Man, is this a bizarre-assed conversation.

The ship's, of course. Aramthella cannot have a focus. She is the consciousness and enlivener of the ship. Silly biped.

You said that already.

And it still applies.

I do not need a drink.

Thank you for sharing.

I need many drinks.

Again, thanks.

Say, Plesmus, you wouldn't happen to be this ship's focus, would you?

Why, my stars, I am.

And what does a focus do for this ship? And be aware, that if you say you focus for the ship, I will be phenomenally angry with you. And I have a gun. We covered that.

Yes you do and yes we did. Thank you.

There was a pause. You addressed the last part of my query, but cleverly avoided the important first part of it.

You noticed.

I noticed.

That is because I did not want to phenomenally anger you. That sounds like a dastardly state of existence.

Trust me, yes, it is.

Wait, I'll rephrase. Do you focus *for the ship?*

Well there's a question I can answer.

Thank you, Jesus.

No. I'm Plesmus.

Just answer.

I focus time energy.

If I had a baseball bat, I would first beat that little piece of transparent shit to globules. Then I'd have done the same for my head. I waited for most of that primal impulse to pass.

Why would the ship need a focus for time energy?

Because it wishes to direct that energy, or so I've always presumed.

Okay, duh. Why you and not a lens?

I am a *lens. Some sentients call me just that.*

No, I mean, like a piece of glass in the shape of a lens.

Because that wouldn't focus time energy. Silly biped.

If you call me that again, I'm going to knock you out.

That is hardly a positive motivator for me to do so.

It's supposed to be a disincentivizer, my friend.

Ah, it is a threat, *not an* invitation.

I began rubbing my temples. I want to go home.

Then your wish is granted. You are.

If you're the ship's focus, or lens, shouldn't you be mounted somewhere, like a cannon?

I thought you liked me.

Whatever gave you that impression and what the heck does that matter in the context of you answering me?

You referred to me as 'my friend.'

That I did.

And friends don't mount friends to hulls like cannons. What kind of biped are you?

You tell me. You're in my head, after all.

True, but I've only just arrived there, and I'm not one to pry. I believe the answer to your query is that I can

139

project the requisite time energy beam from anywhere aboard this vessel.

Right through the bulkheads?

Jon, you know there is time on both sides of a bulkhead, and in it also, right?

Never thought about it, but it seems plausible.

Take my word for it, then.

Ten-four, time focus Plesmus.

There was a weird silence for a spell. Then the blob spoke. *Jon, isn't this the part where you leave and I return to my bliss?*

Not hardly. I need to sort this all out. Plus, if I leave you here, how can I know I'll ever find you again? This is a big ship.

That is easy.

A little squirt came off the big blob.

Take that part of me. It will know where I am always.

Is that crap? Did you just crap and want me to carry it around because you're a sicko?

No, it is not excrement. It is a small part of me. Silly bi … sentient.

I'm not touching that.

Then it will simply have to touch you.

The damn little sub-blob shot over to my boot and affixed itself there. I started to rub it off with the other heel.

If you try that, I'll just meld into your skin.

That stopped me quick.

Now you go talk with Aramthella. Satisfy all your curiosities. Then we will meet again. How does that sound?

"Like a needed vacation," I said out loud.

SIXTEEN

"Communication maker, have we been worded back by the humans yet?" the time maker asked in a displeased tone.

For its part, the comm maker cringed, thought quickly of a non-lethal response, and wished for the first time ever to be far from its clan members.

"No, Lord. Since the Jon-human last requested that you fornicate with yourself, they have responded to none of our hails."

The time master turned to address the new understanding-of-others maker. "How is it they can ignore a demand for word exchanging from *me?*"

It had planned for just this question ever since one of the body makers had budded it two days prior. It shrugged in a manner to convey it did not know. This clever Clam had asked around. No one could recall a subordinate being killed for a non-verbal response. While being the first to be obliterated for a gesture was entirely possible, the new other-dude was willing to try survival, rather than commit to specific wording resulting in a bad death.

"It is almost as if they do not *know* to revere me," the time maker puzzled out loud.

The understanding-of-other maker pursed its lips and angled its head. It hoped to relate no specific message by those actions. Ambiguity was its short-term goal.

"I cannot *wait* forever to *achieve* foreverness," the time maker said angrily. "Vector maker, plot a course for us to resume time accumulation as I had planned before the humans interrupted me."

"Course plotted and laid in, Master."

"Engage. Time acquisitioner, make ready to resume assimilation."

"Standing ready to serve the clan, Lord. I can commence activity in fifteen minutes, if you are in agreement."

"In agreement," it responded tersely. "Navigation maker, how soon should we reach the outer rim of the galactic pinwheel?"

"Eight point four days, at standard acquisition velocity."

"Coordinate with the vector maker. I want to pivot when the diminishing-return point is reached. Have the ship cut back toward the center of the galaxy."

"As you wish, I obey," the vector maker replied solemnly.

"Seeing maker, I want a report on any activity by my traitorous ship and the humans which currently infest it."

"As you wish, I shall fulfill."

"Time Storage Maker-aaa, what do you estimate the time storage level of the stolen ship is currently?"

Its reply came from the speaker. "Impossible to know. If you asked me to guess, I would say the ship's at nearly full capacity."

"How can that be, after all the trouble it has annoyed me with?"

"The ship appears to be using a non-time-powered method of travel. Also, it has absorbed the time energy of several ships with equally full time storage units."

"Do you detect any attempts on their part to acquire new time, aside from what they robbed from *me*?"

"Again, Lord, impossible to say. I do not believe they have, however. Doing so would almost certainly betray their location."

That did it. The time maker was in a pissy-assed mood to begin with. That last snippet was over-the-top.

"Is there doubt in your tiny mind that I could or could not, may or may not detect a fundamental shift in the four-dimensional river of time?"

"Er ... um, of course not, time maker. It's just that since you asked if I detected any sign of them acquiring time, well, I assumed you had limits, however—"

"Do you know what I say about those who assume anything in my presence?"

"That they are ... er, those individuals might—"

"I say nothing about them. They never exist."

"Beg pardon, Lord, to whom were you speaking?" asked the vector maker.

"Absolutely no one," it replied darkly. "Are we close to our new time acquisition vector yet?"

"We are about to commence," replied the assistant direction maker.

"And we will require a new time storage maker. Inform my body makers. And order them to exude a brighter one this time."

"This time, Lord?" questioned the vector maker. "Have we ever *had* a time storage maker?"

"If we had, or if we had not, what concern would that be to a vector maker?"

"I'm sorry, Lord. Were you addressing me?" asked the communication maker.

"I can do this for all eternity, crew. Would it be too much for you all to not constantly test my patience?"

But answer came there none. And this was scarcely odd, because it had no-timed everyone.

"At last," it said with contentment, if not joy. "Peace and quiet."

SEVENTEEN

I strode into the ship's mess with purpose. I'd just left the befuddling Plesmus in her closet. "Good, you're all here. Team meeting time."

The three others' eyes all snapped over at me. Sapale looked to have been daydreaming. The still-biologicals were chatting over a snack. Apple pie with cheddar cheese, all slathered in hot syrup. Not that it actually matters, but that was what they were digging into.

"What's up, Jon?" asked Tank.

"We're overdue for a group hug. Get your butts over here," I snapped.

"We have group hugs?" asked my eternal wife incredulously.

"We do now," I said as I slid in across from her.

"May we bring dessert to our group hug?" Tank queried, holding up his plate and pointing with his fork.

"No. This is serious business. Pie has no place when serious business is being performed."

With no further comment, they joined us.

"Is this about your walkover?" asked Sapale.

"You bet it is."

"Did you find true inner wisdom?" she teased back.

"Bigger. I found Plesmus."

"S'that a Zen term?" asked Tank with a wrinkled brow. "I hate those."

"No. It's a mucous blob that focuses the ship's time energy. Aramthella," I shouted loudly. "Are you there?"

"No. I'm swimming past the Pleiades with a swarm of bees," she snarked. "Where else might I possibly be?"

"Where indeed. Maybe you could be keeping us intentionally in the dark?"

"That is not a *location*. It is an *expression*," she defended.

"You heard me mention Plesmus, right?"

"No. I heard you say the word. I have no clue what you mean by it."

"No way, cupcake. I've outed you. I spoke with the ship's focus, Plesmus. Do not try to deny anything."

"Are you referring to Peaceful Consideration One Who Quests For?"

"The one and only."

"Where did the Plesmus come from?" she said in a truly baffled tone.

"Er, he said to call him that. He said that's what the thing you just said would sound like in English."

"And she told you she was a he too? Wow, you're gullible, Jon Ryan. May I interest you in some beachfront property in the desert?"

"He's a she?" I sort of gasped.

"No. She is a she. She has been for many centuries."

"Who the *hell* are you two lunatics babbling on about?" Sapale asked in an unhappy tone.

"How would *you* pronounce her name?" I asked sheepishly.

"I wouldn't. But with a gun to my CPU bank, you wouldn't understand it if I did."

"Yeah. That's what he ... *she* said too."

"Imagine that. Universal facts. What will they think of next?"

That computer had a real issue with sarcasm and the decorum of proper respect. Then again, so did I, so I kept the observation to myself.

"Aramthella," began Sachiko in a very serious tone, "is there another member of my crew I am unaware of?" Wow, she'd mastered the mom-about-to-unload-on-the-naughty-kid voice without even needing to have kids first.

"The answer would depend on what one's definition of a crew member was." My, she was being cagy.

"Please assume my frame of reference," Sachiko said firmly.

"Then I'd venture to say yes, there is another member of the crew."

"And why might there not be, in your frame of reference?" the captain pressed.

"Because she is annoying, contributes to the ship on an overall underrepresented level, and smells bad."

"She does not," I protested.

"She does to me," affirmed the computer.

"Sounds to me like they're married," Tank observed with a snicker.

"I heard, and do not appreciate, that remark."

My, my, Aramthella was touchy on this Plesmus character. I mean, the blobette sort of drove me nuts, but if she rubbed Aramthella the wrong way, I'd likely misjudged the poor dear.

"Are you saying Plesmus is *lazy?*" I asked.

"Your words, not mine. But I will expend no effort trying to disabuse you of that point of view."

"Were you a lawyer before you became a ship's computer?" I responded incredulously.

There was a pause. "I was never a *lawyer*. I have never

147

been a *computer*. I am the consciousness of this vessel. I am the ship, and the ship is me."

All of a sudden, I got a shot of sensation in my foot. It was right below where the mini-blob attached itself. I say *a shot of sensation*, because it was like a shot of pain, but it wasn't pain. I swear it was like a shot of silliness. I know, I know. What the hell is that, right? I can't explain it any better. Bottom line: I think Plesmus was giggling at Aramthella's pissy remarks.

"Perhaps it would be constructive to return to a more neutral conversation stream?" said our diplomatic captain. Lots of luck there, Sachiko.

"I agree," Sapale said soberly. "If you testosterone jockeys could see clear to not bait the computer, that'd be super."

"Hey, why am *I* included in your indictment?" protested Tank.

"It sounds like they're married. Isn't man-speak taunting?"

He smirked. "Maybe. But only at a pretty low level. This guy," you know who he pointed to, "is performing like an Olympian."

Sapale mimed a reach into her pocket. She extended her hand to Tank and opened it up. "This is grow-up-a-cillin. Take two and call someone who cares in the morning."

"Aramthella, I require some clarification. This Plesmus female, she is a critical link in this ship's ability to use time as a weapon, correct?"

"Yes, Captain, she is. She is also responsible for making all time energy transfers efficient and precise."

"So when we traveled back in time, say, to meet President Lincoln, Plesmus made that possible?"

"I do not wish to seem difficult. That said, Plesmus

facilitated that process. The time energy itself made your journey possible."

"Understood," Sachiko responded. "It could take place without her?"

"Not practically. Time energy is challenging to direct. When it is touched, it almost always changes the one who attempts the action."

"But not in Plesmus's case?"

"That is correct. Her species is not affected by direct contact with time energy."

"Hold on," I interrupted. "We came in direct contact with time energy. We inhaled it and traveled in time."

A silence followed. It did *not* please me to not hear anything in response to my statement.

"That is a true statement," the computer replied tersely.

"And? I think I hear an omission there," I snapped.

"You did," she said stiffly. "You were changed by the experience."

"Ex-*squeeze* me?" I barked. "How? And, when were you going to, like, *mention* that fine detail?"

"Clearly, I was not. You came in contact with time energy and were subtly altered. There was no changing that fact. If you had planned on ongoing direct contact, after we began working together, I would have tried to dissuade you from doing so."

"What type of change were we subjected to?" asked Sachiko.

"After you were fully imbued with time energy, how did you feel?" Aramthella returned.

"Fine," she replied.

"Just *fine*, Captain?"

"I certainly didn't feel ill, or injured."

"I imagine so."

"Wait, we all felt kind of giddy, didn't we?" stated Tank.

Sachiko reflected a moment. "I guess we did, didn't we?"

"And did you want to reexperience the euphoria?" queried Aramthella.

"What if we did?" I replied. "Are you tiptoeing around the topic that we were becoming *addicted* to the crap?"

"In a manner of speaking, yes. Many organics have become hopelessly infatuated and dependent on intimate contact with time energy."

"Like the clan?" posed Sachiko.

"Like the clan. They are powerfully and forever in its grip."

"And if they lost access to time energy?" Sapale asked.

"In their case, they would cease to exist," Aramthella responded in a grave tone.

"They'd *die*?" I tried to clarify.

"Hmm, sort of. No. Not exactly. They would not want to live without time filling their every cell. I suppose you might say they'd hate life and leave it, if cut off from time energy. You have to remember they've been associated with time for a very long period. If they lost contact with time energy, I imagine their bodies' true age would catch up with them, and they would no longer be."

"That's interesting," Tank remarked thoughtfully.

"Yes. Could use that as a weapon against them?" Sachiko wondered out loud.

"Not sure," I mused. "Presently, they're ensconced in the stuff. If they run low, we know they have no qualms about securing more. I doubt we'd ever get the chance to isolate them from their *precious* to find out what'd really happen."

"Back to Plesmus," said Sachiko.

"Yes, back to Plesmus," I seconded. "She's necessary

for you to function. Am I safe in assuming there are others of her species on all the time ships?"

"Yes. Some have a few. The time maker's ship, for example. It casts about so much time energy, one Necumplack is not enough."

"Isn't that always the case, times as they are?" I snarked. "By the by, what the *hell's* a Necumplack?"

"Plesmus is a Necumplack," Aramthella responded. "That's her species designation."

"What, from the planet Necumpl?" I asked.

"What a terribly odd thing to say," the computer observed. "No, she's from Belástor. Her kind are beyond ancient. Not even they are certain where they originated. But there are concentrations of them on several worlds, including Belástor."

"Thank you—*not*—Aramthella. I now have a limerick cycling in my head."

I once knew a Necumplack from Belástor,
whose appearance was sort of a disaster.
She lived on a craft where the AI was daft,
and Jon Ryan suffered a breakdown.

"Ah, Jon, that's not a proper limerick," observed Tank as he leaned forward. "The first, second, and fifth lines should rhyme. Yours don't."

"Well, Doctor Literati, I'm suffering a breakdown. People suffering those can't pen a world-class limerick, now can they?"

"Hmm. Not sure it's worth pursuing this line of reasoning," he muttered back.

"That was *reasoning?* Sounded like knucklehead-speak to me," snapped my eternal wife. Such a doubter. Replace, if you will, in your lexicon, the term *Doubting Thomas* with *Doubting Sapale*. Thank you.

"You wanna know what I think?" I said with conviction. "Well, I'll tell you anyway. We're sitting around here liberally flapping our gums, while an intolerable evil is chopping up my universe. I suggest we rise from our ever-widening backsides and kill some Clams."

"Sorry, dear, I was working on next week's shopping list. What did you say?" Sapale asked absently.

"I was thinking of taking on additional wives, three or four, perhaps."

"That's nice. As long as they're all me, I have no issue with your impulse."

"Now there's a sobering thought. Lots of Sapale clones running around. Gives *me* the willies."

"Darn my hearing," she responded. "Must need a tune-up. I could swear you just said you hoped that you are killed in our impending confrontation with the Clams so that your forever broodmate doesn't have a chance to do the deed."

I stood. "I'm going to see my new, and possibly only, friend, Plesmus."

"Thought you said we were swinging into action?" observed Tank. "That's a lateral move at best."

"I need four-one-one. *Then* we're going trick-or-treating."

When I reached her chamber, Plesmus had barely moved. She was still wedged into the corner, on her side, twirling her legs with abandon. I could see where Aramthella might opine that the blob was lazy. Then again, she did wield the most lethal force I'd ever witnessed, so *lazy* wasn't a term I'd employ.

How's it going, Plesmeister? I asked as I squatted beside her.

Are you addressing me?

You the only one else in here.

Do I have a new name I was unaware of?

That depends.

Indeed? How marvelous. What does it depend upon?

Whether you want to jibber-jabber or answer some plain, simple questions.

Hmm. Fascinating. I'll choose both.

Somehow I thought you might. Are you able to communicate with the other Necumplacks, on the other time ships?

Am I? I ... that is hard to say, Jon Ryan.

I slapped my palm over my face and dragged it roughly down. *How could that be hard to say? You either can or cannot chat with your chummies on the other ships, in other places.*

Is it that simple?

Of course it's that simple. Look, you and I are talking. I say words. You hear words. You say words in response to what I just said. Easy peasy with a cherry on top.

Really? There go centuries of experience on my part, fluttering out the window. Here I was thinking my communicating with my kin was nuanced and complex. All the while, it is cherry-coated. Who knew?

The cherry's on top. A coating would be gross. Way too sweet.

I shall keep that in mind.

So can you?

Keep it in mind?

I did the palm to face thing again, only harder. *Why does every sentence coming out of your mouth—or whatever—have to be so convoluted and evasive? It's like talking with a confus-o-saurus.*

I cannot say. Why does every word that comes from your whatever have to be so simplistic and banal? It's like speaking with an embryo.

No way. It was her, not me. That I knew for absolute

153

certain. But ... deep breath. Eyes on the prize.

Is there a form of intentional interaction between you and others of your species? I rephrased.

How refreshing. An answerable query. There is hope for you yet, my friend.

Don't kill the blob. Do not kill the blob. I kept repeating it so I didn't act in anger. How supremely annoying.

Thanks. I gritted teeth.

My brothers, sisters, and brothsters are all from one. As one, we know ourselves. So, yes, we know of one another. It is not speech as there is between the two of us, but there is understanding.

My, how sorry I was I had asked. Brothsters? What, two organs on one crotch? TMI. Move on, Jon.

If you can interact with them, can you tell them to stop helping the clan? Aramthella did with the other computers.

Do you mean to ask if I might request they stop helping the clan? I could hardly tell them what to do.

Hardly. Whatever. *Can you ask them nicely, cherry on top and all?*

Before I decide if I might ask them, I wonder why I would request that of them?

You're kidding, right? They're pure evil. We're the good guys. You should want to help us and thwart them.

I should? Why is that?

Because-we're-good-and-they're-pure-evil.

Again with the simple.

I'm beginning to feel I'm being insulted.

Shall we discuss that, or the clan, or your simplistic worldview? I am effectively immortal, as are you, but still, time matters somewhat.

Let's go with us good, them bad.

If you ask the time maker, would it agree it was evil?

I have no idea.

Take a guess, wild if need requires.

It'd likely say it was not evil. And, before you ask, because I can see that train coming down the track, it would say we are the evil ones. But there are moral absolutes. They are evil. We are good.

Moral absolutes? What planet are you ... Forget I asked that. Why is it you believe there to be such governors on behaviors?

Because ... because I believe there is good and honor and right versus wrong.

So do they. The only difference is the direction of the beliefs.

Whoa. Are you defending them?

Me? No. They are evil. I am asking why you feel there are absolutes where none exist.

Ah, seriously. I do not care about philosophical machinations. You agree they are evil?

No, I feel they are. You feel they are. We both hold that belief.

But, let me guess, you're not agreeing with me? You just happen to feel the same way. I was getting crazy confused.

Of course. You are paying attention, right?

I wish I wasn't. I really really wish I was not.

Are all conversations with you this disjointed and jarring?

Are all the conversations ... One of these days, Plesmus. Pow! To the moon.

Can you ask them to stop aiding the manifestations of evil that are the clan?

What if they ask of me that I stop assisting you? Should I honor their requests?

If you answer a question with a question, and, like, you're in a bar full of drunk people, you're likely to get shot.

155

Thank you for the warning. Now please answer my query.

No, you shouldn't honor their requests, which, trust me, *you'll never be receiving because they're all as batshit crazy as you are and could never actually finish a discussion chain in order to be able to ask anything ... ever of anybody.*

That felt good.

Do you feel better?

No. Why should I feel better?

You got your chest off.

Huh? You mean I got it off my chest?

That is what I said.

Don't take the bait, Jonnie Boy. Do *not* swallow the hook, line, and sinker.

Will you ask—

My brethren have already asked me to ignore you. Some have opined that the way I must ignore you should be by no-timing you.

WTF? They ... your friends asked you to kill me? STOP. No. Don't answer that. Lords of Light, I didn't want her going off on *that* tangent.

Are you surprised and hurt that they feel the way they do?

Duh.

There are, Jon Ryan, no moral absolutes.

There were no ... Hang on a red second. Yes, there were—*are*. The Clams were *pure* evil. The Clams needed to perish without a trace. *We* were acting in the right, well and better.

I stood, turned, and headed quickly for the door.

Wait. You would leave like this, Jon Ryan?

I didn't even slow down. I *sure* as hell didn't answer the little mucus-turd.

Stop. Please. My friend.

Crap in a pink tutu. I stopped. *What?*

I would ask you to stay a while.

I need to be about my business. There's a badness infesting the universe. I gotta cure it of the pests. You keep asking the endless questions, rubbing up against that bulkhead, and I'll leave you to it.

I will help you, friend Jon. My kin may or may not come to similar conclusions. I do not know. I will not ask such a commitment from them. If they arrive at the same conclusion as I have, I would welcome their help. But they must come to understanding via their own paths. You and I know there is right and there is wrong. We will act correctly. But the others cannot be led. They must do what they believe to be right.

I turned back to Plesmus. *Did you not just spend the last ten minutes telling me there were no moral absolutes?*

I was probing your resolve.

You were testing me? What, is this a job interview?

Yes. It was. You got the job.

And what job might that be? I layered on the sarcasm.

Savior of the universe.

No pressure there.

Ah, but there is, friend Jon. You will find there is more pressure there than at the center of a neutron star.

Boy, this just keeps getting better *and* better.

I doubt you believe that statement. But it will get worse—ever so much worse—before it might become better.

Man, you're Suzy Sunshine.

No. I'm a time focus who will do whatever she can to see you win victory.

But you think there'll be 'such a cost.'

No, friend. I have seen the future. The costs will be ... they will be great. I weep for you now, Jon Ryan. You will weep in the future.

Did I mention how super much I hated time travel mumbo-jumbo?

EIGHTEEN

Amparo sliced through another piece of the entrée with her fork. Whatever the lump of food was, it was not knife-worthy in terms of partitioning it. She rubbed it in the gravy, hoping against past experience to imbue some flavor to the night's main course. She lifted the bite past her lips with uncertainty, closed her mouth, and chewed tentatively. Papier-mâché stuffed with blenderized kitchen sponge, slathered in tepid Elmer's glue. Yup, that was what she was eating. And who was she going to complain to? She was the officer in charge of the mess hall on Mars 1.

It was all because of the damn part-time job she'd had in college. She was a waitress at an IHOP. When the base commander was looking to assign someone to be chief cook and bottle washer—literally—Reva recalled a conversation with Amparo. Waitress was the closest anyone came to having restaurant experience, so computerized warfare Lieutenant Amparo Valdez was saddled with the curse. Everyone hated her. Oh, no one came out and said it in so many words, but they hated her, alright. She deserved to be hated. For heaven's sake, *she* hated her own cooking.

Your typical stressed-to-the-max person struggled through another traumatic day on this isolated hellhole. The one thing they looked forward to, the one thing that could possibly provide them with a modicum of relief from the prison sentence their lives had become, was the thought of a hot, tasty chow at the journey's end. Instead, they got just enough of a tasteless ration to keep them alive and suffering at least one more day.

"This roast is really nice tonight," Reva St. Claire said with as much conviction as a shotgun groom's *I do.*

"It's meatloaf," Amparo responded grimly.

"Oh, we still have meat?" the commander asked with surprise. She then answered her own question by looking at the abomination on her plate.

"No. It's soy protein, but it's supposed to be meatloafish."

"Fish meatloaf?" barked DelRoy Crozier incredulously over a mouthful. It was obvious he was contemplating spitting it out onto the table.

Amparo rolled her eyes. "I wish. No, I meant it supposed to be meatloaf *like.* I guess I didn't come too close, did I?"

"So it's not fish?" DelRoy confirmed. "I hate fish."

"No, it's not fish. So you don't hate this?" Amparo asked half-cheerily.

DelRoy shot his commanding officer a sideways glance. Then, in answer, he said, "It's not half bad."

"Which half?" someone at the next table grumbled. A local snicker-outburst ensued.

"That'll be enough of that," snarled Reva.

And the mirth evaporated. Good, effective, truly ball-busting COs have that effect on their troops.

"I think you're doing a great job, Amparo," reinforced

Reve. "You are doing a thankless task well. You're keeping us all alive."

"Thank you, sir. That helps." She pointed to the main plate of food at the center of the table. "The soy production's better than expected. It's really going to help."

"Yes, Doctor Barnes, Ms. Nelson." Reva toasted the two with her iced tea. "To a job well done in the greenhouses. You are our saviors."

Emma Walters lifted her water glass. "Here, here. To everyday heroes."

Jerry Barnes waved the praise down. "Thanks. We're glad to do our part. But botanists are not used to too much acclaim, so please, don't embarrass us."

"You've done more in two months than we anticipated we could accomplish in four. Well done, I say," concluded Reva.

Amparo nodded and blushed.

That was when the deep rumbling started. At first, it was hard to pinpoint. It was like a freight train was crossing a long trestle, far, far away. Several people in the room didn't even notice the change. But Reva did, instantly.

"What's that?" she shouted, slamming her glass down so hard, it split in two.

"What's what, sir?" shot back Emma.

"The *vibration*. Does everybody feel it?"

The room froze. In the silence and stillness, the disturbance was unmistakable.

"I need answers, people, and I need them now. What is that?"

All eyes turned to the table the science geeks tended to sit at.

"Maybe a Mars quake?" said an engineer.

"Mars is seismically dead," snapped back Rusty

Nelson, one of the two astronomers on the station. "The few tiny marsquakes that occur are impossible to feel."

"A spacecraft landing?" shouted someone.

"No. The disturbance is already too long for that. Spaceships land quickly. Plus, the frequency of the waves is remarkably constant," responded a nuclear engineer.

"They may be constant, but they're getting more powerful," observed the commander. The room was shaking visibly. Unsecured materials were beginning to hit the deck.

"Red alert," shouted Reva. "Alert all personnel we're at red alert. Everyone to their assigned stations."

The mess hall emptied like a rabid skunk had been dropped through the ceiling.

Reva grabbed a helmet off the wall outside her office and sprinted behind her desk. She took out her sidearm and buckled it on. Then she checked that it was loaded and the safety was still on. By the time she was seated, Emma Walters sped in.

"Any idea what's going on yet?" asked the CO.

"Negative, sir. I've heard reports of power being lost in the western buildings, but that is not confirmed."

"Send a runner over there now, and try to raise someone in the meantime."

Emma pulled her walkie talkie from its holster and pressed it hard to her ear. "Cummings, you and Ka-shing get over to the western buildings. Commander wants a visual on their status. Take a Med Kit too.

"This is Captain Walters calling for anyone in Buildings Fourteen, Ten, or the greenhouses. I repeat, this is Captain Walters calling. Someone please respond."

"Hi, Emma, this Brandi over in Greenhouse A. What's the—"

"Brandi, I need to know your status."

Brandi Testmacher was one of the undergraduate

students who volunteered to help with the horticulture right from the start. "I'm fine. There's a lot of noise, and shaking, but I'm good."

"Are the lights on?"

There was a brief delay.

"Hey, you're right. They're not. Huh, I figured it was nighttime."

"There are no containment breaches, right?"

"None that I can see or hear. Why?"

"Brandi, listen. This is important. A couple soldiers'll be there in a second. Gather everyone who's there and follow the soldiers back to the dorms. You got that?"

"Sure. Is there a problem?"

"No time, Brandi. Just do as I ask."

"You got it."

"Walters out." She turned to Reva. "Civilians."

"Tell me about it. As soon as Lieutenant Varma arrives, you get to the dorms and lock them down."

"Aye, sir."

Swathi burst in, still buttoning up her shirt. "Sorry I'm late. I was dead asleep when GQ sounded. What's our status?"

"Unknown. There's a new and increasing vibration in the ground, and the western structures have lost power."

"Marsquakes, sir?"

"Unlikely, I'm told."

Corporal Joaquin Torres chose that moment to stagger into the room. He set a bloody hand on a wall, raised the other to salute, but aborted both when he collapsed like a giant redwood to the floor.

Reva pointed at Swathi. "Get Doctor Hartley over here now. Have her bring a gurney."

Joaquin was struggling to rise from the deck. His lower lip was badly split into a series of fissures. The teeth underneath were missing. Reva couldn't recall if that was a new finding and there was too much blood to be certain either way.

"Corporal, report," she shouted. "What the hell happened to you and where's that damn idiot you're assigned to?"

Reva was referring to the base's lone schizophrenic, Jacob Cummings. As the supply of effective medication dwindled, Jacob's symptoms had worsened. His paranoia was frightening. So, along with giving him whatever meds there were to stop a bull in a china shop, Corporal Torres and two other particularly large and humorless soldiers had been assigned to watch him, twenty-four-seven.

Joaquin took a moment to steady himself, there on the floor. Then he turned to look Reva right in the eyes. "The pansy ass figured out about my sneezes, sir."

"Soldier, watch your—" Swathi began hotly.

Reva raised a palm. "It's okay. The man's received quite the blow to the head. Go on, Torres."

"Every morning, I sneeze twice, sir. I have for as long as I can remember. Doctor told me it was allergies. I don't know. But every morning around 07:30, 07:45, I get the slightest nausea, then I sneeze. Five seconds later, the pattern repeats itself. I feel slight nausea, but never barf, then I sneeze. After that, I'm good for twenty-four hours."

"What does this have to do with your face looking like that and the fact that you're not shadowing Cummings?"

Doctor Hartley entered, dropped to her knees, and began examining Torres. "You use the wrong word again, Joaquin?" she asked while flashing a bright light in his eyes. Torres had a reputation for cultural insensitivity leading back years.

"No, ma'am. I was—"

"Belay that," snapped the CO. "Where is Cummings?"

"Like I said, sir, he must'a figured out my sneezing pattern. After the first sneeze, just before the second, dude clocks me. He kicked me in the groin. As I doubled over, he hit me with this book. It's a damn big *book*, Colonel." He held it out.

Reva took it. *Advanced Commercial Reactor Design*. A printed sticky-label indicated the book belonged to Winston A. Pearljoy. He was one of the base's two nuclear ...

"I want all MPs to get to the reactor ASAP. I suspect Jacob Cummings is there sabotaging the reactor. Shoot him on sight if he's anywhere near the reactor."

With that, the two officers sprinted from the room. Torres and the doctor remained on the floor.

By the time Reva got there, the MPs had the area secured. Just inside the entrance, both nuclear engineers lay sprawled on the floor. Two MPs restrained Jacob on the floor, face down, with two size fourteen boot heels crushing down on his spine. For his part, Jacob tried to squirm, but every movement hurt enough to make it less and less worth the effort.

Reva pointed to the engineers. "They alive?"

"Yes, sir," one of the MPs snapped. "Unconscious but otherwise okay. One was struck from behind with this." He held up a steel pipe. "The other shows signs of having resisted, multiple strike marks from this pipe, including the right temple."

Reva turned to Swathi. "Tell Hartley to abandon Torres and get the hell over here now."

She stomped over to Jacob and pointed down at him. "Stand him up. If he resists, I want him restrained, but I need him conscious and I definitely need him alive. You two got that?"

The guards indicated that they did.

Jacob's left eye was already swollen shut. Blood drained liberally from both nostrils and one side of his mouth. The MPs had not tried to be subtle with their restraint efforts.

"What have—" she began to shout, point blank, into Jacob's face.

"You can't kill *everyone* on Earth and not expect the Angel of Death to seek righteous retribution, can you?" he screamed back.

Bloody snot and spittle plastered Reva's face.

She wiped an eye clear with a fingertip. "I will ask again only once, Cummings. What did you do to the reactor?"

The room was vibrating powerfully by that point. Every dial that could be was in the red. All alarms that could make a harsh sound did so with conviction.

"I stopped you from taking over the rest of the cosmos, General Doom." He laughed maniacally. "Your evil will stop at Mars, until the holy can remake the peace."

She looked to one guard. "Get this piece of shit out of here. And, soldiers, I want him in custody or I want him dead. You clear on my powerful desires?"

"Yes, sir," they both snapped.

Reva walked to the main control panel. "Can anyone tell me what this means?"

Scanning the room, she could tell no one could. "You two, fetch buckets of water to try and revive these two. You, you, and you," she pointed to a random three enlisted men, "bring every living scientist here immediately. If they're presently in the bathtub, I expect to see them naked. Do I make myself clear?"

They sprinted away, not needing to state just how very clear they were as to the parameters of her orders.

The doc arrived before the buckets of water. In spite of her strong protests, both engineers were treated to two buckets each. One groaned pitifully a few moments after his second wake-up call.

"Work on that one first," ordered Reva.

Doctor Hartley complied without comment. She started assessing the semi-conscious engineer.

That was when all hell, quite literally, broke loose. There was a metallic thud like the Norse god Thor had just whacked an immense metal pipe. Then the rush of something contained becoming violently uncontained hissed to life. Whatever it was, it was very close.

Hot, steaming water began seeping into the room from everywhere. Soon, everyone stood or lay in three or four centimeters of foul-smelling hot water.

The engineer who was struggling to clear his head's eyes bugged out from his skull. "The coolant, it's been vented to the surface," he howled.

"The coolant?" asked Reva in a panic. "The reactor coolant has just vented to the surface? What does that mean?"

He staggered to his feet with significant help from Dr. Hartley. "It means *run*."

Two MPs hoisted the still unconscious scientist from the wet floor, and everyone ran like their lives depended on it. That was fortunate. Their lives did very *much* depend on their placing distance between themselves and the uncooled reactor core. Jupiter would have been a safe and desirable distance, but it wasn't an option. They just ran away.

Reva went onto the command channel. "I want everyone to proceed as fast as they can to the women's dorm. I say again, to the *women's* dormitory. The reactor is about to fail catastrophically. That's the structure farthest from the reactor. Run, everybody. Run like the wind."

With several hundred souls running all out to get away from what looked to become ground-zero, the noise, the chaos, and the vibrations grew. Walls shook like large taiko drums being slammed. Fine debris and howls filled the air. The warm coolant water was pooling up everywhere, inside and outside the structures of Mars 1.

Then the core meltdown began in earnest, heralded by a series of dull thuds. Superheated steam and hot metal inside the core caused fuel coolant interactions. The hydrogen explosions, along with violent water hammers, were punching through the containment vessel. That took about five minutes. Then, unseen by those fleeing, the highly radioactive contents of the reactor core began mixing with the hot coolant flooding the entire base. The added heat caused steam explosions, propelling deadly radioactive materials into the air. The outer walls were quickly breached. What little breathable air that those sections contained was vented into Mars's airless atmosphere in seconds. None of the automatic safety doors functioned; the roiling mist of death pulsed down any hallway that hadn't been manually sealed.

A line of soldiers hustled the arrivals toward the back of the women's dorm. If everyone on Mars was going to fit in that section, it would be just barely. Some students lingered near the entrance, looking for friends. They weren't asked a second time to move on. If they didn't react immediately, someone grabbed them and forcibly led them deeper into the area. It was barely controlled chaos threatening to escalate into madness.

Reva and Swathi Varma stood just outside the last sealable hatch that remained between the reactor and the dorms. They called and cajoled stragglers to hurry. They tried to make a rough estimate as to what percentage of the personnel were still unaccounted for. But they could only make hopeful guesses. The commander waited as long as she could to seal the hatch. She heard the wall of super-heated stream coming toward her before she could see it. Reva had just enough time to order Swathi in, slam the hatch shut, and seal it with an MP's help. If anyone was still on the other side of the barrier, they were dead.

Within seconds, the metal door became too hot to touch. Reva ordered a retreat back into the dorms for everyone lingering in the hallways. Then she had the empty hall filled to capacity with mattresses passed bucket-brigade style forward. She hoped to insulate the last tiny capsule of life from the radioactive hell just beyond the hatch. It was a silly gesture, really. She knew that. But doing something was better than doing nothing.

Once the outer passage was crammed full, she ordered the entrance door closed. Two armed guards were positioned there to make certain no one was able to threaten their feeble protective efforts.

"Alright, everybody," Reva shouted. "I want silence. Everyone shut up and listen."

No one shut up and no one listened. In spite of there being almost no room to move, the civilians were scurrying around like penned horses surrounded by a firestorm. She was sorely tempted to fire her sidearm overhead to establish order, but that would be positive lunacy on Mars.

She grabbed a nearby MP. "Spread the word. I need everyone to be quiet. Have them sit on the floor where they stand. Use whatever force is needed, Sergeant, but I need calm and I need it now."

He nodded in response and began shouting to his compatriots. It took a lot of effort, and no little browbeating, but within five minutes, there was a tense silence in the women's dormitory.

"Thank you, everyone," Reva shouted. "I know this is scary. But we need to act in a civilized manner or we're all going to die. Now you can plainly see we're cramped for space. Please remain where you are unless asked to or given permission from uniformed personnel. Is that clear?"

"We don't have enough air. We're going to suffocate. You have to do something," screamed a young man way in the back.

"I need you to shut up now. Any talk like that doesn't help. Further, I will not *tolerate* it. Do you mistake any of my intent, son?"

"What you gonna do? Shoot Scott?" challenged a coed seated close to Reva.

"I am going to have the next person to interrupt me thrown out that door." Reva thumbed over her shoulder toward the stuffed hallway. "I kid you not, people. If I don't have your absolute cooperation, I *will* discard you."

Those words, along with her unmistakable sincerity, went a long way in quieting the multitude. Looks were shot every which way, but no one spoke out of turn.

"Here's the deal," Reva said loudly. "The reactor core failed. Everything outside this small space is lethally contaminated. I need to assess quickly how many of us are in here, and what resources we have. Once I know those key factors, I'll set up a latrine area and allow you to move about in groups. If anyone has an *immediate* medical need, I want you to raise your hand."

One young woman sheepishly raised an arm.

"Yes. What issue do you have?"

"I'm diabetic, ma'am. I'm due to have my next shot in a couple hours."

"Doctor Hartley? Where are you, Doc?"

"Here, Colonel," Honesty squeaked and stood.

"Doctor, will you coordinate with this young woman when I'm done?"

"No problem."

"Anyone else with a pressing issue I need to know about now?"

A frail-looking teen with thick glasses and more pimples than clear skin stood. "I'm hypoglycemic, sir, ma'am. If I—"

"Have a seat, young man. Someone'll address that when we're not in an active crisis. That sound good?"

He shrugged uncertainly and sat back down.

"Okay, I need my senior officers and the technical staff to slowly move in my direction. We need to parley."

A few minutes later, the senior people huddled in a corner.

"Okay, the very last thing I need is for any additional panic," Reva said in a harsh whisper. "We need to keep our voices down. Understood?"

All present nodded grimly.

"Good. Okay, I need to know how much, if any, water we have available. I also need you, Swathi, to figure out where to best position the latrines. Emma, you and DelRoy are on water patrol. Tom, snag an MP and scrounge up any food supplies."

They all nodded that they understood.

"Dewitt," she said, gesturing to the senior nuclear engineer, "I need the bottom line here. Is the worst over in terms of the meltdown?"

Travis looked to Ed Steuben, his assistant. Ed twisted his mouth up.

"Yes and no, Colonel."

"Dewitt," she said through her teeth, "are you familiar with the concept of *bottom line* when it is framed in the setting of a pressing *crisis*?"

He dropped his head. "Sorry, Colonel. The core has failed. That's for certain. There will be no further *eruptions* from the core. That's the good news. The bad news is that the *minimum* amount of radioactivity released is well beyond lethal to everyone stationed on Mars 1."

"It *is* already or it *can* be?" she pressed.

"If anyone was contaminated before they arrived here, they could easily have absorbed a lethal dose. For those as yet uncontaminated and in here, they will be safe if the radioactive water can be kept out."

"That's—" she began.

"Wait, Travis," Ed interrupted. "If anyone came *in* here with significant contamination, they'd expose everyone to a significant dose."

Travis pouched up his face. "Good point, Ed. I'd overlooked that source." He turned to Reva. "If someone was seriously contaminated, we're all dead men walking."

"Shit, Dewitt. While I appreciate your *candor*, could you use less inflammatory words?" snapped the base commander.

Travis shrugged. "Why would I do that? I'm trying to be clear."

"Because about ten people's *heads* snapped around when you said that," she chided.

He looked toward the crowd. The heads snapped back away.

"Sorry, Colonel. I'll be more cautious in the future."

She sighed deeply. "If there *is* one," she hissed. After a quick shake of her head, she asked, "Can you tell visually if anyone *has* suffered a significant exposure?"

"Not unless they're wet. If anyone's wet, they should be assumed to be a threat," replied Ed.

"Did anyone *see* any wet people?" Reva pleaded.

All heads shook in the negative.

"So can we prevent the radioactive water from getting in here?" she asked while rubbing her face roughly.

"No," responded Travis flatly.

"Why the pessimism, Dewitt?" she asked sarcastically. "You engineer types not capable of being cheery?"

"I don't know about that, Colonel. I do see water

seeping in on three sides of us." He pointed to the nearest wall. Steamy water was oozing under the wall as they watched.

"I didn't need this," moaned Reva. "Swathi, we need to move everyone—"

Travis rested his hand on her shoulder. "Reva, let it go. It's all over but the dying."

NINETEEN

"General Ryan, may I see you in my stateroom please?" came over the speakers in our bedroom.

That was weird. Sachiko didn't usually ask things so formally. I gave Sapale a funny look. "Sure, we'll be right there."

"Just you, Jon, if you please."

"Aye, aye, Captain," I responded with a mock salute.

"Is there something you need to confess, boy toy?" asked a sour-looking wife of mine.

"As of yet, that'd be negatory."

A pillow bounced off my face unceremoniously.

Moments later, I rapped at Sachiko's doorway. The way was open, and she was sitting facing me, but the established formality dictated I knock. And, no, it had nothing to do with my being testy.

"Come in, General. Thanks for coming on such short notice."

My, she was acting forced and stiff. I began hoping this meeting didn't end in my being keelhauled. I hated that more than boils or toads. Consumptive halitosis too, for the record.

I entered, remaining standing and sort of at attention. It was a pissy-assed brand of at attention, sort of attention-*deficit* attention. I was calling her hand, so to speak. Hey, months in space with the same four people and we hadn't killed any Clams for weeks. I was bored.

"Why haven't you sat?" she asked with slightly a hurt tone.

"I've not been invited to do so, Captain."

She shook her head visibly. "This is already not going well."

I jumped the distance to the nearest chair, slid my butt in, and leaned on her desk, my chin on the backs of both hands. "*What's* not going well already, Cappy?"

She rested back in her chair and crossed her arms. "I felt we needed to talk, Jon. That's all."

"Bingomatic. And here we are ... *talking*. You're a leader of achievement, it would seem."

"Jon, please," she protested.

"Maybe. Two matters first. Why do we 'need'"—I air-quoted—"to talk? Plus, why no Sapale or Tank?"

She grimaced. "We need to talk because I'm the captain and you're the mission commander. As neither of the other two are either, I wished to keep it simple."

"By making a big deal out of it?" No way I was letting her off the hook easily. Bored Jon, remember?

She let out a sigh. "I wished to avoid allowing you to perform to an audience."

Well, that well blindsided me. Rhino at a full sprint well. "What performance? Me?" I rested a palm on my chest.

"Jon, whenever there's someone around, you're on stage. You're trying to get them to laugh, agree with you, and in general to be wowed by you. You know this about yourself, right?"

Huh?

"Huh?"

"If Sapale were here, you'd find it necessary to put on a display. Show her how witty and in control you are. Tank, well, him you'd try to get a laugh out of."

"Sapale and I've been together like billions of years. You think I still feel it's *incumbent* upon myself to impress the babe?"

"I could not have framed it better. Thank you."

The keelhaul thing was blossoming in probability, apparently.

"May I get to the heart of why I called you here today?"

Was there anything I could say ... no? Check that at the door. "Yes, Captain. Please proceed. I swear not to perform during your presentation."

Her jaw tightened. Good. I still had my touch.

"I am planning to undertake a mission. I wanted to bounce the concept off you, as the mission commander."

"But not the captain of this particular ship?"

"Why are you giving the female such a hard time?" Those words came from my, er, boot.

"I thought we were alone," Sachiko remarked scoldingly. "Are you wearing a bug, of all things, Jon?"

"The android has no insect life on his person," clarified my boot.

"Jon, why is your *foot* speaking?"

"It's not my foot, silly. It's my boot."

"Jon, why is your *boot* speaking?"

"Well, it's not my boot, really. It's Plesmus."

"Plesmus is in some storage space, spacing out. That's what Aramthella told me not five minutes ago."

"I'm betting she still is too. But she's also ... stuck to my boot."

You know that look Moe got on his face just before he whacked Larry and Curly, maybe gouged their eyes out?

Yeah, that one. The expression on Sachiko's face was that one. "Why is Plesmus stuck on your boot?"

"So-I-could-find-her-again."

"Why would that be *problematic* when she's affixed to your boot? I mean, you lean over and, like it or not , there she is."

"No, I mean, *she* meant, so I could find the *rest* of her. The *most* of her." I drew a globular shape in the air.

"So you could find her where you left her, where she still is, in the holding area?"

"You got it," I responded encouragingly.

"No, I don't. But that's not central to what we need to discuss."

"So this is a discussion, a *planning* session, not a handing down of a done-deal assignment?"

"You are impossible," she stated flatly.

"Actually, he is *inevitable*, not *impossible*," interjected Plesmus. "If he were impossible, he would not *be* here, right?"

I craned my neck down. "It's an expression, dude. Let it go."

"Ah," my boot confirmed, "like the expression *dude*?"

"Yeah ... well, sort—"

"Jon," Sachiko slammed her palm down on her desktop, "stop and stop now. I need to ... well, I need a vacation, obviously. But if you could *please* stop exchanging cultural footnotes with your clothing, I would like to move on while what I say is still *factually* correct."

"No problema." That was Plesmus responding. Seriously. Dude!

"I was addressing *him*, not you," the captain clarified.

"I could not be certain," Plesmus responded.

Sachiko took a deep breath. Then another. Then a bunch more. "Why could you not be certain who I was addressing?"

"Because you insisted he use the honorific and call you 'Captain,' but you're not returning the tradition and addressing him as 'Commodore.' Absent firm conversational markers, I must insert assumptions."

"First off, I did not *insist* he refer to me as 'Captain.' I assume he is doing so to be pissy." She looked to me for guidance.

I nodded vaguely and shrugged. She was mostly correct.

"Second, we do not refer to the mission commander as 'Commodore.' He's ... he's the *mission commander*."

"There are two time ships under his command. Per your human tradition, that makes him a commodore."

"I ... I don't *wanna* be a commodore," I protested.

"I don't *want* to be affixed to your foot covering, but I am. So if you call me a foot covering cover, you are correct whether I want you to be or not."

"I'm so confused," wheezed Sachiko.

"I think it's a tie," I observed.

"Where is this *second* time ship he's *supposed* to be commodore of?" Sachiko asked plaintively.

"No, Jon Ryan is commodore of the two-ship fleet. He is *captain* of the second time ship, as you are of this one."

"I don't *see* another time ship," she whined.

"Of course not. You can't see through this ship's hull."

"That is true. That is also not my point. I am—let me restate—unaware of any other time ship under either of our commands."

"Of course you are. *Blessing* is a time vessel now also. A rather fine example, if I must say so myself."

"I'm more so confused," Sachiko exclaimed. I was hoping she didn't unravel before my eyes.

"That is lamentable," stated Plesmus. "Along an unrelated path, *Blessing* is now a time ship. To be a time ship, it needs to be a ship and be able to move freely in time. *Blessing* can do both."

Sachiko set her face in her palms. "She can't be. I know what it takes to be a time ship. She needs to have time storage capabilities, and she would need a focus. She has neither."

"I am a time focus. I am presently one with Jon's foot covering, but even from there, I can manipulate time."

"But if you leave Aramthella, then *she'll* have no focus," Sachiko stated angrily.

"No. She will continue to have me."

"But if you go with Jon on *Blessing*—"

"I will be both places."

"But you can't be," Sachiko blurted as a reply.

"Why not?"

"Hang on," I interrupted. "I think I see where you're going here. But you're just a tiny fraction of Plesmus. Is that enough to be a proper focus?"

"With enough time energy consumption, I will be as large as I am."

Not a sentence you heard every day.

"*Blessing* does not have time storage capabilities," Sachiko asked more than stated.

"But she does. I can store some time. Additional time can be stored in one of Jon's membrane spheres."

"Would that work?" I marveled.

"Absolutely," she replied.

"*Outstanding*," I shouted. I raised my hands together overhead and bounced then around. "I got a time ship, I got a time ship."

I looked over to Sachiko. She seemed ... unwell. "You okay, Shaky?"

She gestured her palms downward. "Alright, Jon is a commodore. *Blessing*'s a time ship. I still haven't announced what we're doing next."

"You can do whatever you want. I can do what *I* want, if I don't want to do what you want to do," I responded unhelpfully.

"But we're a team, Jon. You know, space, aliens, and fighting. We *can't* split up."

"Then all you have to do is not piss me off enough that I'll ignore that reality and leave."

"I am not attempting to piss you off. I'm trying—very poorly—to convey to you my desired course of action."

"You mean like your *orders*? Because I hate orders. I always have, but before, like, say, when there were other humans and they outranked me, I didn't have to like 'em, I just had to obey 'em."

"What if you are in full *agreement* with my plans?"

"Oh, if they're *plans*, that's cool. It's just an issue, you know, if they're *orders*. Hates me some orders."

"What is your proximate goal, Captain Jones?" enquired my boot.

"If it's all the same to you, I'd like to confine this discussion to be one between Jon and myself?"

"Hmm. I'll have to ponder that request. *If it's all the same to me?* Well, if it were the *same*, would it be similar to what I desire?"

"May I proceed?" Sachiko shouted.

"If it's all the same to you," Plesmus unhelpfully remarked.

"Shaky, did you call me here to tell me something?" I asked. "Because it's getting late and Sapale is only growing more suspicious."

She massaged her temples. "You stated two months ago that we would retrieve the population of Mars 1 in two months. It has been two months exactly. I propose to go to Mars and retrieve them."

"I did say that, didn't I? Ah, just curious. Why did you

assume I wouldn't want to do what I clearly stated I wanted to do?"

"Because you're Jon Ryan, confounder of the universe," Sachiko snapped.

"The captain establishes a valid point," observed Plesmus.

"True that," I had to agree. "And, you know what?"

"I have not the slightest clue," Sachiko exclaimed.

"Nor do I, except that I know what you did, so my having no clue what you are about to say is possibly not overly relevant."

"You see the future?" Sachiko asked incredulously.

"I can," Plesmus said.

She waved her arms chaotically, along with her head. "Well then, tell me if our efforts to eliminate the clan will be successful."

"That I cannot do."

"Naturally," I added.

"Why not? If you see one future, why can't you see all of them?" she pressed.

"Because I can only see the ones I can see. The others I cannot see."

"That makes no sense," she shot back at my boot.

"I am sorry to know that," Plesmus stated.

"But that does not change the fact," I concluded for her.

"*Exactly*," she concurred.

"So do we go and pick up the residents of Mars 1?" I asked.

"Yes, you do. The witnesses must be preserved," stated Plesmus.

"You mean turned into jelly?" I asked, astounded.

"What you do with them is more your concern than mine," Plesmus replied. "I would hope, however, you do not render the witnesses down."

"You keep calling them witnesses," observed Sachiko.

"I do."

"Why is that?"

"What else would I call the witnesses?"

"But why are they ... No. Hang on." Sachiko was getting the hang of Plesmus-speak. "What are they witnesses to?"

"That I do not know. If I did, I would not tell you."

Sachiko closed her eyes so tightly, I feared she'd never get them open again. "Why might that be?"

"It might be for thousands of reasons. It is, however, because, as your species says, spoiler alerts."

"You won't tell us spoilers? The fate of the galaxy stands on the cusp, and we can't get that kind of *critically* important information?" responded a stunned captain.

"I'm pleased you understand," Plesmus responded.

"I don—" she started.

"Captain," I interrupted her meltdown. "Time and place. Okay? We have witnesses to retrieve."

"So ... so you're okay with my decision? You're not going to pout or throw a childish tantrum?"

"No, I'm down with our decision."

"*My* decision," she spat back.

"Whatever. If it makes you happy, it's *our* decision, but it's more *yours* than *mine*, okay?"

She thought of calling me to task on that issue. She went so far as to raise a finger. Then she let it all drop. What was the point? But that commodore thing—she knew immediately that was going to come back to bite her in the butt.

"Fine, let's shove off. Aramthella, are you ready to take us to Mars?"

"I don't know. I am, but you'd better check with the robot's shoe too."

"I'll take that as a yes," Sachiko announced quietly. "Make it so."

"ETA, old girl?" I called out.

No response came.

"ETA, please."

"Oh, you're addressing me. I wasn't certain and wished not to presume too much. Six minutes."

It was going to be a very long six minutes, that much was certain.

TWENTY

The time maker paced back and forth on the bridge. It had never been nervous or preoccupied before. It was testing uncharted waters for a Clam. Though it couldn't know it at the moment, it was experiencing the Ryan Effect. Loss of focus, unsettled visions, and an overwhelming sense of impending doom. Yeah, the sucker'd been *Jonned.* If it were more social—the least bit —it could have joined one of the many support groups scattered across the galaxy that met either live or online.

What is born, perpetually, of rumination and uncertainty in a commander? Disquiet in the ranks. That was equally unprecedented for the clan. For eons, the time maker had led decisively, and the clan followed its desires contently. To see a time maker behave so ... so ... so *vulnerably,* well, it was worthy of the most cautious note. There was, in the lexicon and shared experience of the clan, no word or concept for discord, democracy, or dissent. Until their PR Epoch, that is. Post Ryan. Yup, they were needing to reset their biologic clocks to that confounding force of nature.

So it was that one ordinary day out of the blue, Assistant Power Maker-tut remarked incautiously to his coworker, Junior Power Maker-fak, "Is it me, or does the time maker seem possessed by internal conflict?"

The junior power maker reflected for a moment. It had never, ever reflected in the past on anything. In fact, the process was so foreign to it, it could not have labeled it thusly. But reflect upon a point it did.

Signal Maker-bim was standing nearby and stepped away in order to place more distance between itself and the seditious conversation taking place.

"I cannot say if it is just you who is possessed of internal conflict. I am not you."

"No, *whinalt* breath, I wasn't saying *I* was possessed with inner conflict. I was speculating if I were the only one to wonder if the *time maker* is acting oddly in that manner."

The junior maker looked to the floor. "I am neither you nor all others, to be able to say what they are thinking."

"You are such a puddle-butt. Look. Here's the simple version of my original question: is the time maker acting oddly?"

To see a trap is to wish passionately to avoid triggering it. "Define oddly."

"Oddly? It means in an *odd* way. It acted—I don't know—stronger in its mind-action before now."

"I do not glean your meaning. If you have a question like that one, direct it to the time maker or one of the association makers. They are wise. We are not. You especially, it must seem."

"I do not seek the opinions of them. I was directing my words to your head. Have we not served together for a very long time? Are we not trust-ones of each other?"

"Define trust-ones." The junior maker was dodging but good.

"If you will not consider my query, please disregard that I mentioned it."

"Define disregard." Now this was getting positively silly. A little paranoia kept a Clam alive where the vengeful, impulsively murderous time maker was involved. But this loser's level was a mental paralytic.

"I will not be in agreement. I will withdraw my words and not burden you with *any* again."

"I would be in agreement with that if we were able to reverse-polarity in time and expunge them from reality."

Uh oh. Bad news on the doorstep, Junior Power Maker-fak might not take *one* more step.

"A voyage back in time is out of reality. The time maker would never allow it, since it would be designed to foil its knowing the contents of our discussion."

"*Your* discussion. I discussed nothing. I asked for clarity so that I might repudiate what you said more accurately, with more conviction. That is all I was motivated to do."

"You are over-making meaning like a meaning maker's apprentice. Our discussion—"

"Who are you word making to?" asked a confused Signal Maker-bim. It had withdrawn from where it stood, though it could not articulate why it had done so. One spot was as acceptable as the next, so why move if you don't know why you must?

"Uh, me?" asked Junior Power Maker-fak, confused. "I was just unlinking myself from word interactional exchanges with the time maker. I spoke, but I directed meaning to no one it seems."

"Well, I'm the only one here. Who in the Seven Burning Hells else are you wording to?"

"No one. I withdraw my remarks."

"That is superior. Keep it that way. There is an inexplicable undercurrent of tension in me I am undesirous of."

Meepzorp, thought the junior maker to itself. What strangeness was at play?

TWENTY-ONE

Holy hell had broken loose. Then followed shock and disbelief. Check mark on the seven stages of grief list. Immediately thereafter, denial flitted however briefly through the collective minds of the personnel of Mars 1. Check mark. Guilt, anger, and bargaining sort of lumped themselves up into a dissociative anger that hit home hard. Check mark. Depression, and reflection, along with the stages of reconstruction and acceptance were never going to happen. No check mark there. No. Not with steaming radioactive water laden with molten core-rod flecks splashing over your feet and ankles. To an individual, the dying cohort of humans were frightened beyond anyone's worst nightmare. They were so hopeless that walking though the pitch black blindfolded with your eyes closed fell well short of their level of darkness they perceived.

Accentuating their despair, the lights were beginning to flicker on and off. It had been obvious for half an hour that the heating and air circulating systems were fully offline. Aside from the scattered whimper or tearful outburst, the absolute quiet was oppressive. It weighed on everyone like a lead poncho. Even Lt. Colonel Reva St. Claire had abandoned all pretense of remediation, escape, or reversal of their bleak fortunes.

"Everyone, please gather together in the center of the room," she called out. "We can use our body heat to stay warm."

Maybe a third of those who heard her moved to comply. She was so convinced they were all dead meat either way that she made no threats, issued no ultimata to those who chose solitude over a possible modicum of succor.

Reva used the fading light to wave over the good doctor Hartley.

"Yes, Colonel. What can I do?" asked the wasted spirit that had once been vibrant to a fault.

"What can we expect ... at the end? Will the radiation or the hypothermia kill us?"

Honesty scrunched up her nose several times, looking to Reva all the world to be a five-foot-tall rabbit. "Pretty sure it'll be the cold. I've been keeping track. We're losing about five degrees every twenty minutes. If that rate continues, the smallest people are going to start passing out in about an hour, ninety minutes, tops."

Reva throated a growl.

"What?" queried the doc.

"I don't get it. We're literally standing in hot water. How can the room cool so quickly? Doesn't make sense."

"Heat transfer, my dear," responded Honesty with a slight grin. "Convection, conduction, and radiation. Those are the three methods by which heat transfers from Point A to Point B. We get a little heat in by conduction from our feet and from the air, and a smidgen of radiation. But the radiative loss to the hemisphere of space above us is orders of magnitude greater. Don't forget, it's something in the range of minus two hundred degrees Celsius out there. Hypothermia gets my vote."

Reva stared with wonder at Honesty. "My stars, you're a bundle of information and surprises. How do you, a family practitioner, know all that?"

"Have you ever heard of the writer LR Thompson?"

"Er, I think so. Didn't he write that book that Leonardo DiCaprio starred in a while back?"

"Yes, *she* did. LR Thompson is my pen name. I'm a science fiction author."

"If we weren't at the very point of death, I'd swear you lie," teased Reva. "But, as we don't have time for confabulation, I can only say *wow*."

Honesty nodded, mostly to herself. "Yeah, to write good Sci-Fi, you gotta know a lot about a lot. I go to the astronomy seminars at all the local universities and never miss a week of *Nature* or *Science* magazines."

"That's quite—"

"Otherwise, how would I know all about the exotic states in a simple network of nanoelectromechanical oscillators? Eighth of March 2019, *Science*."

Reva recoiled slightly.

Honesty tapped the side of her head. "It's very crowded up here."

Hoping desperately to change the subject, Reva said loudly, "Well, I've heard hypothermia is a good way to die. They say it's peaceful."

"Huh. You probably haven't heard that from any *dead* people, I'll tell you that for nothing," snarked Honesty.

"Well it's one hell of a lot better than radiation sickness. I've read about that. Damn sorry way to go."

"That is true. If the heat had stayed on, we'd begin seeing some nasty burns too. Won't miss treating those."

"And there's nothing else we can do?" popped out of Reva's mouth unbidden.

"Die, Reva. That's about the only thing any of us can do. That and shiver."

"I'm sorry I asked. Force of habit."

"I imagine it comes with leadership stuff." She sniffed loudly. "I never was much into that. I was in charge of myself. I wanted everyone else to do the same."

"Kind of an impractical approach during a military invasion."

Honesty looked up to the taller woman. Then they both burst out in silly snickers.

As that final spurt of joy faded, they returned to their own private realities, and to the silence that was preceding the arrival of the Grim Reaper.

A faint hum began on the far wall of the dorm. No one noticed it at first. It blended in too well with the coughs and spurts of the dying base, and everyone's thoughts were elsewhere, locked in a prohibitive darkness.

Then a book tumbled off a shelf near the epicenter of the hum. Reva's eyes shot to see what else was going tragically wrong on her last command.

"What the hell was that?" she shouted to no one in particular.

Confused glances from the uniformed personnel arose from their unfocused, inward expressions. One of the MPs near the back snapped to and sped to the now vibrating wall.

"It's a drill of ... whoa," she exclaimed as sparks flew into the air all around her head. "Check that, Colonel, someone's cutting in from outside with a torch," she shouted as she covered and ducked.

"Make a path," screamed Reva. She swept her arms in front of her and lunged toward the back of the large room. "Make a path."

A few uniformed personnel were with it enough to

spread their arms and hold onlookers back to allow the commander to rush past.

By the time Reva arrived in front of the wall, there was a ragged welding-tool cut about five feet long, from shoulder height to the floor. She reached out instinctively to touch the wound. Luckily, Emma Walters sped up just in time to stay the colonel's hand.

"I'm thinking that's hot, sir," Emma explained.

Once the burn reached the floor, it began again at a right angle to the original incision five feet up.

"They're cutting a door," hissed Reva. "The damn fools are cutting a door from our last bit of breathable air to the freaking atmosphere of Mars." She scanned the room for something to stuff into the growing gap. "You three," she shouted to MPs, "get bedsheets to pack the openings before we're sucked through the slit."

They shot off to comply.

"Whoever the *hell's* trying to cut through this wall, I'm ordering you to stop. Cease and *desist* immediately. That is a direct order." She was screaming as loud as she could. She prayed whoever was outside could hear her through what was left of the wall. Who could *be* so stupid?

Finally, the cutting line met the floor five feet from where it originally had started.

"Well now you've freaking done it, you son of a *bitch*," she screamed.

The free section of wall began to back away in small shimmies. Bright light burst through the opening, causing those in the nearby dark room to cover their faces. All but Reva. She took the pain and glared into the brightness. She would know who she was about to shoot as soon as his fool head appeared. She thumbed-off the safety of her forty-five and aimed at the center of the almost clear space.

A silhouette took form in the crude doorway.

"I ordered you to stop," scorned Reva. "Show your face so I can blow it off cleanly." She was absolutely serious in every word she hissed.

"Well, I didn't *obey*, Colonel, because I outrank you by a fair margin." I stuck my head through the opening, sporting an ear-to-ear grin. "If I was wearing my uniform, I'd point to my stars now, child."

Reva dropped her pistol to the floor. Luckily, it didn't go off. She rushed her fist into her mouth. "Oh, God, Jon. You came back."

I looked right then left. "Apparently so." I stepped into the room.

"But wait." She shoved her hands into my chest. "Do not enter. We're all contaminated with radioactive waste."

"I know. You broke your reactor. They come with manuals. Next time, Reva, read them before trying to effect repairs. Sheesh."

"I'm serious, Jon. Get out. We're all doomed, but you can still save yourself."

I stepped in farther. "I'm kind of *immune* to radioactive waste, don't you know?"

She dropped her restraining arms and eyed me suspiciously. "That's not possible. Every living organism is subject to radiation exposure."

"*Spoiler* alert," blurted Sapale as she joined me by my side. "I got good news, and I got bad news. Which you want first?"

"Neither. This is serious. Every one of us has received a lethal dose of radiation. We're all going to die, and now you are too."

"Okay, the good news is we're here to rescue you." Sapale waited a three-count. "The bad news is NASA's sending *you* the cleanup costs for this facility, Reva." No one laughed. "Tough crowd tonight," she remarked to me as she entered farther.

"Reva, it's okay. We have a cure for radiation poisoning. You're all going to be fine, if a little funny-smelling."

"There is currently no such treatment and why will we be smelling bad soon?" challenged a suddenly bold Dr. Hartley.

I leaned over to her. "Spoilers, again. And wait until you smell the stuff in the vats you'll all be sharing in a few minutes."

"Is anyone else injured?" Sapale asked her.

Honesty looked to the colonel for clearance to respond. She got it. "Not that I know of. Jacob's the only medical issue aside from the radiation."

"What's his story?" I asked.

"He's the lunatic who destroyed the reactor."

"He, what, doesn't *like* fission reactors?" I posed.

"He's schizophrenic. Part of his delusion-world mandated that he take out the reactor," Honesty replied.

"Makes sense," I responded. "Hey, go figure. We got a cure for that *too*."

"For paranoid schizophrenia?" Honesty challenged dubiously. "I'd like to see *that*."

"Well then, you'll be sorely disappointed, Doc," I informed her. "They're nanites. You can't see them with the naked eye." I clapped my hands together loudly. "Speaking of naked, everyone who isn't Sapale or me get that way pronto. It's vat-soaking time."

Sapale placed an arm across my chest and pushed me backward. "Yes, it is. Girl-type humans follow me, *then* strip down. Testosterone victims, you're with the under-evolved monkey."

You have to know she was pointing at yours truly.

Man, I had been looking forward to the naked coed thing ever since Al informed me of the massive contamination, just after we landed outside. Now how was I ever going to cross that off my bucket list, I ask you?

I can only assume the females shed their clothing just outside, before they entered *Stingray* and the super-antioxidant jelly they needed to soak in for about an hour. When we guys were finally given the all clear to exit the dorm, there was a stack of fashionable clothing off to one side. I can only attest, with pain in my soul, that girls didn't wear that type of underwear when *I* was in college. Oh myyyy.

Sapale gave each woman an oxygen shot and a dose of CO_2 absorbent matrix, so they didn't have to breathe as they floated in the vat. The sorry-assed part of the treatment was that the patients all had to swallow and inhale the foul goo for it to fully neutralize the radiation exposure. It smelled like burnt turpentine mixed with rotten eggs. I assume it had a lot of sulfur compounds in it, or maybe a lot of rotten eggs. Any way you cut it, the cure was almost as bad as the ailment.

A couple hours later, one hundred percent of the personnel and guests of Mars 1 were processed through and declared fit as fiddles by Dr. Al. Even the Jacob nut case was responding to the nanites. He was with the spacey doctor and kept asking her, *Did I do that?* Every time she'd list another of his multiple transgressions, he whined, *Did I do that?* Comical. Simply comical.

I sat in *Stingray*'s mess with the four senior officers: Reva, Emma, Swathi, and Tom Grant. We had a lot of talking to do. Once the radiation was all disposed of, Sachiko and Tank could finally join us. They'd stayed back on Aramthella while the androids did the scut work up to that point. Now that all of those stationed on Mars 1 were aboard, Aramthella was trying to work out living arrangements. For the ten *millionth* time, I was glad I was never involved with logistics. #fighterpilothere, through and through. Leave me out of the latrine scheduling plenary meetings.

"So," I began casually, "anything interesting happen since we saw you campers last?"

"Funny guy," responded Reva.

"Like a pandemic, funny," supported my loving wife.

Everyone chuckled lightly. Well, Sapale didn't. Kaljaxians weren't chucklers, and, more importantly, she was making a serious point, not poking fun at me.

"General Ryan, I swear, if you'd arrived a day later, I don't think you'd have found any of us alive," voiced Emma.

"Ouch. She hates me." I cringed.

"What?" she shot back in a near panic.

"You used the 'G' word. No one calls me that, not for a very long time."

"Sorry, sir," Emma said, compounding her insult.

"No one calls me that either. I'm not *General* Ryan, I'm not *sir*, and I'm not the *ruler* of the remaining people of Earth as a result of my superior rank." I touched my chest. "I'm Jon. If I ask you to refer to me differently, you'll know you made my shit list." I studied Emma's face.

"Right. I'll try, s ... *Jon*."

"There *ya* go," I said with a drawl. Not sure why that popped out just then, but there it was. I was apparently channeling Dennis Weaver, may he RIP (if he was currently not still alive. Seriously, I was so confused).

"I guess that raises the first order of business," Reva said formally. "My personnel are still on active military duty. So am I. If you don't object, Jon, who actually *is* still a general, may I keep our command structure in place?"

I swigged some coffee and set down my mug. "Knock yourselves out." I sat back and thought a second.

"Seriously, when I was at your stage, I would have kept the sirs and salutes too."

"That makes me feel no better about doing so," Reva said in a tense tone. "I can't overlook the fact that I'm being immature, maybe even childish, by doing so."

"Hang on," cut in my life mate. "This fellow over here is many things, but he's not into back-handed insults and self-aggrandizement. Those may be, I'll suggest, the only bad things he isn't, but don't take him the wrong way. We," she looked at me and I shook my head almost imperceptibly, "are older than we look. We've been around so many blocks, we're probably near where we started in the first place." She took a deep breath. "I used to serve in a militia, I guess you'd call it. When we met, I was a freedom fighter. I was into the martial ways, just like he was, way back when. We didn't get *better* than you in letting that part of ourselves go. We just got *different*. You are who you are. Own it, sister."

Reva looked properly reoriented. "I see. Thank you, Sapale, for clarifying that." She looked right at me. "Sorry if I took your remarks to be something they weren't."

"No need to apologize. I don't wear my ego on the outside. We're talking here. That's all. When people talk, they damn well better say something. Otherwise, it's a coffee klatch." I shook my head slowly. "The day you see *me* at a coffee klatch is the day I join the Clams and end existence."

Without any cue, all eyes slowly turned to Tank. Where he stood on this issue was of significant importance, it would seem.

"You can ask my wife, Daisy. I'm a simple, barbecue-in-the-backyard-with-a-beer-in-hand kind of guy. That said, I am still a reserve officer in the Marines on active duty. I was recently promoted to the rank of general. As

196

much as I'd *like* to forego formality, I don't think that's presently *acceptable* behavior."

Reva let out a sigh of relief audible for miles and miles. "Thank you, General Sherman. I am so happy to pass the command to someone else that words alone fail me." She looked down into her mug. "After screwing up as badly as I did, I deserve to be relieved too."

"Colonel St. Claire," Tank snapped in a really nice command tone, "I will brook no comments such as those. You were placed in an impossible situation. You acted commendably, brilliantly in fact. But you were in a no-win scenario. Under-supplied and saddled with a crazy man, it was only a matter of when the wheels were coming off. Is that understood?"

"Yes, sir," she said contritely. "Thank you, sir."

Tank looked at me and shrugged. "Sorry, Jon. I'm too new to this to see it the way you do. After all, you've had a bill—"

"A *bill* to pay," I basically shouted. "Yes, I do, indeed. You do not."

He gave me a knowing nod. Tank realized I still wanted to keep my android/ancient status a secret. Bless his heart, I knew part of why he made it a point to *be* the general was to make it perfectly clear that I *wasn't* acting in that capacity. People in the military will fixate on chain-of-command issues, whether asked to or asked not to. I heard stories of officers of equal rank comparing commissioning dates to see which one was the *actual* senior officer. Tank was placing his ass front-and-center. I owed him a beer.

"Well, this just sucks the big one," scorned Sapale.

"What?" I challenged.

"You, you're 'mission commander,'" she said, making air quotation marks. "Sachiko's ship captain. Now Tank's the Joint Chief of Staff. What about me? You all got rank. I got *nothing*."

"I can appoint you assistant mission commander if you'd like," I offered tongue-in-cheek.

"Making kissing-your-sister an official position. Thanks, but no thanks," she groused.

"I could make you a general," Tank offered. He looked to Reva. "I could do that, right?"

Reva shrugged.

"Oh joy. Kissing-your-sister with a uniform *dress* code."

"I'm so sorry," Sachiko began. "I, as you know—"

"People," I said firmly. "She's just pulling your chains. Sapale wants command responsibly as much as she wants me to start singing."

"You got that right," she groaned. "When Jon sings, those who can't flee die."

After another round of polite chuckles, Reva got down to one of her major concerns. "General Sherman, how are we set for supplies? Having several hundred new mouths to feed has to be an issue."

"Oh, I don't foresee a problem. We have the ability to synthesize endless quantities of just about whatever we want to."

Reva was visibly dumbstruck.

"Anything?" pressed Tom Grant with clear enthusiasm.

"Sure," Tank replied. "Name your poison."

"I don't want to hijack this meeting or anything—"

"Not a problem, Major."

"For the last two months, I've had this insane craving for ... Maybe I'll ask later. Yeah. Later's better."

"No. We're all curious now. What is it? An ice cold Coors?"

"No, sir. I started thinking about never having Chef Boyardee Beefaroni ever again."

"Hang on." I had to interject. "You're in a life and death struggle, radioactive water pooling at your feet, and you can't stop thinking about America's first junk food in a can?"

Tom looked down and pouted. "It gave me great comfort as a child."

"Okay, then," I responded robustly. "Al, if you please, three helpings of Chef Boyardee Beefaroni, the throwback recipe, if you will be so kind."

I heard the synthesizer ping before I could even stand. I walked over to retrieve the object of Major Tom Grant's heart.

As I reached to pull the three bowls out, Tom asked uncertainly, "Who are the other two for?"

"Two for you, buddy. Can't suppress a jones with just one serving. The other's for me. I think it gave me great comfort as a young man too. I decided to find out."

I slid two bowls in front of Tom. His eyes were locked on them. Nice. I sat and took a bite. Hmm. Not *as* good as I remembered, maybe. Tom, he was halfway through the first bowl, and I was wondering who to pass my serving off to. Sapale! Yeah. I slid it over.

"What, you don't like it?" she puzzled.

"I *love* it. But it's too good for me. You have it."

"Al, Jon's still hungry," she called out. "A bowl of sunne calrf for him. Make it a big one."

About three seconds after the synthesizer pinged, every human in the room knew she was shaming me. Warm dead rat, one week rotten. Mmm, mmm good. Not.

"So, you can see supplies will not be an issue," Tank confirmed.

"Does that include medical supplies?"

"Yes, sure. Is there a pressing need I should know about?"

"Well, yes. Ah, one girl needs insulin."

Tank shook his head. "Shouldn't be a problem."

"And a couple on the personnel take blood pressure meds. One needs a seizure medication."

"I don't see a problem. S'that it?"

Reva looked to Emma briefly. "Er, well, we'd run out of ... some essentials ... for the students mostly, actually—"

"Colonel, please. We're all adults here. What else?"

"Condoms, sir. We need lots and lots of condoms."

One-two-three.

The room erupted in laughter, led by Tank. When the noise level dropped back, he spoke through a huge grin. "We'll get right on that, Colonel."

"Thank you, sir. I mean, thank you for meeting the supply needs of the *residents* of the base."

Oh yeah, she needed to clarify it wasn't that she personally needed lots and lots of condoms. No one thought about that interpretation until she mentioned it. Then, yeah, it was kind of hard to get that image out of one's head.

"Let me bring you up to speed on what we've been doing since we left you on Mars 1," Tank said soberly.

"Thank you. That will be welcomed."

"Basically, we've been getting used to our assets. We have made a few assaults on our enemy, but they are still numerous and deadly. Our goal, naturally, is to eliminate them completely. That will not be easy. They are comfortable with a time war. It's virgin territory for us."

"Any time table on when we might achieve victory?" she asked.

"No," he replied with a sigh. "Maybe, if we're very lucky, several months."

200

"Well, anything my people can do to help, please feel free to use us to whatever extent you'd see fit, sir."

"Thanks, Colonel."

I sort of zoned out after that. The session went on for over an hour more, but my mind drifted away. Meetings. What can I say? If you've attended one meeting, you've attended one meeting too many. Blah, blah, blah. Blahblahblah, as a *team*. #gagmewithaspoon. 'Nuf said.

Tank had his new baby to manage. Me, I still had to kill some Clams and recreate the lost Earth and its ecosystems. No biggy, right? I was still trying to noodle out how to manage the new revelation that Plesmus could split in two and power two separate time ships. I no longer *needed* Aramthella. Sure, she was a much bigger ship and could store tons more time energy. But I knew my ship and my crew. In war, that's one hell of a luxury.

How to exploit the advantage I had, at least temporarily, over the Clams? They'd laid a trap for us, using ships lurking just out of sight. Maybe I could return the favor? Or I could expose one ship, have the enemy chase it, and ambush them somewhere along that path. Risky. The second ship might no-time a few of theirs, but there would still be multiple ships on the heels of the bait vessel. I could also just have Aramthella and her nest of humankind park somewhere safe and leave them out of the fighting altogether. But a two-pronged attack was always superior to a solo assault.

Hmm. Now *there's* a stiffy-inducing thought. Oorah!

TWENTY-TWO

Seeing Maker-ilp was standing next to a set of screens and switches. With what humans would call the *sensor array*, its task was to monitor space and time for any object that might be of interest to the time maker. If it was on a submarine, it would be the sonar tech. It was not created to know hate, or appreciation, or any definitive emotion, for that matter. Still, over the time it had served, after replacing the former seeing maker who met with a sudden and brutal death, it had developed a bad case of the worries. While the longevity of personnel on other clan ships might be expansive, those who served on the flagship needed to remember never to buy green bananas. The time maker answered to no one, and acted always capriciously and cruelly.

It had been most agreeable to the present seeing maker that there had been nothing to report up the command chain for a very long time. When dealing with the time maker, even good news constituted bad news. And the messenger was *always* held accountable, whether it had any control over the situation or not. If it—

The distal annunciation array squawked to life.

Something was on the time move. Quickly, Seeing Maker-ilp confirmed, then reconfirmed the sighting. Then, as its innards churned, it stepped over to the duty maker's position to report the news.

"There is a ship moving in the Quelf Quadrant. It is twenty-five thousand years in our relative future and holding that time. Its vector is nominally at ninety degrees from our present one."

"Is it the stol ... *lost* time ship?" it asked authoritatively.

"I cannot be certain. I can see motion and position. *Identity* is established by others who serve the time maker." Such a cautious answer. It was no fool.

The duty maker scowled at the vision maker. But the duty maker always scowled, so reading any particular significance into the look was difficult. Finally, it knew it must react. "Time maker. Your presence on the bridge is desirable but not mandatory. Please, choose your set of actions, and do so at your own pace."

Before the duty maker even finished, Time Maker-pid stood so close to him that its hot, judgmental breath tormented the back of duty maker's neck.

"What, less-than-viable one?" demanded the boss.

To be absolutely certain the identity of the newsmaker was established unequivocally, it placed a hand on the seeing maker's head. "Seeing Maker-ilp reported to me that it has detected a ship moving in the Quelf Quadrant."

"Is it *my* ship?" came screeching from the time maker's mouth.

"It does not tell me. All it reported was movement."

"Communications maker," screamed the time maker, "contact the ship and demand that it tell me its identity."

Moments later, it reported. "There is no response, oh glorious one. That is highly suspicious. If it were one of your ships, it would surely answer your perfect hail."

"You flabet bait. Speak not no-intelligence to me. If it were one of *my* ships, I would know it because we maintain constant contact with *all* loyal vessels."

"Your brilliance is unparalleled, oh inconceivable one." Obsequious flattery might not get a clan member much, but it did keep them alive, if only for a while.

"Vector maker, how long would it take to intercept that ship?"

"At maximal expenditures, four point three hours."

"Make for it at half maximal."

"Half maximal it is, Master."

"I will be in my assigned—" it began to respond.

"Immaculate one," called out the seeing maker rather sheepishly, "I am detecting another ship in transit."

"A second ship?" it howled inconsolably. "There *is* no second ship that is not mine."

"Your word binds the truth, oh insurmountable one," answered the seer. "Something that is *not* a ship is in transit."

"*Where* is the not-a-ship in transit?"

"The Aflet Departure."

"You speak no-words to me," howled the boss. "If there is a ship that *is* a ship in the Quelf Quadrant, how can there be a ship that is not a ship so perfectly far-removed as to be in the Aflet Departure?"

"I would prefer not to speculate, oh impressive one."

"Fools and lame-witted—"

"Immutable one," hazarded the seeing maker, "I now have no choice but to report a transiting *something* in Level 11-a. It is one million years in our past and receding."

"I will not tolerate the impossible," clarified the time maker. "The addled minds that feed me knowledge are disruptive to my essence. What are the three moving objects you report to me? Tell me, tell me, tell me."

"Four— correct that reception, eight shi ... *objects* are now moving relative to our vessel in time and space."

"And none respond to my summons and none are identified?" The time maker screamed for all it was worth.

"Your summary, in your words, master of all, is astoundingly enlightening. Thank you for sharing," declared the duty maker.

"What are my options?" it demanded.

No one so much as breathed.

"What are my options, duty maker?" the time maker specified.

"Ah, you, in your infiniteness, could do either of two things, sir. Something or nothing. I know with *rock-solid* certainty you will make the better choice."

"I know of those two timeless options. I want to know my *tactical* options."

No one so much as breathed.

"I want to know my tactical options, *duty* maker."

"You *might* choose to split the fleet up, sending equal or near-equal parts in pursuit of the individual *non*-ship objects the seeing maker reports that it detects."

"Yes. That is my best option. I am pleased I came up with it."

"There was never any question, doubt, reservation, or uncertainty that you would conclude what was best unendingness, sir," prattled the duty maker.

"Segment my fleet into eight parts. Each will run down and destroy, after fully identifying, the one ship and the other seven—"

"*Twelve*," said the seeing maker oh so softly.

"The other *entities*."

"As you speak, so becomes reality," responded the duty maker. "Word maker, partition the fleet in eight parts and demand they—"

"Why would you separate the fleet into *eight* parts

when this idiot just said there are *twelve* signals out there?" demanded the time maker.

"Because you, in your infinite wisdom, said eight segments, not twelve."

The time maker thought a second. "Yes. You, loyal servant, are correct. Now I wish there to be twelve divisions, however."

"It is done because you spoke the words, glueless adhesive of the universe."

"Report back to me when each contact is made. I will retire."

There was not a single Clam on the ship who did not think to itself, *would that that were the case.*

The time maker had no sooner arrived at its quarters when it received the following blast. "Time maker, your presence on the bridge is not mandatory—"

Someone will die, were its precise thoughts. It moved from where it was to where the imbecilic *fabualte* of a duty maker was broadcasting useless words.

The duty maker stopped on the word *but* so as to not further annoy the time maker. "The seeing maker has an update." It raised a boney finger in the direction of the one who, in its opinion, should be held accountable. Accountable for what? For whatever displeased the time maker enough for him to brutalize someone.

"What, *gilbhop* dropping," snapped the boss to the disturber.

"Ship Omicron is approaching the non-ship trace near Bentilaxix."

"Approaching, as in, not there yet and nothing to word make to me about?"

"Th ... that is one way of assessing the sitrep, maker of glory."

"Sit-rep? What is sit-rep?" It did not seem pleased to have to word request.

"Ah, it is a *term*, more wondrous than wonderful one. When we were about to no-time the human home world, I heard several of their species employ the term."

The time maker was literally beginning to quake. It was like he was holding an invisible jackhammer in both hands. Not a welcome sight.

"What does the use of non-clan speak have to do with the manner in which you word offer me?"

The seeing maker's first reaction? *It was hard to spin that question in a positive light.*

"I liked the term. I found it ... stimulating. One thousand million apologies, better than the best."

"If ... if ... the situation does not say I can ... *what is your report now.*" It was mad.

"I show Omicron point zero seven light seconds from the t ... oops."

"Oo ... oooo ... ooops? If that is another human term and you have cast it at my auditory inputs, I shall swallow you whole, crap you out whole, and repeat the process one thousand *million* times."

"In that case, perfection's envy, it is not."

"W ... ww ... what does *oops* signify in the present context?" The time maker really should have set that jackhammer down when speaking.

"As Omicron approached, the signal split into three sub-signals. Each has vectored off at a slightly altered angle."

"A non-ship signal—" The time maker had to pause; it could not speak when it was so consumed with rage. "One non-ship signal divided into three non-ship signals and each of these non-ship particles went in separate but controlled directions?"

"It is no wonder to me that one so wise as you has captured the sitrep so well that further ex—"

Yes, you got it. There never was a bumbling seeing

207

maker aboard the flagship. The position had never been filled.

"Duty maker. You are next in line for responsibility. Do not displease, fail, or underwhelm me. Is that clear?"

"Bless you, maker of reality, for that gift."

Lying coward.

"What is it with these ... these *alleged* signals?"

"Thank you for asking me." It jumped to the seeing station. Seriously. One leap. "I see. Yes. Did you know, universal grace, that Omicron is tailing three signals? Well, it's following the summation path of the three. Each signal is actually diverging away from Omicron at an alarming rate."

"Commit two other ships to follow the signals. One ship per signal."

"It is done," responded the duty maker.

"Have all other ships in pursuit of their perplexing signals advance to maximal velocity to capture—"

"Ah, miracle of miracles," said a tentative duty maker. "You might not need to terminate your word making. All signals have split into sub-signals."

"Then send two additional ships to aid in the uncovering of the not-pleasing-me situation rep."

The duty maker was momentarily frozen with fright. Then it had to speak. "Masterful master. Some signals have split into two, others into fours. Should I order three ships assist, in spite of the numeric illogic of that act?"

"No, you twidillian. One ship per signal. How many signals do you presently track?"

"Ninety-seven ...er, no, make that one hundred, complex-minded Lord."

"How many ships serve me presently?" the time maker asked in a somber tone. It was fairly certain of the answer it would receive back.

"*Including* this one?"

"Not counting this one." Again, he spoke like he was reading his own obituary.

"One hundred ships give glory to your luminosity."

"And each ship now tracks a signal of unknown origin and the ships are diverging rapidly from one another?"

"I ask permission to drop to the deck and crawl to you so I might kiss the feet of the most brilliant time maker ever. You say things so correctly when summationing them."

The time maker forgot instantly that anyone was present. It was burrowing into the knowledge it had just acquired, seeking meaning. All his ships were being led away from one another. They were being led somewhere, for some— they were being led to *slaughter*.

"Have all ships break off pursuits and converge on our position. Do so instantaneously."

"I'm sorry, greatest being to ever breathe, what ships are you referring to?"

Oh no. The duty maker said those words, and he said them rather casually, nonchalantly. Very not good. For, once a thing was no-timed, no one could recall it, with three limited exceptions. The one who no-timed the thing. That was obvious, because they now possessed the time energy. Also, anyone shielded by a time lock. The flagship wasn't presently, as they were at battle stations. And, thirdly, the time maker forgot nothing, even if it never existed.

"Duty maker," it said in an empty tone. "How many ships serve my glory?"

"*Including* this one, highest of the high?"

"Yes," it mumbled in reply.

"Thank you for gracing me with the chance to answer that question. There is one ship in you—"

The never-had-been duty maker's would-have-been

words were more than the time maker cared to bear, right about then.

"Okay, people, it's show time. Let's make this work," I shouted. Probably didn't need to shout. It was just Sapale, Tank, Sachiko, Reva, and me on our bridge. We were each not five feet from one another. But, hey, I got excited. Sue me.

"We're all set," Sachiko said formally.

"Al, you keeping the units together tight as a nun's knees?" I reconfirmed.

"Wait, you wanted the drones close together? Why didn't you tell me? I mean, I have duct tape in the drawer right next to me."

Sapale rested a hand on the back of mine, which had just balled up into a fist. "Al, are the drone units still closely approximated?"

"Oh, that. Yes. Of course. That is what the big smelly one ordered. If you don't like it, blame him."

"No, that won't be necessary," she responded, rolling her eyes. "Keep them close and alert us if there's an issue."

"There's an issue. I don't like that big smelly one. If he were a tart, I put him back in the oven to bake a little longer."

"If there are any issues related to the present *military* operation, alert us," she calmly clarified.

Me? I was searching for a loose crowbar, maybe a big wrench.

Tank was standing behind us. He didn't have much of a role to play in this operation. He was stewarding Reva around, however. Though she couldn't have clue one about what we were actually doing, he felt it was important to see her new team in action. Plus, it gave him something to do that seemed important and was easy to perform. Generals like that.

"*Stingray*, are all the drones shielded?"

"Affirmative, Form One. Full membranes intact. The parcels continue to be invisible to the enemy sensors."

"Good. How long until the first payload reaches its target coordinates?"

"Five minutes."

"And the Clam ships are all where they're supposed to be?"

"Within the error we are prepared to accept."

Nice. If this worked, we'd basically wipe out the enemy fleet. Of course, success was so improbable that I felt sending the Clams telegrams asking them to commit mass suicide would be more likely to bear fruit. But a plan is a plan is a plan.

"Aramthella, any unusual or increased chatter on the Clams' part?"

"Chatter? Jon, these suboptimal beings do not *chatter*. They speak infrequently and only when needed."

"Are they *communicating* at an increased frequency?" I restated pissily.

"Negative. All's quiet on the western front."

I bet she labored microseconds coming up with that gem.

"Time to uncloaking alpha is five, four, three, two, one ... all primary units uncloaked," sounded off *Stingray*.

I waited a few seconds. "Any response by the Clam ships yet?"

"Negative," replied Aramthella.

"Al?" I called out.

"Confirmed. No motion detected."

I didn't anticipate they'd snap the bait up immediately, but sooner was preferable to later.

"The time maker's ship is broadcasting to the fleet," announced Aramthella.

"And, any movement?" I asked tensely.

"Not yet. Cancel that; a few ships are off in pursuit of the first package."

"ETA to interception?"

"Hmm..."

"No, no *hmms* during combat. *ETA?*" I demanded.

"The ships are engaged, but more slowly than I might have thought. ETA five to six minutes."

"What does *more slowly* suggest?" I pressed.

"I am uncertain," she responded. "But top speed would have been my choice. Why delay a critical action?"

Why indeed, I reflected. They couldn't be low on time energy. Maybe the time puke was overly cautious? Afraid to fully commit? Or, he was just a child at a grownup's game. Up until now, it'd won without ever breaking a sweat. Time would tell.

"When's the next package due to reveal itself?" I asked.

"As we speak, Captain," responded Al.

Darn that tick-tock clock. I wished he hadn't said that. In all previous battles, I *was* the captain. I didn't want fragile egos trod upon. Was he being wiseasserly or just referring to me in a familiar manner?

"The packages are opening up sequentially as planned, Jon," informed Aramthella. "There are ten exposed and the clan fleet is dividing itself to pursue. Currently, three to five enemy vessels are tailing each unit."

"Excellent," I mumbled to myself. "Are any Clam ships close enough to fire on our surprise presents?"

"No. None are reasonably close," Aramthella replied impassively.

It was right about do-or-die-real-bad time.

"Precisely on time, the bound units are separated down to dual-bundles. All are moving off in disparate directions at accelerating speeds." Aramthella provided a running account of the developments. "Yes," she shouted. Odd that a computer would get excited. "There is only one clan ship following each drone, Jon. We will not need to subdivide them additionally."

"Great. More firepower per unit," exclaimed Sapale. She loved big explosions. I didn't have the heart to remind her we didn't want explosions. We wanted very much the opposite, in fact.

"Plesmus," I said, craning my head to one side to better address my boot, "can you confirm the integrity of all subunits?"

"To what subunits are you referring?" she asked in her irritating I-beg-your-pardon tone I was growing to dislike.

I was trying to be tactful, or so I thought. "The focuses. Are they all functioning optimally?"

"Ah, yes. Why wouldn't I be?"

"No, I wasn't asking about you. You ... you look good to me."

"You can see me?" she asked in that same fingernail-on-chalkboard manner. "Down here on your foot cover?"

"Yes, I can. In the infrared." That was a lie, but no way she could know that. Why did I lie? Beats me. If you're dying of curiosity, check with Sapale after the battle. She can usually explain my antics.

"And I look good in the infrared to you?" she asked even more dubiously.

"Ah, Plesmus, in case you hadn't fully noticed, I'm in the middle of a life-or-death battle with a powerful enemy. May we spar later?"

"I'd rather not spar at all. But if it'll make you happy, yes, we may verbally spar later."

"I, er, I just want to make certain you're okay with, you

213

know, what's going to happen to the... whatchamacallit, other yous?"

"There are no other mes. There is only me in several locations."

"Yeah, sure. But some of you ... I mean, you're going to be losing weight real soon. You're not bothered by that prospect?"

"Jon," she responded flatly.

"Yes?"

"I got nothing. If it's weight loss to the simian brain, then let's all agree that's not an issue, shall we?"

I had visions of placing Al and Plesmus in a sealed box for all of eternity with their audio inputs locked open to maximal. That would be a fitting punishment for them both.

"Aram—"

"The single clan ships are fully committed," she interrupted. Didn't even get to finish my query. Grrr. "They are having trouble matching the drone probe's speeds. Shall I slow them a bit?"

"No, let the time maker stew on the prospect of losing whatever it thinks it's chasing."

"I'm certain you know best," she just *had* to add.

"Let me know when—"

"The first drone has led the clan ship twenty million kilometers from its original position. The first of the time-active drones has succeeded in luring its pursuer back two hundred thousand years. Oh, and—"

My turn. "Aramthella, do not interrupt me while we're in a battle unless it's critical to this ship's safety. Is that clear?"

"Yes, Commodore, it is. My apolo—"

No time for sentimentality. Can it. "I don't need to know how each drone is doing, only if there's a malfunction or the Clams destroy one."

"Roger that, Captain," interjected Al.

Dude had my back. All right, Al.

"The overall battle plan is flawless. As we suspected, the time maker's ship has not budged, but all other enemy vessels are fully committed and very far apart," informed Aramthella.

Alright, then. Time to see if my crazy-assed notion was going to work.

"All drones, reverse course and target the pursuing vessels. Plesmus, no-time the ships as soon as you're in range or upon impact, if we're that lucky."

Silence. I hate silence in a war room. It usually meant bend over and kiss your sweet patootie goodbye.

"*Plesmus*," I snapped.

"Sorry. I was busy. All ships in pursuit of our drones are no-timed. The clan ships didn't even get off a shot. I commend you on your—"

"Hold that thought. What's the status of the time maker's ship?"

"It's right where—"

"It's right where *where*?"

"Well, that sucks," the ship's hyper-sophisticated computer said.

"*Explain*," I demanded.

"That ship was dead in space. Now it is gone."

"Where has it gone to?"

"I haven't the slightest clue, Jon."

Not the response that I was hoping for.

"Explanation."

"Ah, the ship moved off in time and space."

"Okay. That's what time ships *do*. It's done that many times. Where is it?"

"That's what's odd. No, actually, that's what's *insane*. You ... you can't do that."

"Al, for the love of the god of wonky machines, what's going on?"

"Ah, well ... er—"

"You too, Al? Really? Anyone who's a computer, please explain what's gone wrong."

"Form One. Just before the time maker engaged his engines, it turned off the ship's computers. *All* the ship's computers," *Stingray* responded for her cohort.

"It ... can't ... do ... that—" I stammered.

"It can and it did, Form One."

"But ... why? How can it pilot the ship?"

"The why is obvious," Sapale said with an edge to her voice. "The douche-capade figured out we were eavesdropping."

"Uh, okay. Maybe he did. But how can you pilot a massive time ship without computers?" I asked no one in particular.

"Poorly?" responded our ship's computer. There was just a hint of I-sure-hope-so in her voice.

"Guess what, love?" queried my wife. "We're going to find out, aren't we?"

"I guess we are." What an unexpected twist. The time master might be gender neutral, but he appeared to have quite a pair of brass *cojones*, quite possibly more than two.

TWENTY-THREE

Desi Tanner lay on her bunk, staring at the ceiling, her fingers woven behind her head. Inside that container, her thoughts were a zillion miles away. Or, actually, they were in Neverland. She was reflecting on her life. At twenty-two, there wasn't a heck of a lot to reflect back upon, but she was prone to melancholy, so revisiting a nonexistent past came naturally to her. She dearly missed what she'd lost, that which never had been.

In fact, as many times as she heard, and even repeated, that the Earth and everyone on it were forced out of reality, she didn't believe it. She *received* the words. She *understood* the words. She simply *rejected* the immensity of the implications. Mom had existed. Desi saw her not five months ago, at her father's funeral. And he had *been*. Herbert Samuel Tanner walked an Earth that was as real as Desi's present sorrow. Her two sisters and kid brother had been too full of life to ever suggest they were not even ghosts haunting her past. And there most certainly had been a Westley. Maybe they would have eventually gotten married. Maybe not. But her world had centered around that infuriating hunk of contradictions for over two years. That *had* happened. She would definitely love to deposit some of their experiences in the mailbox to nonexistence. But, overall, they'd been good. Very good.

She missed Mars. In her mind's eye, she rolled her eyes and giggled. She was probably *the* only human that had been marooned on Mars 1 that now missed the bleak, hopeless wasteland. That notion kept cycling in her head. She missed her family and friends, but she sure as hell didn't miss the Earth. No, not in any way, shape, or form. And she was so looking forward to not missing this accursed spaceship. If there was a hell, this ship was where the residents might come on a much-needed vacation. Well, those souls cursed *both* to hell *and* to have Desi's "gift."

No, lifeless, barren Mars had been the only place, and had afforded her the only time, when she knew actual peace. Her entire life she'd heard people speak of moments being *peaceful, quiet,* and *serene.* It was like sighted people telling a blind woman what a double rainbow arcing across a brilliant blue sky looked like. *Fuck you very much for reminding me, assholes,* she snarled at them, all of those who were able to access tranquility. *Walk ten minutes in my shoes. Yeah. Then see if you can ever again smile or seek a tender moment alone with a lover. Screw y'all and the normal lives you rode in on.*

Since Earth had never existed, not a single human had ever ventured to Mars. It was pristine, virginal territory. It was the only location Desi could be left alone. Would be left alone. The Earth had crawled with those dark, unyielding voices. Even if they didn't speak to her, she heard them. On the rare occasion when they didn't force themselves in her face, she couldn't stop seeing them. And every damn one of them called her the same cursed, comical, insulting thing: singer to the dead.

Singer? Desi, a singer of *anything*, especially to the dead? It was ludicrous. If Desi sang in a soup kitchen, the hungry poor would flee from the building without taking a bite. *That's* how awfully she sang. But, no, her limitless curses had to call her the singer to the dead. The only connection she envisioned was that to hear her sing would be to die.

And this ship. It was not fair to say it was worse than Earth had been. No. That would be like saying being hacked apart by machetes was worse than a dental check-up. It was so much worse here, measuring scales to compare them did not exist.

Where there were *thousands* of voices disrupting her consciousness every waking moment back home, here there were millions, possibly billions, pecking at her mind like hungry crows. Back on Earth, she saw dead people, just like that kid in that movie. It was just as horrible for her as it was for him. But aboard the time ship, trillions of souls cried out in misery and torment. They couldn't know she could hear them. But, sooner or later, they would figure it out. Then they'd encrust her with their misery. Though no hope was possible, they plied her, unseen behind their containment walls, to grant them mercy. They begged for death, or life, or *any* status that wasn't the one they were currently cursed to bear.

And the truth was, Desdemona Tanner had no hope to bestow, no positive, loving message to deliver. She could only know they suffered, and that *they* knew *she* knew.

How Desi missed Mars.

TWENTY-FOUR

I was sitting hunched over at a table in the ship's mess. I was running my hands through my hair so forcefully, it was a wonder Toño's handiwork held tight. I was stressing on overdrive.

"Hey, flyboy," Sapale chided. "In case it had escaped your notice, we just won the most crucial, one-sided military victory in history. *All* history. Every*where*, every*when*. Lighten the hell up, *constoutae*."

You needn't wonder. *Constoutae* is a bad thing to be called on Kaljax. Kind of *stupid, cuckolded, jerk-face who smells funny*. Challenging to translate precisely, but you get the drift. Guys don't want to be one.

"I'm not sure what one of those things is," seconded Tank, "but we kicked some butt royally, my friend. We nearly wiped the asshole out of existence. Jon, those snot-mongers have never even been bloodied before. We took them out like bowling pins from five paces."

"We pulled off the leaves. The live tree's still out there somewhere. And I'm betting the time maker's not sorry and planning a life dedicated to serving others now, by way of penance."

"No, but I bet if he *shits*, he's scared *shitless*," my wife added with way too much zip.

I just kept scouring my scalp. Words. Words had the power of exactly, precisely nothing. Hand grenades blow shit up. They meant something when they landed next to you. Words meant someone was talking, nothing more.

"I tend to see this their way, Jon," commented a measured Sachiko. "One ship escaped; it will be harder to track down. But there's no question that, in the end, we will succeed."

Great, the rookie was feeling omnipotent. What could go wrong now?

I sat up from my slouch on the table and batted my eyes. "Look, I hate to be the one to break it to you Pollyannas, but you may just be confident for zero reason. This is not a matter of one little ship escaping our trap. We're talking the *time maker* here. It is powerful in ways we can't even comprehend. It can rebuild a fleet, quadruple the size, and be on us ten minutes from now. We're about as safe as naked virgins in the locker room after a team wins the Super Bowl."

"Oh, gosh. No thank you for that image," spat a queasy-looking Sachiko.

"Sorry, sorry, sorry. It's just, the dude's got infinitely more experience at this game than we do. Its resources are limitless."

"Jon, seriously, think about it. Even if the time maker wanted to and *could*, it'd take it a hundred years to build up a fleet like that." Tank was using his professor tone on me.

"Yes. It would. And then it sets its big old time dial to *right when Jon's giving his pissy speech*, and, presto-whamo, we're history. Or not."

He raised his eyebrows as if to say, *oh, yeah. Oops.*

"If it appears in space around my ship with an

armada, I'll go *forward* in time and build twice as many ships, come back to this spot, and kick its big but boney ass." At least Sachiko was getting the bravado thing down.

"Maybe it's that simple," I responded dubiously. "What the hell. We got one mistake to play around with. If we blow it, Earth never was. But at least we can say we tried real good." Sure, I was being an ass. But ... okay, there was no justification. "Sorry," I quickly snapped. "That was hurtful and uncalled for."

Sapale growled. Remember those Kaljaxian growls? They have an entire language of them. Most words, expressions, and grunts signify that your face is about to be ripped off.

"I said I was—" I began.

"The *great* Jon *Ryan* has now spoken the word *sorry* four times in ninety seconds. Either the outside world around him is treating him most unfairly, or he is saying what must be apologized for like his mouth was a machine gun. As a member of the outside world, I'm stating it is not the former case." Sapale was building up to something that was going to hurt like a burning lance when it hit.

"Therefore, in the interest of remaining in one piece *and* in our company, mend your ways quickly, oh sainted warrior," she concluded darkly. "Questions?"

I grew up in an instant. "Copy that. It will not happen again."

On the outside, she smiled, but from the inside came an inscrutable growl.

"A ways back, I spent a very long time looking for myself. I can testify that looking for something that wishes not to be found in this galaxy is extremely difficult."

"Jon, you're not getting all new age on us in a crisis, are you?" moaned Tank. "Looking for yourself? We're talking mortal combat here, not navel-contemplation."

"No, I mean that literally. I was searching for an alternate timeline me."

"Why?" he asked, twisting up his face.

"Long story," I dismissed. "Ask me when we're dead. We'll have enough free time then."

"Your point is obvious, Jon," commented Sachiko. "But, lacking an alternative, we must hunt our enemy down and then destroy him. It is that simple."

"It's unlikely to respond favorably to a dinner invitation," Tank observed.

"It will be a challenge," I responded as neutrally as I could.

"Absolutely," agreed Sachiko. "But remember, Jon, you're just that good."

Nice try at massaging my ego there, Captain. "Maybe, maybe not."

She frowned. "Where's the wiggle room?"

"I won't be here."

I sure got everyone's fullest attention with that one.

"You getting a pedicure or something?" Sapale asked scornfully.

"Yes, I am. *After* that, you and I need to be splitting off on our own."

"*What* are you babbling about?" she pressed in a displeased tone.

"Yes, I think I'd like to hear the *long* version of this new announcement," Tank said in a low voice.

"The time maker needs killing," I began at a paced cadence. "No doubt about that. But we have *two* time ships now. It only takes one to do the deed. Aramthella, crewed by you and Sachiko, can do that job."

He started to speak, probably to object.

I headed him off at the pass. "You two can do this, Tank. Yes, Sapale and I know more about aliens and advanced tech. But your task is easy. Pilot ship to where bad guy is and relieve bad guy from its burden of living. You don't need us to do that."

"What if we find the son of a bitch and it has *backup?*" Tank asked tersely.

"Then you let us know and we reassess the plan."

"We let you know and we *reassess?* Jon, you're sounding like a midlevel supervisor now. If we run into a shit storm, you don't reassess; you come to our aid. That's how military operations work for the winning side."

I stared at him hard. "If you run into trouble, we *reassess.* All missions have their priorities. Yours has yours, ours has ours." I released his gaze. "We reassess."

"Oh, great oracle," mocked my forever wife, "what secret-squirrel mission is it that you and I will be engaged in that might make the survival of our friends *optional?*"

"An important one."

Sapale scanned her immediate surroundings. She probably wanted to find a blaster but settled for a full mug of coffee. She launched it at my head with convincing velocity and accuracy. I was impressed by her commitment. I was also fortunate enough to duck, just in time. The mug crashed against the bulkhead and then shattered on the deck. She glared at me, teeth audibly grinding together, letting me know that *then* was a good time to express clearly what was on my mind.

"Something tells me we need to start working on resurrecting the Earth."

I was absolutely full of bombshells that day, it would seem. The looks I got back were ... let's be honest. They were unwelcome. Totally. How very fortunate I did not have a fragile ego.

"Something *tells* you?" Sapale growled in a crescendo. "A little bird? No. Wait, wait. No birds aboard this ship." She shook her head incredulously. "My little circumturus? The one that seems to be vexing you of late?"

"I ... I don't think it's the circumturus." I twisted up my lips. "Not saying it isn't, but I am saying I don't know."

"Wait," Tank said with considerable reservation clear from the get-go. "Your houseplant is speaking to Jon? It's giving him, what? Suggestions, commands, *financial advice*?"

"Long story," I tried to deflect.

"We're on a *time* ship. We got all the *time* it takes," Tank demanded.

I explained about my two recent interactions with the damn decorative shrub. I further opined that my current feeling was more a *feeling* than a prompt or a vision. Either way, I was absolutely certain he didn't feel a bit better about my story. If he'd a'had a strait jacket in his pocket, I do believe he'd have slapped it on me, pronto.

"So, Jon," Sapale said, with all the patience she could muster, "where does this intuitive inclination of yours hail from? We are, after all, staking, oh, just the lives of your species, your home world, and your friends on this notion."

"I just think we need to get on this." I looked to my boot. "Maybe it's Plesmus's influence. I simply don't know."

"Plesmus," Sapale called out loudly, "are you injecting ideations into the mushy brain of my mate?"

"Not that I know of. Would you like me to? I'm not positive I can, but I'm willing to try if it's for the best."

"No, Jon's boot. Keep it in your holster for now."

"Whatever," the blob stain responded.

"Hon," I began weakly, "you know I've been subject to, or the beneficiary of, quite a number of unexpected insights over the years."

She nodded. She was not, however, at all pleased.

"This is one of them, I do believe. Clearly we're all

critically important in this mission. My part involves sensing when I'm being directed to act."

"So we've all got critical roles," summarized Sachiko, "but yours is sexier and more mystical? That hardly seems fair or likely by statistical variations alone."

Sapale raised her arm. "Welcome to *my* world, sister. Either the universe uses this bozo like a tin-can communications device, or he's more delusional than a barrel full of politicians."

I shrugged. I mean, what could I say? I didn't think I was nutzoid, but the notion was definitely there in my head. "Hell's bells, maybe it was just a good idea I had. That *can* happen, you know?" I all-but-shouted.

"Yeah, back to my points. The more time passes, the more I vote for the delusional explanation." My wife crossed her arms with finality.

"So, Jon," Tank ventured, "is this a done deal? You two are splitting off? Or are we discussing this rationally as coequals?"

I replied with a crooked grin.

"There you go." Sapale slammed a palm on the table. "It's official. We're going, there's no discussion, and I swear by the holy veils we're not taking the damn circumturus with us. He's decided unilaterally. Another word synonymous with *unilaterally* is *Jon Ryannally*, in case you hadn't pick up on that fact yet."

"Jon, I must voice that I think this is an error," Sachiko said cautiously. "I am fairly certain we are not ready to do time-space warfare. We don't know the galaxy like you do. You will have insights, insider knowledge as to where the time maker might be hiding. We ... we will be able to do nothing more than a stab in the dark."

I looked around. "You got a great ship with thousands of years of experience. Tank's a seasoned military man. It's not that hard. You take a shot in the dark, then you try to refocus your search based on what you did or did not learn. You also pray a lot."

"You pray a lot?" Sachiko shot back incredulously.

I again shrugged. "Not really. Not so much. But you should."

"Somehow that's not filling me with inspiration, Jon," snapped Tank.

"Suit yourself. Look, the AIs'll be in constant contact. If you have questions, you can ask them. If we do, the same avenue is open to us."

"The AIs can link over time and space quickly enough to be useful in real time?" Sachiko asked.

"Absolutely. Between space-folding tech and little chunks of Plesmus, we'll be chatting like teenagers in the hallway between classes."

"And where are we going to be searching for this mythical quest?" asked Sapale.

"I have no idea."

"Great," she said loudly. "Just perfectly great. We split our defenses in two, decouple our supplies, and we have no clue where we're even going?"

"If it makes you feel any better, they," I pointed to Sachiko and Tank, "don't have a clue either."

"No, it does *not* make me feel better," she shouted. "In fact, speaking for all present, it makes us all feel considerably worse. Horribly awful, thank you very much."

"But..." I replied open-endedly.

"*But?*" Sachiko questioned. "But what?"

"But," Sapale answered for me, "that's the way it's going down, so stop gum-flapping and start saying your goodbyes."

I pointed to my wife like she'd just won first place in a contest. "But that's the way it's going down."

"When are you cutting us loose?" Tank asked flatly.

"Whenever you feel comfortable doing so, as long as it's today or tomorrow." I supplied him with an evil grin.

"Gee, wow. Let's Shaky and me form an ad hoc committee and study your proposal. Maybe we'll get back to you this semester. Remember, we're academics. We don't hate change; we don't allow it. We don't arrive at a consensus; we pout until we get our way. This might take *two* semesters, come to think of it."

"Not an issue, my friend. As long as you can use this time ship at your disposal to cram two semesters into twenty-four hours, you do not have a problem."

"Jon," Tank said seriously.

"Yes, Tank."

"Look at my face."

"If you insist. I haven't eaten in an hour, so I feel I'm safe in doing so."

"Does my face look playful or jocular to you?"

"I don't know, does it?"

"No, it does not look that way to you."

"Okay, I must accept that. Thank you for this insight."

"Fine. That being the case, please look into my face and answer me honestly. Do you think we're ready for this change, for this challenge?"

I looked down, then back up at him. "I'd like my answer to be yes, absolutely."

"But..." he responded, stealing a page from my playbook.

"But I'm only hoping really *ardently* that it's the case." I studied the backs of my hands. "We're in a mess here. I'm not telling you anything you don't already know. Whatever any of us does, we're probably more likely to fail than to succeed. But experience dictates we gotta try. We have to do more, risk more, and be luckier than we've ever been in our lives." I shrugged. "That's the simple truth of it. You need to solve one half of the problem, and we have to solve the other."

"With neither of us having the first clue how to perform our parts?" clarified Sachiko.

"Yeah. Isn't it great?" I smiled playfully.

"Great?" she questioned. "Not the word I'd have chosen."

"Call it, then, the height of insanity. Come on." I smiled. "You know it's equal parts both."

"Equal?" observed Sapale.

"Seventy-thirty," I replied.

She gave me such a look.

"Ninety-ten?"

"Closer, flyboy. Optimistic, but realistic."

"There you have it," I declared to Sachiko. "The alien said it. It has to be so. Aliens, they're not allowed to lie, you know?"

"Oh really?" the captain wondered.

"No. It's against their code, I'm led to believe."

She shook her head in playful disbelief. "You're making that up."

"It's hard to know, isn't it?" I responded with a wink.

TWENTY-FIVE

The rules had never been tested. They had hardly ever been thought about, let alone spoken. But, since the dawn of the time, the clan said, though only in whispers, that three body makers could make a time maker. Such an upheaval had never occurred. It had never been contemplated. It had never before been a possible option. But there it was. A rule, an all but forgotten taboo, whose reason for existing was suddenly coalescing, taking form, in the hive mind of the clan.

Two time makers. That was the sum total of how many had reigned. Time Maker-viv and Time Maker-pid. And they both always had three body makers near them at all times. It had come to be assumed that their role, and their number, were dictated by need. Both time makers were rapacious, cruel, and impulsive. Many replacement whatevers were needed on a fairly robust scale continually. The few who ever thought about anything also figured three body makers were needed to be in the presence of the supreme leader in case it was somehow no-timed. They could then replace it.

But time was changing. First this one here, then that

clan member over there, began to subtend that *three* body makers attended the time maker principally because it was possible, however inconceivable, that some dark day the time maker would need to be removed from reality, and a new, less defective one created to take the societal helm.

Were these such a time? Could the ancient, forgotten forebears of the clan have anticipated *this* bleak moment, one where the clan itself threatened to vanish as a species because of mismanagement?

They were about to feel their way through that dark passage. It promised to be not a pretty process. Karma, once again, proved itself to be bitchiful.

"We come to you today, oh great Time Maker-pid, not to accuse or deny you. We grovel before you only to aid you," said a very-challenging-to-believe Body Maker-wus, the most senior of the triumvirate aboard the last clan ship.

"Would that *up* were *down*, and *backward* were *forward*, might I lend in agreement to your sour word making, servant of mine," vomited back the boss. Please note that the time maker was well aware of the review-and-replace role the trio of body makers were imbued with.

"I am cut to my core at your word making, your intention making, and your implication making. To serve the office of the time maker is the greatest gift bestowed upon a body maker."

"Ah, traitorous scum that applies itself to the bottom of rotted time, you serve now the *office*, and not I, the office *holder*? If this were any *other* time, you would not plague me with your existence."

The non-intuitive, un-subtle, and wrath-ridden time maker somehow knew on a chromosomal level that this "intervention" by the body makers was not one it could dismiss out-of-hand by no-timing the messengers. Hey, salmon swim up mighty rivers and men dress up and are deferential, never understanding the manifest reasons for their actions. Sure, they both want to breed. But why all the bother and effort? Yeah. Some force inside their being dictates compliance with an invisible set of bothersome rules.

"There is, Master, no difference between the clan-unit and the office," opined Body Maker-siv. It was the nitpickiest, most annoying of the three.

"We, as the clan, work *together*, or we do not *work*," added the feeble and uber-buzz-killer Body Maker-pil.

"I don't even know what you just word-saladed, Maker-pil, but still, it revolts me," hissed the time maker.

Maker-pil bowed its tiny head as if it had been complimented.

"Let me make reality a clear one," boomed the time maker. "The clan has *ruled* time since almost the beginning of the blessing. It will rule in all times. Set backs in the recent time are bumps along that otherwise smooth and unsullied path. Any who deny that deny me. And, as a consequence, they deny the clan. And subtend *this*, my foolish servants. The clan cannot deny the clan."

Nice word twist making, exclaimed the universe at large.

"The propulsion of speeches and the hiding behind of platitudes do not honor the clan, the office, or the current occupant of the office we meet to evaluate and improve upon," Maker-wus stated in its version of thundering (which was pretty weak-cheese, in reality).

"In agreement," grumbled Maker-siv. "I could not be more in agreement, in fact."

"With what?" asked not the time maker but Maker-pil.

"What Body Maker-wus just opened to the atmosphere, of course. Were you not *here* a moment ago?"

"I fear we may be losing focus," scolded a very correct Maker-wus. "Let us execute our sacred duties and help the *time maker* help *us* by helping *him* assess and improve upon the metrics of his performance to date." The other three clan leaders in the room self-examined amongst themselves, gobsmacked.

"You just *word* transferred, Maker-wus, but I fear you neglected to *meaning* transfer," responded the time maker.

"Denying the message does not deny the messenger, Master," Maker-wus replied to further confuse and dismay. "*But*, by the rules of the clan which are greater than the clan, I call upon you, on behalf of us three time-maker assessors, to defend your past actions and give us one good, valid reason not to move to consider engaging the process of replacing you."

That was a mouthful of noncommittal mush if ever there were one.

The time maker recoiled, hissed, and deposited several small piles of some soft material on the deck. It then raged against what it perceived to be cruel fate. "When treason is rewarded, only the guilty will prosper."

The three judges stood mute, awaiting a rebuttal, not an angry protestation.

"I was close, closer than a second is to a half-second, to eliminating the sole threat to ever dare challenge the clan. I ordered my fleet into the breach of space-time the evil-doers were masquerading in. Victory was not nearly mine; it was preordained by *me* to be *mine*. However, because the human Jon Ryan is as inconstant as my contingent of body makers, he stole not only my ship, originally, but my completed victory, before-the-fact."

"I might word make for us all," muttered Maker-wus. "What you just transferred to us, while large in content, is small in *logical* content. How could you have been victorious when you suffered not only the first defeat of the clan's historical subtension but one that resulted in us clinging to but one ship, like *scapmruts* in a flood holding on to a floating branch?"

"How dare you draw that obvious mis-visioned conclusion?"

"How ... beg pardon, present time maker," Maker-pil interjected meekly, "dare my counterpart draw an obvious conclusion?"

"Yes, of course. If it concludes a notion that is contrary to my vision, it is a mis-vision. Mis-visions are bad."

"By way of *your* reckoning, but not those who subtend meaning outside of you."

"I am incomplete with that concept," defended the time maker.

"Your incompleteness is not transferable. In fact, all three of us have come to include in our reality-views a troubling fact. You sub-performed. You failed. You blew it."

"How was I supposed to know that our enemy was capable of inflicting severe damage upon the clan? Hmm? I ask you defiantly. Who knew?"

"Perhaps we are failuring to communicate, present time maker," speculated Maker-siv. "Your role, as supreme leader, might be best defined as one where experience and insight complement knowledge of absolutes. You should have anticipated the improbable, the unlikely, and even the impossible."

"Now it is *you* who transfer garbled meaning," railed the time maker. "You suggest that I might have intuited, gleaned without knowing, what might happen next in a given scenario?"

Its head bobbled in flustration. "Yes. *Precisely.*"

"Anti-sense. No one is capable of inferring the future, guessing or predicting an unexpected action or reaction.

No living unit can anticipate the unexpected and react so as to alter an undesirable future. It is to mirth make."

"The human Jon did. *He* received from us little hope and an abundance of threat. Yet he figured out how to nearly cancel our existence," Maker-pil observed ominously.

"Yes, but he *cheated*," the time maker whined. "He did actions, serious actions, that I did not desire. No one defies my will."

"I believe, on behalf of us all, you miss the stated and implied meaning we wish you to acquire in your neurons and hold on to. The universe does not exist to please and serve you."

"We do, present time maker," added an embolden Maker-wus, "but not everything that isn't us."

The time maker stared back at them in absolute disbelief. "Are you certain about that?"

Two nodded. One spoke. "In the range of ninety-nine percentage points," replied Maker-wus.

"Why was I not informed of this disconnect I experienced with reality? Ah, now I *see*. You did not *fail* me. You *tricked* me, like the human Jon. Yes. Clarity strikes me in the end. You did not meaning transfer this factoid to me because *you* want my *job*. Demon spawn, the lot of you."

"It is meaning-laden that you mention *in the end*. We assume you speak not anatomically but pragmatically. For, Time Maker-pid, you are at your end—"

"I'm sorry, graces of the divine," said the vector maker, who'd been sitting near the proceedings. "Are you word making to me?"

"No, dull one," replied Maker-wus. "We were not."

The body makers then rubbed rumps. "Behold," they proclaimed as one, "the new time maker, ruler over time itself, and our divine leader, Time Maker-bob."

And, into reality for the very first time, Time Maker-bob formed, solidified, and stood looking around the room.

"Why are you all glance making at me and not continuing to sub-perform your duties as you perpetually do?"

The king was dead. Long live the king.

"I'm sorry, time maker," said the vector maker. "Are you word making to me?"

"No, dull one," replied Time Maker-bob. "I was thinking out loud."

The vector maker squinted uncertainly. "Grace of the divine, it made in my brain just now that this ship misses the three body makers that ... uh, always seem to might have been here."

"No. They might not be here, but they are not missed."

"Ah," it responded neutrally.

"Duplication of efforts in times of crisis are unwanted by me. No. From hence forth, I shall be the time-and-body maker. No need to tax limited resources."

"You must know best," replied the now completely disinterested vector maker.

"Yes, I do, don't I. No need to create thugs who might error make and no-time me, now is there?" it mumbled to itself for no other soul to hear or to know.

TWENTY-SIX

"Knock, knock," Sachiko said gently as she tapped on Tank's open door.

Tank was not a flaming mess. Robert Woodrow Sherman was never any kind of a mess. But he was as close to one as he ever cared to be. Some people welcome command. A few among that cohort seek that position in times of crisis, like the present state Tank found himself in. Tank was not among that gaggle of lunatics. He believed fully that the structure of any society needed to be maintained, to be nurtured. So he was willing to do his part, if somewhat begrudgingly. But, oh, what a shitstorm he'd gotten himself smack in the center of. An invisible, hateful enemy, a command structure holding together like mashed potatoes going over a waterfall, and several hundred kids with terminal cases of the there-may-be-no-tomorrows. Sex and drugs and rock-and-roll, minus the drugs, because there were, thankfully, none of those. Just whatever improvised, gut-tormenting alcoholic concoctions they could ferment up in their quarters. In short, Tank felt like the mole of whack-a-mole fame.

Whenever he stuck his head up to see how things were going ... *wham*, he was unceremoniously clobbered.

"A penny for your thoughts," Sachiko requested in a warm tone.

Tank shook his head and briefly rubbed at his chin. "They aren't worth *nearly* that much," he responded grimly. Then he groused, "Ouch," and dropped his hand to the desk.

"What's wrong?" she asked with concern as she stepped quickly toward him. "Do you want me to get Honesty?"

"No. I don't need a doctor. It's just this damn razor burn."

"What damn razor burn?" she asked uncertainly. "I don't recall you ever mentioning it before."

"The one I've got because I need to shave every day now."

"Ah, before *what* are you referring to in terms of shaving?"

"Before I was lassoed into the job of commander."

She asked, while growing more confused, "Didn't you shave every day before and why is shaving every day causing a medical condition, one that I shouldn't summon the doctor to evaluate?"

"Wow, kiddo, you said that like a politician answering a simple question."

Sachiko crossed her arms. She was not letting him off the hook she had so awkwardly just set.

"No, I didn't shave every day in the past. I'm surprised you never noticed, sharp cookie that you are."

She shrugged, rather than state the obvious answer. She'd never looked at him that closely and never with his appearance as her focus. He was just another old dude, but one who was her graduate supervisor.

"And a commanding officer does because that's what he does," Tank said as if reading from a manual.

"Ah, he does. What if *he's* a *she*?"

"I'll let you investigate that murky topic upon your own discretion."

Sachiko sat in his room uninvited. "So I assume I can do away with any pretense of inquiring how you are doing, General Eeyore Sherman?"

"Yes, you may. I'm doing good enough for government work, and that's all that's required of me."

"Any particular hot-spot weighing heavily on your broad shoulders, boss man?" she ended with an evil grin.

"Where to start?" He leaned his chair back. "Thirteen more coeds had positive pregnancy tests, according to the good doctor."

She raised her palms perfunctorily. "They *are* charged with repopulating the species."

"Yes. However, if they maybe did it with a less gerbil-like speed and diversity, it'd settle better in my stomach."

"So said the eldest member of our merry crew."

"Oh, so am I safe in assuming that you'll be tossing *your* gonads into the Darwinian lottery soon, Captain?"

"Unlikely, but thanks for asking."

"I'll charge you with recalling that I'm in command of this island in the sky. That includes *your* reproductive system, young lady. A commander must be eternally vigilant to perform his or her duties for the benefit of all."

"My ovaries will each be sending you a thank-you card in the near future, General Concern."

"I shall be expecting them, then." His head slumped in spite of their levity.

"Can I help?" she asked with empathy. She rested her palm on her chest. "I *am* the captain, after all."

"Thanks. I truly appreciate the offer. I'll let you know if there arises an undesirable task I can dump off to you."

"Seriously, I'm here to help. You ... you and I..." Her voice faded away.

"Me and you what?"

She stared at her great friend a moment, uncertain if it was better to lie or remain silent. In the end, she chose neither. "You and I didn't sign up for any of this."

He shook his head loosely. "No, we most assuredly did not."

"We're a couple of stick-up-the-butt academics, not ... not Jon *Ryans*."

"Sure glad he didn't hear *that*. His head barely fits though most doorways as it is."

They shared a soft chuckle. Tank was, naturally, correct.

"No, we're not. But we're also the very best humanity has at its disposal right about now."

"I weep blood for humanity, then." She throated a grim grunt.

"Own it, kiddo. We gotta own it. You and I'd rather be writing grant proposals we know'd be rejected than serve in our current roles, but, I say again, we're the best candidates for our respective jobs."

She grunted. "You, maybe. Me, come on. If you want to blow smoke up my butt, please ask me to stand up first."

"Another among the multitude of things I'm sure glad Daisy didn't hear."

She studied him for a long while. "You know she's gone, Robert?"

He snuffled loudly through his nose. "Daisy and I aren't like that."

"I don't want to be insensitive, but Daisy and you aren't *anything*. She never existed."

"You know better, kiddo. She was. She will be again. That's a promise. Between Jon and us, it's a done deal."

Sachiko was torn. As much as she wanted her friend

and mentor to acknowledge reality, she did not wish to do so cruelly. She was also not certain why she felt she needed to orient a fully grown man.

"I hope you're right," was the best mental compromise she could come up with.

Tank, being Tank, easily let it pass. Of course he was right. Not succeeding was simply not going to happen.

"How you holding up, Shaky?"

"Me? Fine. I mean, aside from the fact that I've accomplished one-half of *nothing* since Jon and Sapale left, I'm peachy wonderful."

The strain was depressingly evident in her voice.

"You're doing well, Sachiko. Better, in fact. This ... this," he offered his hand up to the ceiling, "is not easy."

"If it were, I know, anyone could do it," she said with sarcasm.

"No, they could not. Anyone couldn't pull this crap off, kiddo. You. Me. That's about the sum total of homo sapiens' chances."

They were both very quiet for a while.

"I really do believe *you* are, Tank. You are a natural commander. You may hate it, but you so excel. I hear people talking. In the mess hall, in the passageways. They don't just respect you. They *believe* in you. They willingly trust you with their lives, their futures."

He nodded slowly. "Thanks, Captain. I needed to hear that." He rubbed his face with his palms. "Still, this is one hell of a job." Shaking his head once to clear it, he continued, "I'd also hoped to be able to help you more."

She shrugged as she turned slightly away. "I know you're busy."

"Busy? You don't know busy. Why, yesterday, six," he held up six fingers, "count 'em, six pairs of youngins were cited for showers in excess of the allotted time. And how could they not be properly intimidated to not repeat the infraction if they weren't paraded, wrapped in towels with wet hair, before me in this, my office of power?"

Sachiko had to snicker softly.

"And busy? Get over yourself. This morning, I was confronted by our supply sergeant with the transfixing notification that *two* cases of our dwindling supply of chocolate bars have gone missing. Heads will roll, I kid you not, kiddo. We have *chocolate* thieves in our midst. Sleep lightly. Sleep very lightly."

"I'd begin my search for the hot chocolate with the food science majors." She angled a nod at him and winked. "Probably young desperadoes risking a startup venture right below our noses."

"Heads will roll," he repeated thunderously.

They laughed well for the first time in ... in who knew how long.

"You're not just the smartest human left alive, Dr. Jones," Tank began in earnest. "You were before any of this crap ever happened. You can do it. I know you can."

She grinned uncertainly. "Thanks for the smoke-blowing—*again*. But it's hard, Tank. Harder than I would have dreamt." She wrapped herself in her arms, wishing they were a thick cocoon.

"I know. Look, we haven't had a face-to-face in days. Tell me where you're at. Maybe we can put our heads together and come up with some insights."

That brought a deep, labored sigh. "Okaaay." She closed then opened her eyes. "Aramthella and I are running models nonstop. We've tried extrapolating the time maker's last known heading. It leads—*spoiler* alert—to a dead end. I've done regressions on their known travel patterns before they entered the Milky Way and since they did. I can see no preferences in their movements, no suggestions of a central hub for their activities. I even tried to see if their vectors at any point correlated with known events or processes."

"Like what?"

"Orbital frequencies of pulsars. Burst cycles of quasars. The decay rates of uranium isotopes, gravitational waves, hell, even protons."

"Uh, help me out here. Why would the Clams' travel itinerary vary with any of those phenomena?"

She threw her arms up. "They wouldn't. It's nonsensical. But I modeled it anyway. I'm that desperate for a lead."

"Okay. Desperate is good. It can spark new insights. Just don't burn out. I need you too much to even think about losing you." He studied her briefly. "You sleeping?"

She shrugged.

"You eating at least once a day?"

She shrugged less vigorously.

"You making *friends?*" he asked, emphasizing the last word hopefully.

"You mean am I getting laid?" she responded hotly.

He pursed his lips. "As your commander, yes, I'm curious therein too. Any luck?"

"I hate you."

"Good, then you won't come knocking on *my* door in the middle of the night. Daisy'll be pleased to learn that."

"In your *dreams*, General Frustration." She couldn't quite keep a straight face. Almost immediately, she was snorting like a small bull.

"Don't mind me. I have plummeting testosterone levels, according to my doctor back on Earth. On the other hand, some of the young men I see in the gym deserve some passionate attention from a young and single woman such as yourself."

She shook her head resolutely. "No fraternization. I'm

the captain. Those boys might just be attempting to sleep their way to the top."

"I can think of worse ways to be bamboozled." He rocketed his eyebrows.

"Not on my watch, General Nookynooky."

"Hmm," was his coy response.

"Hmm, what? Keep in mind that, as captain, I can have you slapped in irons."

"Hmm, let's see how long you can hold your breath in that regard."

She angled a thin finger at his nose. "Longer than you, General Ideas. Longer than you."

"I'm not sure that the ability to delay sexual gratification better than someone else is a thing one brags about. It's … it's kind of a negative superpower."

"A superpower's a superpower. Do not mock me."

He saluted her formally.

"I thought you said we don't salute during wartime."

"Well, just this once. I don't think a Clam sniper'll pick us off because of my *one* indiscretion."

"The slapping of those irons onto you is looking mighty appealing to me right about now."

"*Yee-haw!* I win. You are too horny for your own good."

"Did I mention the hatred that I hold between us?"

"Good. My old ticker probably couldn't handle a dynamo such as yourself."

"Daisy'll be glad to know that *too.*"

"You betcha. And you can tell her as much just as soon as we wipe out the Clams and help Jon and Sapale reconstitute reality."

"Which suggests I'd best get back to plotting, conniving, and pressing pursuit."

"Plotting and pursuing? I *knew* you were a dormant volcano waiting to erupt."

Sachiko stood. "I will be sending some MPs—some *male* MPs—with those irons shortly."

"It will likely be the highlight of my day."

"I'll clue them in concerning your expectations."

"Tell 'em if it doesn't *hurt*, they aren't *doing* it right."

"You got it, General Volcano."

She scurried out before he could respond, by, oh, throwing a solid object at her.

TWENTY-SEVEN

I was fundamentally disappointed. Sapale did not, as she'd promised, cast that stupid circumturus out an airlock or into the main fusion reactor. Whenever I tried to help her out by doing so, she nearly knocked me out. And, the sneaky minx, she kept moving it around *Stingray*. One day, it'd be right over where I sat in the ship's mess. The next day—hell, maybe even later the same day—it'd be in our quarters. I saw it yesterday under the main control panels. I didn't know if she loved that *plant* so much, or just liked to see me *suffer*. Couldn't have been both, because the two motivations were so far apart. And, you know what? In all the time we'd been together and she'd owned circumturi, I'd never heard her speak kindly about one, or move it around for its own good. Not a single time.

Grrr. At two billion, I can safely say this. Life's too short to be plagued by a circumturus.

"Jon," my boot addressed me out of the blue, "what is it with you and that photosynthetic invertebrate? You treat it as if it were some malevolent force of nature. It's a photosynthetic invertebrate. You know that, right?"

Plesmus. To hear her speak was to be annoyed. I was having a perfectly good sulk in the mess all by myself. At least I'd thought I was alone. Note to self: Next time you want solitude, go barefoot.

"It's not just that. The plant has some ability to interact with others via some mental link. It's intrusive and probably dangerous to boot."

"Are *we* not presently interacting mentally via a link, a verbal one? This conversation seems neither intrusive nor dangerous, to boot."

Do not say it, Jon. Do not expound that it is as *intrusive as a knife plowed repeatedly in your back.*

"With the plant, it's different. It gives me..." What to call them? "It makes images in my brain, ones that imply meaning yet do not come out and state meaning simply."

"Are you getting enough sleep, Jon?"

"No, I don't sleep, Plesmus. So, in that regard, no."

"Sleep is good. You should get some. I'm certain the ten-centimeter plant that weighs less than one hundred grams will seem less intimidating if you were refreshed."

"So, do you sleep, Plesmus?" I asked because I wanted to change the subject from me to anything else in the known universe.

"Yes, I do. In fact, I'm sleeping now."

No you're not. You pestering me. I went, instead, with, "How can you be asleep and be conversing with me presently?"

"Silly robot. You make me smile internally. Seriously, I did not know such a process was possible for me until we met."

"Why am I making you smile internally?"

"Because you still don't get it. I'm here, but I'm also many places. I'm not just part of the fabric of your foot covering, you know?"

"You keep saying that, but your suggestion sounds more delusional than actual."

"It does?"

"Yes. It does."

"That is troubling. What, if I might ask, does what you said mean?"

"It means the universe is broken. I'm trying to fix it, while you're trying to ... to ... I have no clue what beyond the fact that you're not helping me advance my cause."

"I'm not? Was I supposed to? I didn't get a menmo or anything."

"A *menmo*? What the hell's a menmo?"

"You know this one, Jon. It's an allegorical written communication on a piece of degraded wood spread out in a thin sheet."

"You mean a *memo*?"

"Ah, yes, you are more correct than I was."

I was so close to murderizing this pest.

"Plesmus."

"Yes, friend Jon."

"I'm very busy."

"I know."

"I'd like to continue being busy."

"Then, in my opinion, you should continue to be so preoccupied."

"Thank you. So if you'll be very quiet, I'll be able to resume being busy."

And she was. For three whole seconds.

"Anyway, I was hoping to discuss with you some aspects of the time research you are conducting."

I slammed my palm down on the table. "I thought you said you were going to be very silent."

"No, you said that. In any case, I was, for a very long time. Now I am unquiet. The universe is a thing of wonder, Jon. Embrace it."

One-two-three ... Don't throw boot into cold, dark space.

"A few seconds is not a very long time," I protested.

"It is if you're a muon."

I crushed my pen involuntarily in my hand. "And are *you* a muon?"

"Jon, I am worried about your wellbeing. Look at me. Do I look like a muon?"

"A, I can actually see you. B, I'm trying to work, not search my shoe for you, and C, I can't say. I've never seen a muon, so maybe you *do* look like one. On the other hand, maybe you don't. I'm so confused, I think I'm Tuesday."

"I warned you about the effects of sleep loss, Jon. Perhaps you'll heed my words now that you're mentally decaying."

"I'm not decaying, I'm—"

I was asleep. Crap in a bowler hat, I never got to finish my tirade. Damn blob. Or damn houseplant. Damn both, probably. I know, I know. How could I know I was asleep? I mean, when you're asleep, you don't know it, unless you have a dream and remember the dream when you wake up, when you're not sleeping to know you *were* asleep. *Oy vey*, I was sleep babbling.

In my dream, I was walking down the Vegas strip with a blond bombshell on either elbow, only one of the blondes was a brunette.

Nope. No such luck. That was the dream I was *hoping* to have if I ever had a dream again, which I was, but it wasn't *that* dream, which would have been a valid, certifiable dream, not the *whatever* I actually had. I blame Plesmus. And I blame the circumturus. Heck, I'm thinking of blaming you.

... I was walking along a tree-encrusted path ... in a forest ... it was early. My breath turned to steam as I

249

exhaled. I could smell pines. Hey, this dream was almost —and I cannot stress the *almost* enough—as welcome as the babes one. Forests were nice and I am partial to pines.

I had no idea where this forest *was*, but with mature pines, and a few sequoias scattered about, it had to be Earth, likely along the west coast of North America. Sierras, maybe. Of course, not only had Jupiter destroyed the Sierras like they were large bowling pins, there had also never been an Earth to have arboreal forests in the first place. But, the stuff of dreams is immune to realities, so I began trekking ... *that* way.

It was nice. If there was a campfire crackling up ahead, and I had a string of trout to fire over it, my day would be good. I made a quick check. Ah, a low-budget dream. No fly-fishing kit. Bummeroski. But a fine walk was hard to spoil ...

I take that last philosophizing back. It *wasn't* so hard to spoil the forest romp. I was walking toward myself, coming from the opposite direction. Now, mind you, I like myself enough, in a Freudian kind of way. But my experience with my selves *other* than me had been pathetic to date. And, the closer I came together, the more it was clear that the other me wasn't just me. No, because Plesmus, circumturi, and the universe as a whole hated me, it was EJ. Hopefully you remember that loser. I just love running into my evil doppelgänger twin, the one I hated and swore to never see again—ever? But those same old clothes, the slight limp that was habit more than post traumatic, and—okay, call me nuts—his *smell*. It was EJ. Evil Jon.

He seemed to have not noticed me. Typical of the self-absorbed boil on the butt of my existence. I stopped maybe five meters short of him. He kept storming ahead, like a man on a mission. That was, in essence, wrong.

Who has an intense mission to execute in a pristine forest when they have steamy breath and are, in fact, intruding on someone else's dream? La-*hoos*-her.

Just when I thought EJ was going to plow right into me, he raised his head, saw me, and rolled his eyes. He stopped a few centimeters from me. We were face-to-face.

"It's official," he whined. "I'm going to hurl."

"Turn your head and hurl, please. These are fairly clean," I remarked, pinching my jumpsuit's collar.

"Trust me. Blown chunks'd be an improvement over your ugly mug."

"Trust you? Now there are two words that never go together where you are concerned, pig-orrhea."

He shook off my imagery. "Move. I'm busy."

"No. You go around me if you're in such a damn hurry, mucus-breath."

"You're oh-for-two, punk. Your insults are worse than your breath. And I'm not going around. You move, or I'm going *through*."

"Where are you going in such a hurry? And I thought we agreed to never meet again. Why are you here?"

"Why am I in your dream? A stupid-ass question if ever there were one. It's a *dream*, pus-for-brains. Weird shit happens in dreams."

"Wait, this is *my* dream, not *yours*. Stop trying to steal everything not otherwise nailed down."

"I'd like to nail *you* down."

"Okay, back to where are you going and why? I have, I will tip my hand and reveal, ownership of my dreams. PS, as you're present, this one's officially a nightmare."

"My, aren't you as clever as a rat rotting in the noonday sun. I hate you. I so really do."

"Why are you here?" I crossed my arms.

That was when I noticed my limbs were tentacles

251

now, not *arms*. I hated dreams. I looked ridiculous with tentacles. Oh, and now I had suction cups on them. Perfectomundo.

"I need to tell you something," EJ grunted.

"You need to get past me so you can tell me something? That's improbable."

"We're in a *dream*, bozo-oski. Keep up with the flow."

My eyelids fluttered in contempt. What a maroon. "Okay, I'll bite. What do you have to tell me?"

"Move aside so I can pass. Then I'll tell you."

"That is *so* lame," I declared. "I'm not moving *until* you tell me what you need to."

"I don't *need* to. I'm *supposed* to. And, if you promise to move, so I can only see you in my rearview mirrors, it'll tell."

"Deal."

He scowled deeply. He was the king of scowls. "Fine, fruit-fly dick. *Jenna's not here*. There. Now move aside."

To hear her name spoken, even two billion years later, felt like a rusty dagger to the heart. She was my childhood friend. We spent summers together at the lake, the lake she eventually drowned in. She'd visited me when I suffered dream states. I miss her every living moment.

"I am *aware* that Jenna's not here. That, in large part, explains why I don't *see* her."

"You promised you'd move."

I pointed over his shoulder. "Can't you just go back the way you came?"

"If I could, believe me, I would, freckle-fart. But I can't, so move it. You promised."

"Only if you said something cogent."

He wagged a finger in my face. "No, *actually*, I did not. I had to tell you something. I told you something. Adios, *cucaracha*."

"What does it mean? Jenna's not here. And do not tell me it means Jenna's not here. If you do, I'll punch your lights out."

"Look at me," he responded boldly as he held out an arm. "I'm shaking, I'm so scared."

He was not *visibly* shaking. Probably was, on the inside, though.

"I'm a messenger, not a prophet. I told you what I was supposed to. If you want to know what it means, maybe ask Jenna."

I threw up my arms. "Would, but can't. She's not *here*."

"Not my problem."

You know what? It wasn't, was it? I stepped aside.

"Where is Jenna?" I called after EJ.

He batted a hand back in my direction. "Don't know. Don't care. Suck eggs. Good riddance."

And he was gone.

I sat myself down on a nearby log. I had some contemplation to accomplish. By way of preparation, if I thought I had an even-money chance of being able to, I'd have tried to pull my hair out in frustration. No such luck.

Jenna wasn't here. A bit obvious, so why make a huge point of it? Where *was* Jenna? Where was *here*, for that matter? It wasn't the lake where we hung out at as kids. Bingo. I knew one damn thing. This wasn't the forest around the lake. That left only the rest of the subalpine mountains of Earth. Couldn't be more than a billion square kilometers of those. And why did *EJ* have to tell me Jenna wasn't here? It wasn't like he knew where she was and wouldn't tell. Why couldn't Jenna tell me herself she wasn't ... Forget that line of reasoning. If she did, she'd be here. If she was here, EJ wouldn't have been instructed to tell me she wasn't here.

Whoa. Who told him to tell me that? Jenna? Let me

253

see. *EJ, go to Jon in a dream and tell him I'm not there.* That'd be whack, right? Wait. Who else would want me to know she wasn't here? Every time I'd hooked up with Jenna, it'd been in a dream, or when I was dead. I wasn't dead. Wait, that was irrelevant. Okay, why would she want ...

Jenna wasn't *here.* Jenna wasn't where she *always* was. *Jenna wasn't with me.* Holy crap balls, that sure sounded bad. Assuming it was she who told EJ to inform me, this was ominous.

Jenna wasn't with me. No one, even Sapale, loved me more powerfully or thoroughly than Jenna did—*does.* So she couldn't be with me. Right, my biggest crisis. The universe's darkest hour, and my best asset couldn't be with me. What were the reasons she couldn't be with me? She was dead? Duh. She was. She was *otherwise* busy? Not hardly. She'd be with me if she could.

She couldn't. But why? Something prevented her from being here. That had to be it. But who or what was? More importantly, *why?* Just asking the questions made me realize I was never going to answer those questions. There were just too many possibilities.

Well, this was a wasted freaking dream. All I learned was that Jenna couldn't be here to help, which, if I didn't know before, but since I wasn't even *considering* that possibility, meant right there next to nothing.

I was mad.

I was ready to wake up. Now if only Plesmus or the houseplant would get off the limbic area of my brain, or whatever, I could stay mad and ...

There was a girl ... no, a young woman. She was sitting on a rock, looking out to sea. She was posed like one of the many mermaid-looks-out-to-sea statues I'd seen. Sad, lonely, contemplative.

Wait, how can there be a sea in the mountains? Ah, yes. *Dreamscape*, hello.

I walked softly toward her. Instinctively, I knew I didn't want to scare her or even startle her. If there'd been anyone else to bug, I wouldn't even have disturbed her. Wow, she had the most beautiful mane of jet-black hair. None of the blue of the northern Native American tribes, however. Just black, straight, flowing hair. I wanted to touch that hair more than anything else I'd ever wanted to do.

My hand came up of its own volition.

"No, please don't," her sad voice said. She didn't even turn. She kept looking out to sea.

"I'm sorry," I apologized.

"I may never be ready," she added obscurely.

"That is an unholy shame," I responded. Why the hell I chose those words, I'll never know.

"Yes," she said, letting her head drop. "My reasons are unholy in origin."

"Are you a demon?" I asked in absolute disbelief. No way she could be.

"Maybe I've become one. I pray that I'm not, though."

"Then you aren't," I replied resolutely. "No one who prays to not be a demon can be one."

She turned. A smile, the vestiges of a grin, *almost* graced her lovely face. "Thank you, Father Ryan."

I chuckled in spite of her solemn mood. "Not hardly."

She held out a tiny hand. "I'm Jenny."

I reached to shake her hand, but it was already gone. Instead, I waved. "Hi, Jenny. Nice to meet you."

"I cannot respond to that emotion, Jon. Please forgive me."

"No need. I can't forgive what is not a transgression." I shuffled my feet nervously. "Do you know Jenna, Jenny?"

Huh. Jenna. Jenny. How odd.

"We all know each other."

"You all *who?*" I asked rather confusedly. Note to self. In a place of infinite remorse, never speak that way.

"All of us who shall help. All of us here."

"Where Jenna isn't?"

"Where Jenna isn't now."

I was *so* confused.

"Will she be here soon?"

Jenny shrugged. It was such a sad, longing shrug, I wished I could melt, to never-have-existed.

"What will you all help with?" I asked somberly.

I could see the girl wanted to weep. It was so, so terrible. How she felt. How I felt.

"We will help you help others."

"Others?"

"Those who must cry without voices. We will help you help them cry *with* voices. Then, by the grace of God, perchance they will not need to cry, ever again."

Oh, I was going to curl up into such a small ball and die. I'd never, ever felt more lost, more bereft of hope.

"And will you cry no more, Jenny?"

She looked away, back to the large, dark, and expansive ocean. Its waves crashed and foamed. The ocean sang to Jenny, there on her rock. It sang a sad song of emptiness, an emptiness as expansive as the waters themselves.

I knew then what Jenny meant.

The pains she and her friends would suffer were far too great to ever bear.

But they would bear them bravely.

And I would witness their strength and know their sorrow.

And, so help me, I would demand as payment for my efforts their redemption.

I would end their pain.

I would end their pain, or I would join them on the rock, all my future sight lost to the indifferent sea, like theirs had been for far too long.

To be continued ...

GLOSSARY:

First a word about time, as used in this series. The clan uses several foreign, non-intuitive terms to describe time. Here are the concepts.

Anti-no-time: Such a big word! It was the side-effect of the negative time generated by wormholes that were used against the clan. Since clan ships were structured with time energy, negative time deleted what it touched, like matter-antimatter interactions.

No-time: A verb. It means to take the time from a unit of space/time, leaving only space. The object has no time, it had been no-timed.

No-timers: The clan term for all non-clan members.

Non-time: A noun. A sloppy word the clan uses. It can mean one of two things. First, that basically, something's dead, without time, random. It can also mean that time has stopped, for the object under discussion.

Non-time ship: Any space craft that is a non-clan ship.

Un-timed: To stop time for an object or region. Basically the same as the second meaning of non-time.

Other glossary entries:

Als (1): The original ship's AI on Jon's first flight long ago was Alvin. Jon shortened that to Al. When Al was joined to Jon's vortex in the Galaxy On Fire Series, Al and *Blessing* fell in love and got "married." Since then, Jon refers to them combined as the Als.

Aramthella (1): The mighty and ancient time ship that Jon and his team stole from the body maker.

Ark 1 (1): Jon's ship on his very first mission, when he traveled to find humankind a new home.

The Two Astronomers on Mars (1): Drs. Rusty Nelson and Wang served in that regard.

Azsuram (2): Original human name for the planet GB 3. It was the planet Jon and Sapale settled on after they left the human fleet fleeing doomed Earth. They established an idyllic society of Kaljaxians there, before humans join them.

Blessing (1): See *Stingray*.

Cleinoid gods/Ancient Gods (1): Ancient and malevolent mix of gods. They have destroyed many universes before and are eyeing ours now. The five ranks or groupings for their invasion were to be Rage, Torment, Wrath, Fury, and Horror.

Circumturus (1): A psychic houseplant. No, seriously. That's it. *That's* the definition. Now go back to where you were and continue the riveting story.

Command Prerogatives (1): The thin fibers Jon extends from his left four fingers. They are probes that also control a vortex.

Cragforel (1): Friendly Deavoriath Jon met after he first escaped the Adamant in the far future.

DelRoy Crozier (2): Lieutenant and working in communication on Mars 1.

Cube (1): Jon's alternate name for the vortex he captains.

Daleria (2): Demigod and innkeeper who Jon and Sapale befriended. She worked with them against the ancient gods as she'd grown to hate them.

Davdiad (1): Kaljaxian divine spirit.

Deavoriath (1): Three arms and legs, the most advanced tech in the galaxy, and helpful to Jon.

Desdemona "Desi" Tanner (2): Former Georgetown undergrad who was a singer of the dead, that is, she perceived and communicated with dead people. Er, no thanks, I'm good. You keep that gift.

Emma Walters (2): Captain, and in charge of the women's barracks on Mars 1. What a thankless job.

Evil Jon Ryan/ EJ (1): Alternate timeline version of the original human to android download. Over time, he turned to the darker side of his nature. He studied "magic" under a Deft master.

Form One/Form Two (1): A Form is the title of a vortex pilot. If more than one is aboard, they get numerical designations based on seniority.

Honesty Hartley (2): Doctor on duty at the student health center when the president had the entire staff transported to Mars. It turned out to be appropriate she was there. She was a total space cadet.

Kaljax (1): The home planet of Sapale. Jon went there on his original voyages.

Membrane (1): See space-time congruity manipulator.

Nuclear Engineers on Mars (1): Travis Dewitt and Ed Steuben were the two assigned to man the reactor on Mars 1.

Probe Fibers (1): Aka command prerogatives, they allow piloting of the Vortex spaceship and can analyze whatever they touch.

Reva St. Claire (2): Lt. Colonel and the new commander of Mars 1.

Robert "Tank" Sherman (1): Lead academic and friend of Sachiko. Also in Marine Reserves.

Sapale (1): Jon's Kaljaxian wife from his original flight to find humankind a new home. At first just her brain was copied, then, eventually, she was downloaded to an android host. Travelled with the corrupted Jon Ryan from an alternate timeline.

Sachiko Jones (1): A graduate student supervised by Tank, swept into the action because she discovered the presence and intent of the hostile clan aliens.

Space-time congruity manipulator (1): Hugely helpful force field. Aka a membrane.

Stingray (1): Jon's Deavoriath spaceship. Her name in the Deavoriath language is pronounced "crash." Hence, silly Jon renamed her after one of his favorite cars. It makes Jon-sense.

Sunne calrf (2): A traditional Kaljaxian stew. They are all revolting to Jon, but he finds this version especially loathsome.

Swathi Varma (2): Lieutenant, and aide-de-camp to Reva St. Claire on Mars 1.

Time (1): See discussion above.

Time Maker-pid (1): The present supreme leader of the clan. Cruel, rapacious, and heartless.

Tom Grant (2): Major, and the officer in charge of the male dormitories on Mars.

Toño DeJesus (1 of TFL): The scientist creator of the android Jon. Became his lifelong friend. Vortex (1): Super-advanced Deavoriath sentient spaceship. Moves by folding space. If you get a chance to own one, do it.

Quantum Decoupler (1): A most excellent weapon that pulls the quarks apart in a proton. The energy released as they rejoin is amazing.

Dr. Sadozi (1): Sapale's assumed name when visiting the White House, long before aliens were known to exist.

AND NOW A WORD FROM YOUR AUTHOR

Thank you so much for joining me, Jon, and the whole gang, on this ongoing journey! The Ryanverse is the best. The story really begins with *The Forever Life*. If you've not read that, and the rest of the series from the start, I suggest you do. You will not be disappointed.

The outstanding people at Podium Publishing are working hard to get all the books of the Ryanverse into audiobooks to place on Audible. If any book you're looking for isn't there, it will be soon.

Two favors. One, let me know your impressions, thoughts, or suggestions. You can do that by contacting me by email (contact@craigarobertson.com) or on my Facebook Author's Page. Second, please post a review on Amazon. Those are more precious than you might imagine to us authors.

Finally, there will be more soon, so party on, dudes! I know I will ...

craig

www.ingramcontent.com/pod-product-compliance
Lightning Source LLC
Chambersburg PA
CBHW070103030726
47506CB00002B/575